PRAISE FOR 'Mu

'If you've got a GSOH, you'll love
novel'

Paul Harriso

'Funny, heartwarming and tender. I really enjoyed this book.'

David Lister. *The Independent*

'Must Have GSOH is charming, moving and hugely entertaining. Full of laughs but with a touching storyline - a must read when you just want to disappear into a book.'

Karol Griffiths. Script editor.

BBC. Warners. Coen Brothers. Author of '*The Art of Script Editing*'

'Love, humour and horticulture come together in this charming, moving and funny novel.'

Bill Dare. Comedy writer/producer. Creator of *Dead Ringers*

'Such a funny, engaging and wonderfully moving novel. The concept is brilliant: a fascinating insider's guide to the business of making people laugh, wrapped up in a delightfully funny and uplifting love story. I really enjoyed meeting the hapless Stephen.'

Stephen McCrum.

BAFTA-winning comedy producer. *Mrs Brown's Boys. This Country.*

'The 40 Year Old Virgin' (well, 27) meets 'Gardener's World'. Laugh out loud as the unlikely horticultural hero navigates the comedic jungle at 'The Killer Comedy Academy' to win the heart and laughter of the woman of his dreams. Blooming marvellous!'

BrOOKS Pinner. *London Independent Bookshop of the Year 2020*

'Proves the author not only has a great sense of humour but a great sense of humanity and empathy. The 'lightness' of the book belies the well-crafted structure of the writing which Mendelson, creator of a string of popular sitcoms, achieves with a master's ease. I absolutely loved this book.'

Jessica Martin.

Actress, comedian, impressionist and graphic novelist.

'So far, every Paul A Mendelson book has been even funnier than his previous one. Stephen Gibson is a wonderful creation, and his story is both moving and brilliantly funny. Mendelson has established himself in the Tom Sharpe league and this novel will disappoint nobody.'

John Bartlett. Writer, producer, director.
The New Statesman. Goodnight Sweetheart. My Family.

'A very entertaining read. As a stand-up comedian I immediately recognised characters from the open mic circuit and laughed a lot at how accurately the line between hobbyist wannabe and professional comic can so easily and hilariously be blurred.'

Philip Simon. Award-winning stand-up comedian.

'Just the light-hearted, life-affirming antidote for all that ails us right now. Mr Mendelson once again shows he must have GSOH - Great Storytelling, Originality & Humanity.'

Paul Alexander. Comedy writer. *Red Dwarf. My Spy Family.*

'Engaging – poignant - seriously funny. I was hooked from the start. (And only the hero doesn't get the gag.)'

Brian Leveson. Award-winning comedy writer.
The Two Ronnies, My Family, The Booze Cruise.

'A perfect antidote for the times we live in and a lovely piece of escapism. You become very invested in Stephen. As ever with Paul A Mendelson's writing, it leaves you with a nice warm glow.'

Francine White. International show-business journalist

'I loved it! Unique characters in a beautifully told story, which made me laugh out loud and brought a tear to my eyes more than once, for both reasons.'

Charles Garland. TV comedy producer/director

'Quirky, very funny and entertaining. A nice dose of feel-good in a cynical time.'

James Hickey, animator.
Paddington. Lion King. Jungle Book.

Must Have Gsoh

Paul A. Mendelson

The Book Guild Ltd

First published in Great Britain in 2021 by
The Book Guild Ltd
9 Priory Business Park
Wistow Road, Kibworth
Leicestershire, LE8 0RX
Freephone: 0800 999 2982
www.bookguild.co.uk
Email: info@bookguild.co.uk
Twitter: @bookguild

Typeset in 11pt Minion Pro

Printed and bound in Great Britain by CPI Group (UK) Ltd, Croydon, CR0 4YY

ISBN 978 1913551 223

British Library Cataloguing in Publication Data.
A catalogue record for this book is available from the British Library.

To everyone who has made me laugh over the years.
Even when the joke was on me.

AUTHOR'S NOTE

The events outlined in the following chronicle occurred in the summer before the catastrophic Covid-19 pandemic.

Or – as one of the persons portrayed here later referred to it – the Great Garden Centre Hiatus of 2020.

Man is the only animal that laughs and weeps.

William Hazlitt

Laughter is the closest distance between two people.

Victor Borge

PART ONE

The Set-Up

ONE

There was this couple that went into the jungle…

The two young people, a man and a woman, are barely breathing.

The man, who leads the way, eases a path through a thicket of rich, green tropical foliage, carefully but confidently, to allow his less assured companion to keep pace. He sniffs with quiet relish the scent of exotic blooms, so she does too. The air is dense with birdsong and so many competing but subtly melding odours, the route ahead obscured by an abundance of plant life. Water drips from a nearby frond, yet beneath their feet the ground is hard and crusty. The man is attempting with every sinew to be as silent as he can. Whilst all around them can be heard the relentless cacophony of rustling.

When he talks to her, it is less than a whisper, as if he is deeply apprehensive. Perhaps not for himself but that he might unwittingly disturb whatever else is here.

"I think we're getting close," he says. "Very close. *Sshh!* … Yes, I'm right. I can definitely smell him."

The young woman can detect a Scottish accent in this person she hardly knows, yet with a subtle trace of what has to be David Attenborough. She suddenly begins to giggle.

Her companion and guide finally sweeps aside the toughest, most verdant branch, to reveal a taller man of similar age, seated at a cheap but tidy desk, head buried in an elderly computer. He wears the not particularly distinctive uniform of the Blooming Marvellous Garden Centre and Nursery, Ruislip, Middlesex.

The new customer, for this is what she is, stares at this curious man, who is now glaring unfavourably back. But his frustrated gaze is less on her than on her companion.

She notices this as she takes in the beige baseball cap, worn as if by design at exactly the angle at which this headwear can cease to look cool; thick glasses that, judging from his squint, appear to be the wrong prescription and stained gardening gloves sufficiently frayed to allow decent contact with a keyboard. The man's face is unusually thin and his teeth are in a jostling assemblage which she is convinced that her uncle, who is a dentist, could have easily straightened out for him, as he kindly did for her – almost free of charge – some years ago.

She has no idea of his background, yet to her own surprise, for this is not her line of work, she immediately assesses him as being both dedicated and neglected.

Surrounded by so many plants and shrubs that he seems to be wearing them, like some sort of gawky wood sprite or a refugee from an avant-garde production of *A Midsummer Night's Dream*, the person to whom this tiny, cramped office belongs appears utterly unamused.

"Do you have to do this *every* Monday, Spike?"

Spike, a slightly runty customer-assistant of twenty-seven, prematurely balding, with a huge, uneven, nicotine-stained smile and broad Edinburgh/occasionally Attenborough accent, shrugs amiably inside his plant-stained, Blooming Marvellous uniform. He nods to his colleague in happy assent, winking at the pretty young woman beside him. (Had she not been pretty, he would most probably still be making the effort, as it is part of his nature and his brief, but might be less invested in the returns.)

The other man watches with some incredulity, as the young woman smiles winsomely back at her grinning guide.

"This is NOT a jungle," continues the disgruntled man, somewhat unnecessarily. And, to the young woman's way of hearing, surprisingly overloud. "THIS is a suburban garden centre."

Unfortunately, Spike appears determined, perhaps even impelled, to stay in character. "Be very careful, my dear, if provoked the beast could charge. With VAT included!"

Now the delighted customer is laughing. Yet, for the life of him, the other man cannot see what is funny. Nor why this admittedly appealing young woman should appear so mindlessly engaged. (He is not even going to bother to remind them that there is no VAT on plants.)

"If this *were* a genuine jungle or indeed a rainforest," the seated man persists, "you would already have been devoured by something further up the food chain."

"Yeah, okay, Stephen." His tolerant colleague beams. "Say hello to Cherie."

Stephen Gibson, Master of Horticulture, adjusts his focus to take in his visitor's agreeable but ever more bemused face. He notices a hint of moisture in her eyes and wonders whether, on Spike's reckless tramp through his masterly horticultured pathway, some of the pointier leaves might have caught her unawares.

"Can I... can I help you, Miss? ...Ms?"

The young woman appears rather hesitant, as if the real purpose of her visit, sidetracked by the jauntier employee's surreal introduction, has suddenly re-dawned on her. "Oh. I do hope so, Steve. I need a plant that'll sit nicely next to my gran's ashes." He catches the tear in her voice. "She was really special to us."

Stephen Gibson nods for a second. In fact he nods repeatedly for quite a few seconds. Spike knows that this is the sign of an encyclopaedic brain at work. Cherie just wonders if the man is all there.

"Memorials," he says, finally. "Very nice thought. And it's Stephen." She looks at him. "Not Steve."

Before she can apologise, not that she has fully decided on this, the capped head is down and Stephen-not-Steve is tapping at his computer, like a giant rodent trying to crack a nut. After only a few seconds, the printer beside him whirrs, rattling the small but rather pretty houseplant squatting on its top. He rips out a single sheet of paper triumphantly and proceeds to hold it close to his face.

"*A boxwood tree sapling in a biodegradable pot!*"

He realises, after some seconds, that his totally justified elation is finding little fellowship in the eyes of his puzzled onlookers. Which astonishes him, as it is patently both obvious and sensational. "Don't you see?" he says, then, after repeating this same rhetorical enquiry, only far louder, explains as if to morons: "*You can plant it right in the ashes themselves!*"

Spike is all smiles, bowled over yet again by his definitely weird yet somehow wonderful colleague. "Told you he was a genius. What did I tell you?"

Cherie is less smitten. The way she crinkles her nose and ruffles her troubled brow clearly only adds to her appeal in Spike's eyes. Yet Stephen can't quite understand why the young woman isn't immediately pumping her fists, that inane gesture which he has observed in his less mature customers, when he has provided them with an inspired solution to their not so common-or-garden dilemmas.

"That sounds a bit much," comments Cherie, finally, once she has processed the suggestion.

Stephen comes back with the clincher. As he usually does. "*Ashes make great fertiliser!*"

"My gran isn't mulch, you know!"

"Well, actually..." considers Stephen.

Out of the corner of his eye, Stephen notices Spike's head flick very slightly to the side and then back, which he has learned from experience is a discreet signal to move on.

"How about a tree? Japanese White Birch. *Betulla platyphylla.*"

"I really don't know," mulls Cherie. "Gran never liked foreigners."

Spike moves closer to his sceptical customer, as if wishing to impart something intended for her ears only. "Trust him, darling. He knows his stuff." His accent has now reverted completely from Attenborough back to Edinburgh. "Man has a green thumb."

Before Stephen can stop him, Spike lunges forward and grabs his seated colleague's right-hand gardening glove. A watering-can wrist, whilst strong, is no match for a wiry, fertiliser-humping arm, and the glove is flung easily to one side. The men can hear Cherie's gasp, as she discovers that just occasionally an expression one has always considered fanciful can find validation in verifiable fact. The thumb, whilst not quite an emerald beacon, is indeed discernibly green.

Stephen Gibson, who is by no means ashamed of his perma-stained digit, is far less content with its exposure at a time not of his choosing. "You know where the trees are, Spike. Find her one."

"Easy, champ!" says Spike. "Just joking." He turns to Cherie, who continues to gawp unblinkingly at the thumb. "Hey, Cherie, what kind of flowers grow on your face?" The young woman snaps out of her mesmerised state and shakes her head. "*Two lips!*" announces Spike, with such boyish glee that she has to chortle, even though it is probably the worst joke she has heard since childhood. She offers him a theatrical groan, which can often be the highest praise of all.

To Stephen they might as well be talking Mongolian.

With a final nod in the direction of his colleague's stern face, Spike escorts Cherie around to the rear of the desk, where a sliding glass door leads outside into an expansive and expertly stocked nursery.

Stephen Gibson's nursery.

“Sorry for your loss,” says Stephen, but the young woman doesn’t hear him. Stephen does, however, catch her half-whispered remark to Spike, as she quits the strangest office, and possibly office-dweller, she has ever seen.

“Bet he lives alone.”

The quiet horticulturist simply shakes his head. How wrong can one person be?

TWO

So these guys were gagging for a drink…

Should a person happen to overhear any of Stephen Gibson's neighbours, as Stephen himself has done on more than one tricky occasion, ruminating on the state of his Uncle Geoffrey's small but crowded semi-detached home in Ruislip Manor, they might glean that it resembles an indoor rubbish tip, only messier. Or, perhaps, prime candidate for a bumper Christmas special of that TV show on compulsive hoarders, the ones who need major psychiatric help.

On the other hand, were you to eavesdrop on his rather fiery Uncle Geoffrey discussing the neighbours, you would simply discover that they are 'fucking Philistines', who need to mind their own business.

Stephen probably falls somewhere between the two camps.

He can, of course, fully appreciate that his uncle might need somewhere to store the massive quantity of antiques, bric-a-brac and arcane memorabilia that he intends to sell throughout the south-east, at fairs and online. Yet he also knows that the majority of items, through and between which he must tread a hazardous and often painful path each day, even to reach the bathroom, were right here in the house when he first landed. Aged three, oversized suitcase in hand and fully orphaned. And have literally been part of the furniture for the ensuing twenty-four years.

Whilst by no means expert in matters antiquarian, the younger man suspects that were a nine-decades-old, badly stuffed and fiercely mouthed grizzly bear, holding a dead yet somehow still grinning cub in her mangy paws, going to sell, she would probably have found herself an eager buyer by now. The same would go for the vintage but dysfunctional arcade machines, mismatched Toby jugs, incomplete sets of *Blue Peter* annuals, and items of furniture withered by age and distinguished only by their shamefully inferior craftsmanship.

Sometimes Stephen believes that his Uncle Geoffrey's sole criterion for purchase is, in fact, age. At other times he concedes that 'under a tenner' might also be an essential component. Whereas many of his fellow dealers report back that their vendors were utterly inconsolable as they watched heirlooms and family treasures depart forever in a heartless white van, a sense of relief appears to figure almost universally in his uncle's purchases.

He has no firm idea how his sole remaining relative actually supports himself but suspects an inheritance from Stephen's own late parents has played a significant part. All he knows is that the older man has always been able to feed and clothe them both – not that either of them have gourmet tastes or a particularly enviable wardrobe – and have enough left over to fill several woodworm-ridden shelves with what would appear to be a constantly updated supply of the most gory horror movies imaginable.

Indeed, should Stephen ever make a mix tape of the sounds of his childhood, not that he would or is even aware of the concept, it would most probably be composed of the clanking of metal, clinking of china, creaking of wood and agonised screaming of assorted D-list actors being slowly tortured to death or devoured by aliens.

It is no wonder that this evening, as every evening, Stephen Gibson heads directly – if this word can be employed solely to describe a sense of purpose rather than the circuitous route he is obliged to take – for that sun-soaked sanctuary at the rear of the small but acutely over-accessorised home.

His greenhouse.

Stephen has no idea where the expression 'out of darkness into the light' originates. He suspects that it is Biblical, but as he hasn't set foot in a church since his moderately observant parents' joint funeral, his religious education has been somewhat brusquely curtailed. Yet it is this phrase that occurs to him every single day, as he turns his key to enter the musty gloom of the hallway, en tortuous route to his green and glassy Shangri-La. Whilst the dust of ages and cursory cleaning swirls with total abandon.

Yet, even today, when his excessively perky colleague's strange but hardly novel behaviour has unsettled him more than he might care to admit, he pauses, as always, beside the cracked and seldom used old fireplace. Above it, next to a precariously dangling mirror too scratched and weathered to reflect anything other than poor judgement, is a small assortment of photographs.

The first is of a couple in their mid-thirties, who appear nothing so much as clones of each other, with the same shapeless white coats and unfashionable NHS glasses, each sporting equally unimaginative hairstyling and expressions that hover on that still uncharted hinterland between passion and lunacy. In their jointly outstretched hands sits a strange plant that is nothing like anything you might find in Stephen's place of work or even in his precious greenhouse, but which Stephen, of course, knows at a glance.

Curiously, as much as one can recognise two proud and indeed revered botanists' devotion to their calling, there is also, in the mutual incline of their heads and angle of their glowing eyes, an equally unmistakeable devotion to each other. This is what always appears to catch Stephen unawares, although he would be hard pressed to tell you the reason. Nor exactly why it causes him to move quite so swiftly on and check out the singular face in the neighbouring photograph. The far more familiar and strangely reassuring countenance of his confirmed bachelor uncle, Geoffrey.

Not that a sizeable quantity of face can actually be seen on this photograph, or indeed on the man himself, obscured as it is by its own particularly roseate foliage. Stephen often thinks, rather fancifully, of New England in the fall. He has never visited that arboreal Disneyland, nor indeed has he ever left these shores, even to meet on home turf those species of plant he so assiduously and expertly sources. Yet he can so easily picture this vast acreage of red maple blended with kousa dogwood and truly believes that ardent leaf-peepers might find something reminiscent in the fiery colouring of his uncle's flowing mane and overabundant facial hair. Grown with the same intemperance as can be witnessed in this householder's relentless purchasing of crap.

It is only as he enters his own inviolate glass cocoon, engorged with botanical miracles which, to an outsider, might appear exotic but to him are simply family, that Stephen recalls this is the very night his uncle returns from his first foreign holiday in years.

"How could I have forgotten?" he asks his nearest and dearest, as he closes the heavy glass door.

Stephen's kinfolk, being plants, do not, of course, answer. And he is not so deluded as to think that they might. But this doesn't for a moment stop him talking to them.

Whilst they may not respond, Stephen would need a lot of convincing to be persuaded that they don't listen. At the very least, he truly believes that a good and focussed chat (or, indeed, firm talking-to) helps plants to grow faster and healthier. In fact, as a scientist of sorts, he *knows* this – and would tell you quite assuredly that it is due to nothing more than the carbon dioxide expelled by the talker. He would add the far less verifiable caveat that the subject matter of any conversation should, of necessity, be of interest to plant life and in no way a threat to the equilibrium of any of the rare and rather beautiful species cultivated in this small but life-enhancing habitat.

"Here we are, ladies and gentlemen," he says cheerily, as he gives them their evening watering, from the supply he has right on hand. "That's it, Terry, drink up. And you, Margo. There's a good girl." Stephen knows that he probably spoils them but tells himself that this is a parent's privilege – or perhaps the simple honouring of friendships unmatched in his experience in the more complicated world outside. How misguided that rather pretty young lady was this morning to suggest that he leads a solitary life.

"Cyril, don't gulp," he tells a particularly fine specimen of *solanum sisymbriifolium*. He suddenly recalls a tutor at college saying to his class, "Never trust a *solanum sisymbriifolium*, the 'i's are too close together." He still has no idea why his fellows fell about at this. As he rarely, if ever, conversed with them, he was none the wiser when his course was over. Too late now, he suspects.

"I'll have to nourish our Uncle Geoffrey," he muses aloud, "when he gets back from Majorca. And I rather think he'll be wanting more than water."

He leans in close to a proudly upstanding *primula auricula*, or 'Harry Hotspur', as it gently cocks its cluster of red-purple flowers in order to listen (although he does occasionally suspect that this might be an inclination existing solely in his mind). "He's probably brought back even more junk, Harry. The man is totally obsessed."

"*Who said people who live in glass houses shouldn't spill their seed!*"

Recognising the voice, Stephen turns round in delight. A rare but welcoming smile takes over his pale, slim face.

Yet, in a second, it has gone.

Transformed into a wide-mouthed grimace of horror, not unlike those on the faces of poor victims in every living-room DVD from *Axe Nicely* to *Zombie Bar Mitzvah*. The powerful hose still in his hand continues to spray uselessly onto the ground.

"Uncle Geoffrey? Oh my God! *What have you done to yourself?*"

Geoffrey Yseult Gibson stands in the doorway, in a crisply cool, linen suit, the like of which Stephen has never seen. On his uncle or indeed on anyone else. The man departed in a scruffy, rust-stained anorak, for heaven's sake, and baggy denims so encrusted with dust and age they could have walked out of the front door on their own.

But it is not this unanticipated presence that confounds the stunned nephew so much as an absence. The large, sunburnt man entering the greenhouse appears, like the small garden some yards in front of him, to have been thoroughly mowed. There's no trace of bird's-nest beard, walrus moustache, long unkempt locks of blazing hue. The visitor, for this is how he seems to a bewildered Stephen, is as neatly trimmed as a whining schoolboy creeping uncomfortably from the barbers. With a tan that has left his newly exposed skin radiating Balearic heat, Geoffrey Gibson of Ruislip appears to Stephen to do nothing so much as glow.

"You've shaved all your beard! Shorn off your hair! *Washed!*" Stephen shakes his head and the hose along with it, drenching assorted cacti that really don't require it. "What happened?"

Save for that time when he first heard about his parents' sudden and tragic demise, a time he can now barely recall, nothing has shocked him as much as what his uncle says next.

"Noreen happened."

Before Stephen has time to decipher this cryptic yet still portentous announcement or demand further clarification, his uncle is joined in the narrow doorway by a being unlike anyone or anything Stephen has ever seen.

A memory cascades into his mind of something he once read – in a rare diversion from matters horticultural. Centuries ago, when the natives of some hitherto unexploited South American coastal region were suddenly confronted with huge galleons laden with Spanish sailors, looming with gargantuan menace out of the Pacific mist, their minds simply refused to process what their eyes were telling them, so inexplicable was the vision, with the result that they happily continued with whatever they were doing. Whilst Stephen doesn't actually continue to water his plants, preferring apparently to drown his shoes and a plastic chair, he finds himself staring blankly at the apparition before him, as if it is some mirage conjured up on the shores of the London Borough of Hillingdon.

The newcomer would be at least six feet tall, even without the heels. With them she has to duck her large, still sun-hatted head to enter his arcadian sanctum. Stephen has no idea as to whether this particular genus of Noreen is African or Afro-Caribbean, not that he is overly familiar with the distinction, although he could tell an *artemisia afra* from an *anthurium cordatum* with his eyes shut. Well, almost shut.

What he does see, in this person's choice of apparel, from scarves in profusion to belts in the plural, enhancing a summery mini-dress that clings like a body painting, whilst amplified by the loudest jewellery he has ever heard, is an explosion of colour with which nature at its very best would find itself struggling to compete. He almost wishes he could borrow the massive pair of bright yellow sunglasses this remarkable lady is sporting, as she gazes around the greenhouse with a look that he can discern is spiced with as much incredulity as admiration.

"Bloody hell!" she says. "What a lot of fookin' plants!"

THREE

I wouldn't say I'm a tiger in the bedroom, but...

"Okay, think of it this way, boy," says the person whom Stephen is struggling quite hard to recognise as his Uncle Geoffrey. The older man tidies up his living room as he speaks. Or, at least, retrieves a couple of dented knickknacks from the floor, one of which is either a nifty umbrella holder or an impractical candlestick.

This minor act of housekeeping would itself be sufficient to jolt his nephew, had his attention not been totally focussed on the fantastical being with the not-quite-so-fantastical northern accent currently standing in the small back-garden. She appears to be smoking a long, brown cigarette that could, in fact, be a rather slim cigar. Even Uncle Geoffrey, normally not the most intuitive of men, can sense that Stephen Gibson is in a serious state of shock.

"Think of it this way," repeats the older man, as he struggles to explain to his charge the new and clearly disturbing status quo, in a way that might hopefully form a precursor to sense. With luck it might also erase that look of goggling bewilderment from the face of his generally ignored yet still beloved nephew. "Yes. *See!* You take two of your favourite plants, not exactly thriving on their own... with me so far, Stephen?"

Stephen just nods, wondering why he is feeling so lightheaded. He decides that it must be about time he had his Monday supper-sandwich – tuna and thousand island. Which, to be honest, is not totally dissimilar to his suppers Sunday through Saturday, as he is usually far too busy in his greenhouse to dine with his uncle, who anyway is normally enjoying an eighteen-rated (or worse) TV dinner on the least lumpy of his chaise-longues.

"So, you cross-pollinate!"

Stephen realises that his uncle is still talking. Perhaps it is the unusual hesitancy and slightly higher pitch in the voice of the older man, but he is finding it quite difficult to concentrate. And he knows that unanticipated sounds can sometimes unsettle him. Perhaps this is one of those times.

"Cross…?"

"Alright, not fucking cross-pollinate," crumbles Geoffrey, losing his thread. He had this all mapped out on the plane. Although, to be fair, he and Noreen had been hitting the Fundador rather hard. "But you… well, you plant them close beside each other and they… sort of intertwine, don't they? And you produce something quite beautiful. And new. And utterly unexpected. Like… like mistletoe!" he concludes, triumphantly.

"Mistletoe – or *Viscum album* – is a parasite," points out Stephen.

"Yes, well—"

"And plants don't suddenly shed their foliage after years and years," he continues, looking out into the garden, "then mate with another species."

"*We're not sodding plants!*" cries Uncle Geoffrey, who is getting rather worn out with this analogy business. And he'd hardly call Noreen another species, but he knows that his nephew can err towards the unduly literal. "Here's the thing, Stephen. Fellers like me – and, well, even you – we're just not meant to be alone all our long, sad, miserable lives."

The nephew just stares at his uncle. He finds that he has nothing more to say.

***

The young man in the cluttered house's smaller, less crammed bedroom has never had any trouble in falling asleep. The moment he slides his long, bony frame beneath one of the crisp Royal Horticultural Society duvets (he has the entire range), he is away.

But not this night.

This night he lies awake, staring at his flaking, lime-green ceiling and wondering what exactly has happened to his poor uncle. Did the man transform his entire appearance, not to mention his personality, of his own volition, solely in order to attract the magnetic and vaguely disturbing Noreen? Or was he simply obeying instructions barked at him by someone into whose tendrils he had already been lured, like an unsuspecting insect on the tip of a carnivorous *dionaea muscipula*?

His musings aren't helped by the thinness of the walls, through which intrude noises hitherto unfamiliar, unless accompanied by the sucking of blood or stereophonic severing of limbs. He finds this distinctly embarrassing and more than faintly disconcerting.

Stephen wonders why he keeps thinking of Spike and that poor bereaved young lady this morning. There couldn't be two couples more different, and anyway, what Spike was doing was simply what he does with every young woman who comes within his ambit – and every older woman, come to think of it. Zimmer frames notwithstanding.

Stephen doesn't like his routine to be disturbed.

He finds it – well, disturbing.

What he finds particularly disturbing are the surprising peals of laughter that accompany other sounds echoing from beyond his wall, against which his confused head now rests. He has, of course, heard his uncle laugh before, although far more often with other people than with his nephew, and he is not sufficiently naïve as to be totally oblivious to what else is most probably going on just inches away. Yet it is the laughter above all that makes him feel what he has either studiously ignored or never actually felt before.

Here, in his tiny bedroom, away from his beloved plants, Stephen Gibson feels utterly alone.

FOUR

Anyone here love their boss? Show of hand.

The Blooming Marvellous Garden Centre and Nursery, Ruislip, is about to open for business.

The Best of British Birdsong CD has been turned on, the costlier leaves have been carefully spritzed and the tempting aroma of freshly baked bread has just begun to filter out via a huge but neatly concealed atomiser positioned just outside the café (where the bread itself is never actually home-baked nor particularly fresh). At the flick of a switch, water features strategically scattered throughout the Blooming Marvellous realm happily begin to channel crystal-clear liquid in an endless loop, over descending slates and illuminated spheres, out of fish mouths and cherubic orifices, at a noise level sufficient to calm the anxious without unduly discomforting the incontinent.

The entire staff have taken up their starting positions, primed and ready to help out enquiring customers and process hopefully well-loaded trolleys. The entire staff, that is, bar three. Spike is leaning on a stand of reduced gardening books and encyclopaedias of World War Two naval battles, chatting happily to a female trainee assistant. Stephen Gibson is nowhere to be seen.

After some minutes, narrowly beating the day's first customer to the newly unlocked door, but stepping aside out of an ingrained politeness, Stephen steams in, flustered and deeply apologetic. The person to whom he must officially make his excuses has not yet acknowledged his presence. But she will.

Spike, however, does notice him or at least hears the anguished panting and tell-tale release of almost antique bicycle clips.

"*Stephanicus Gibsonicus*! You are late, pal. Mrs Dave's bark has already started to bite."

Before Stephen even has time to flinch – and perhaps, for once, he isn't fully concentrating, his eyes being too focussed on how close to the smiling new trainee Spike is currently standing – they hear a familiar voice booming through the public address system.

"*STEPHEN GIBSON!*"

Everyone turns, as if they are all potentially Stephen Gibsons, to see the speaker herself, microphone in hand, striding purposefully out of the main office towards the group by the bookstand. Two members of that select group instantly find reasons to disappear. They might as well have been directing one of the centre's huge, polystyrene '*Just Arrived!*' arrows at Stephen's swivelling head.

Mrs Dave would probably not be considered a large woman. Neither in her own nor in any other Ruislip circle. But if potent forces of nature can't arrive in North-West London garden centres, where can they manifest?

'Hurricane Dave' is scarily resplendent this morning, in one of her many bright green saris, green being the colour she wears most regularly, in a spectrum of verdant tones, because it is meant to signify calm and harmony, but also authority. It is additionally, as she knows, an excellent marketing tool and trademark within the wider community, although the employees of Blooming Marvellous believe her dominant motive in wearing the colours of the forest is so that she can camouflage herself amongst the multifarious trees and plants within the garden centre and leap out when nobody is looking.

Right now, she is out in the open and barrelling down on Stephen, who finds that he cannot move from the spot. He expects a totally justified reprimand, alongside calls for an immediate explanation. Which, whilst it will obviously prove unacceptable, had better at least be good. Yet he is thrown by the unanticipated sadness in her eyes.

"Today of all days," she sighs.

"Is it Passover?"

"No, it is not Passover," she sighs, again. "Well, it may be, but that is none of my concern. Today, Stephen, *today*, we are welcoming a highly top executive from Magnolia Hotels and Spas' head HQ itself, who is coming in to see us. To *consult* us. Coming in to our bloody garden centre. Well, *my* bloody garden centre."

Stephen finds that he can hardly breathe. He is aware that his mouth is open, like one of those gushing fish in the Italianate water feature that tinkles beside them, but there is nothing he can do. *How could he have forgotten Magnolia?* Clearly this is a sign of just how much the spectacular return of Uncle Geoffrey, with his unexpected new look and companion, has unsettled him.

"Oh yes, of course. Big day for you, Mrs Dave. Very best of luck."

He wonders again whether his boss's husband is actually called Dave and the adoption of his first name is an Indian custom. He also knows that he is far too intimidated ever to ask, although in this case he would have doubted that his employer would do anything quite so submissive, regardless of accepted tradition.

Stephen silently acknowledges, with some genuine regret, quite how little he knows about other cultures. Perhaps this

Noreen could provide him with an insight into her own heritage and customs some time. Oldham apparently has some involvement in it, but he has a sense that this isn't the end of the story.

She and Uncle Geoffrey had still been in bed, when he sped out of the house this morning. He had found himself hovering for too long downstairs, amidst the clutter, in the hope that the happy pair might descend, however spent and sated, and offer a more lucid explanation as to whatever is going on. But neither they nor further clarification were forthcoming.

"No, not big day for me. Big for you," continues Mrs Dave, with some irritation. "You are going to talk to her. About sourcing plants and trees for her newest hotel. Which is what you do, Stephen. You are going to win her bloody, soon-to-be-opened Magnolia Spa Hotel and Conference Centre, High Wycombe, business for us. When I say *us*, of course, I mean me."

She notices now that Stephen is looking unusually subdued and shaken. Not that anyone could honestly say he sparkles at the best of times. As sourcing is unquestionably his field of expertise, and the main reason she employs him, Mrs Dave deduces that there has to be another explanation for his currently disturbed state. Her voice softening, eyes resolutely ignoring the thumb that is the exact shade of her favourite sari, she rests a gentle hand on his sleeve.

"Stephen," she enquires kindly, "are you okay, my dear? Is there something wrong – at home, perhaps?"

Stephen lets rip a massive sigh, the tension of the morning leaving his body like a lucky ant from a Venus flytrap. "Well, yes, actually, Mrs Dave. You see, it's my uncle—"

This time she puts a firmly maternal arm around his waist, as she holds up her other hand like a stop sign. "Can I give you a little advice, my lovely?" she says softly. He nods in gratitude. "Don't bring your problems to work. Jobs are scarce and people don't care."

Before he can acknowledge this heartfelt nugget, Mrs Dave has turned her back on him and is addressing the rest of her staff with maximum amplification. The fact that an elderly customer, one of her regulars, has already snuck in to the café beside her, most probably for a read of yesterday's papers and a chew on yesterday's bun, appears to be of no consequence. "Okay, everyone," she exhorts, her hand smacking the microphone and sending thunderclaps around the entire centre, "let's have…"

She pauses, to allow her loyal and devoted staff to pick up their cue. Which they do, with all the enthusiasm of desiccated shrubs: "…a Blooming Marvellous day."

Stephen Gibson, whose days and nights tend to follow a less than blooming marvellous pattern, the relentless consistency of which, until now, hasn't consciously troubled him, can't quite understand why just this morning his crispy, crunchy breakfast has decided to come back up again.

FIVE

So this stunning woman walks into my office...

By midday Stephen Gibson has calmed down.

If not a complete restoration of equilibrium – it has been a deeply troubling twenty-four hours – then at least sufficient to allow him to do what he does best: procuring plants, shrubs and trees for premises, large or small, that demand a touch of customer-friendly greenery at prices that won't cost the earth. (This is indeed a line from Mrs Dave's glossy brochure – not something with which Stephen himself would ever have come up nor stooped down.)

At exactly 12.15pm, as always, he allows himself an indulgent thirty seconds, simply to revolve his chair towards the sliding glass door behind him and allow his gaze to linger all too briefly on the nourishing glories of the open-air nursery. *His* nursery, or at least a nursery for which he is chiefly responsible (because Mrs Dave, according to his disgruntled predecessor, doesn't know her *Arisaema* from her *Elaeagnus*).

Aisle after glorious aisle of high-quality plants and shrubs, of so many deliciously enticing varieties, all informatively labelled and carefully overpriced. Embellished and enhanced by sample trellises, saplings and sturdy garden sheds. His greatest pride is knowing that some people actually come here simply to stroll and stare, as they would a great English garden. At least until they are accosted by an irate Mrs Dave, telling them that this isn't Kew or RHS Wisley and they should at least buy a slice of bloody carrot cake.

Suddenly, however, he notices that the *Thunbergia*, or Black-eyed Susan vines, are curling around each other in ways that could only be deemed romantic. How had he never noticed this before, he wonders. Surely this can't be something they have only just got up to.

A sharp knocking on the door swivels him back to his computer. From the distinctive percussion he recognises that this is no mere courtesy request. It is both an announcement and a warning, just in case he is polishing his thumb, as he must admit that he occasionally does, or is up to something untoward with a plant. (Which he would never contemplate.)

He looks up to find Mrs Dave slapping open his door – of course, in reality, *her* door – to its fullest width, the 'da dah!' hovering in the air but discreetly unspoken. Behind her and towering over her short but formidable frame is a vision so magnificent that Stephen immediately pronounces it, but thankfully just in his reeling head, even more wonderful than the famed blue *jacaranda mimosifolia* of South America. Which, as anyone knows, is about as good as it gets.

The effect is as if someone has just exploded away the walls of his office, or indeed the entire Blooming Marvellous Garden Centre, Ruislip, and bombarded the area with a blinding light. Even the far less uplifting vision of Spike and two of his male colleagues standing just a few yards behind this radiant stranger, leering and gurning and making gestures he can only assume to be vulgar, don't detract from the almost spiritual effect.

Mrs Dave steps aside at this point, allowing Stephen to take in the visitor in her entirety, which is almost too much for him to bear. Despite the rapturous loveliness of her face, with a structure at least one up on perfection, and the swirling glory of her swishing auburn hair, like one of those TV commercials he has caught on his perilous way to or from his greenhouse, it is the eyes that seem particularly to resonate within his suddenly quivering body. And his equally tremulous soul. They are what he could only call golden chartreuse, as might be observed, of course, in the Monterey Cypress. Not that he has ever really taken in people's eyes in the past. Indeed, should you ask him the colour of his Uncle Geoffrey's eyes, he couldn't tell you. Mind you, if you asked him the first name of his Uncle Geoffrey right this minute, he probably wouldn't be able to offer up an intelligible answer.

Fortunately Mrs Dave registers her employee's catatonia and is on the case.

"And this is our resident horticultural expert, Mr Gibson. I grew him from a cutting and now he is virtually taking over."

The rich peal of laughter that greets this puffery, whilst baffling, is far from unpleasant. So Stephen hazards a smile. Unfortunately this remains on his face, like a rictus, causing Mrs Dave, after a few seconds, to attempt to wipe it off.

"Stephen, this lady is Ms Nina Hughes. From Magnolia Hotels head HQ?" The grinning stare remains. "*STEPHEN!*"

Ms Nina Hughes from Magnolia steps forward on her slim and strappy high-heels, lightly tanned right arm outstretched, with a confidence that Stephen finds distinctly scary but simultaneously quite entrancing. Two extraordinary yet quite different women entering his life in less than twenty-four hours is almost too much to bear.

He can sense Mrs Dave nodding to him like a toy dog in a car rear window, so with enormous strength of will he ramps down the dodgy smile to neutral and offers his now safely gloved hand in return. It is only when the young woman's long, elegant fingers meet the worn fabric that he realises that perhaps he should be offering the unsheathed version.

He is, of course, expecting that the apparition's voice will be as heavenly as the rest of her. But he isn't expecting it to be

Welsh. Nor, despite the enviable assuredness contained therein, for it to be quite so soft and musical.

"But, please, call me Nina."

His hand is still holding hers. Which is something he knows instantly that he would wish to do forever. Perhaps even, once they are better acquainted, gloves off.

"And you can call him Stephen," allows Mrs Dave. "Now, I will leave you two young persons alone together. Impress the lady, Stephen. Talking will be a good bloody start."

As Mrs Dave turns sharply back towards the door, Stephen catches a scattering of young males behind her. He doesn't notice Spike giving him a thumbs-up with an accompanying downwards elbow pump and would probably not appreciate it if he had.

Stephen Gibson has absolutely no idea what to do or say next, now that he is on his own with this year's most bloody important guest. A speechlessness which has never before afflicted him, in encounters of a purely professional nature, now suddenly threatens to paralyse. Fortunately, Ms Nina Hughes of Magnolia HQ has the situation under control. Especially when she spots an attractively unusual plant on a shelf beside him.

"How lovely," she says, nodding her beautiful head in the plant's direction.

Without turning, because there is no need, Stephen finally rediscovers his comfort zone. "Yes. That… that's…"

"Ley's Whitebeam," she completes.

If Stephen was speechless before, he has achieved Trappist status in the past few seconds. Nina Hughes appears to be in no particular hurry. She settles herself into the only other chair, with an economic, leg-tucking elegance that makes Stephen wonder if she has been on some sort of advanced sitting-down course.

Finally: "How did you *recognise* her? She's an endangered species."

"Not as impressive as it sounds." Nina Hughes laughs. "My mum moved to Crickhowell in the Brecons after my dad left us. Our biology teacher at school was mad keen on nature and flora and such." She looks suddenly serious, which he puts down to memories of her childhood. But she surprises him once again. "So, what do you say – Ley's Whitebeam? For Magnolia."

"Total nonsense," snorts Stephen, vehemently. "That's the worst idea I've ever heard in my life. A virtually extinct plant – for outside a busy South of England spa hotel! Absolutely ridiculous."

"No, please, Stephen. Say what you think."

"I just DID!" He shouts. "It's rubbish."

"You're an honest man, Mr G. With a strong, clear voice. I like that. Some people would go along with it, just to make the client feel good."

"Why would they do that – if they loved plants?"

With an endearing shrug – not that anything this person might do, save, perhaps, for a frenzied round of nose excavation, could be unendearing – Nina slowly uncoils herself and strides unbidden, on strong, muscular legs, towards the glass doors behind the desk. Turning back, she smiles. "So let's get started. Okay, Stephen?"

She slides open the heavy panel with ease. Still transfixed, Stephen rises and mutely follows.

SIX

What is it with women and flowers…?

The immediate glow of pride on Stephen Gibson's more usually gaunt and pallid face, as he shows off the Blooming Marvellous nursery to his admiring guest, might almost, in its unabashed radiance, be sufficient to incline the heads of his adored sunflowers in a new and slightly more human direction.

He bobs so excitedly just a few steps in front of a bemused Nina Hughes, reeling off the names of plants, shrubs and trees (Latin and English) with such manic, booming insistence, long, bony arms flying in all directions, head spinning repeatedly back towards her, that she wonders for a moment if his entire family might currently be held hostage and one tiny slip or underemployed breath could bring instant obliteration.

Ruislip's own good-garden-guide finally pauses, either for respite or effect, beside a ravishing display of water lilies. It reminds Nina Hughes of Monet's pad in Giverny, which she visited a couple of years ago, during a Paris mini break, with a sweet guy she had met on the plane. She feels the least she can do is nod in genuine appreciation.

"I love lilies, of all sorts," she tells him. "My mother had lilies in her most recent wedding bouquet."

"Many people do," agrees Stephen. "They're also splendid for funeral wreaths."

"I'll bear that in mind."

It is in what she assumes is simply a brief but welcome hiatus that Nina finally notices the other male and liveried employees of the garden centre. They loiter, without any identifiable intent, behind some of the taller shrubs, offering random plants totally uncalled-for spritzes.

This couldn't bother her less. Ms Nina Hughes is accustomed to being stared at, and rarely takes offence, unless it is too leery or the offender too repellent. Yet the recent and indeed continuing attention of this Mr Gibson is, even in her experience, a tad excessive. She feels as if she might almost be a new and hitherto undiscovered species of plant, on which he has suddenly stumbled and can't quite believe his eyes. (Of course, she has no idea of the tragic history behind this simple conceit and possibly never will.)

When Stephen appears finally to have run out of steam or Latin, although she fears he may just be on hold, Nina Hughes decides to root herself in hopefully more fertile client terrain. "This is all great, Steve. Really impressive. Love it to bits. But we'd need whatever you finally recommend to be totally unique to our company. Like a magnolia that blossoms all year!" She accompanies this foolish fancy with a self-deprecating laugh that goes for nothing. "That was a… Fine… Sorry, I *can* call you Steve?"

"No."

"O-kay. Anyway, these are all epic. Thank you for the tour." He just nods and she wonders briefly if he ever removes the baseball cap or, indeed, those tatty gloves. "I hear you are the best. Are you?"

"I've memorised *Archibald's Plant Encyclopaedia*, Ms Nina Hughes. Including the index. Twice. And, by the way, 'unique' is sufficient. You don't need the 'totally.'"

"Agree. Totally."

"But I'd need to inspect your layout."

Unless there is a genus of bush whose natural rhythm has evolved from gentle rustling to stifled sniggering, then the client and the horticulturist can reasonably assume that this Eden is not theirs alone. Whilst Stephen might appear disgruntled, however, at the infantile antics of his colleagues, he is at least relieved to see that his glorious visitor, whose very presence is doing things to his biological system the like of which he has never experienced, appears not to have noticed. She is focussed one hundred per cent on the horticultural wisdom emanating from this strange but incredibly well-informed person, whom she is indeed fortunate to have unearthed. This is quite clear from what she says next.

"Then I think we should meet again. At our brand-new flagship hotel and spa. Fancy lunch tomorrow?"

Stephen stares at this young woman with the entrancing, and currently rather enormous, green eyes. His favourite colour! How did she know?

"*Lunch?*"

"It's a midday meal. Staves off hunger between breakfast and tea."

"Yes, I—"

"Why don't I pick you up right outside? At, say, twelve. We can drive out there. And you can inspect my layout to your heart's content – Stephen." With a smile that pierces his heart, and a tiny wave of the hand that serves to finish the job, she clicks out of the midday sun on those wonderful heels, like a tall and slender wood nymph, and disappears back into sanity.

Stephen finds himself, for the first time in his life, having to lean on a nearby sapling for support. Which, unfortunately, it is quite unable to provide.

***

"SHE LOVES PLANTS, GUYS!"

Stephen Gibson is a man who can usually contain himself. For pity's sake, he is no *leylandii*, sprouting in all directions without control or discipline. But this evening he has rammed back into his dingy hallway, careered through the junk-ridden living room (cracking his shin on a low and massive Indian table, made from the flatbed of a wooden cart, but steaming on), because he has to share his new-found joy with his dearest friends before he explodes.

His uncle's dusty white van isn't in the driveway, so Stephen assumes the besotted fellow has taken his new love to one of his antique fairs or on a buying trip. He wonders vaguely if this rather intimidating and unnecessarily joyous woman is here to stay and whether she will attempt, most probably with little success, to tidy things up. Although she did do a pretty good job on his uncle. To his surprise, Stephen Gibson is thinking rather a lot about women these days and he is pretty sure that at least one might be thinking about him.

"It's fate," he tells Cyril, who is the oldest and by far the wisest in this select community. "Even her own company is named after an ancient genus of flowering plant! And I don't have to tell you, Cyril, that the plant itself was named after the French botanist, Pierre Magnol. What if they called a plant after me – *Gibsonia*? Wouldn't that have made poor Mummy and Daddy proud?"

He looks around until he finds a suitable little pot. With his favourite pruning knife, worn but still razor sharp, he moves confidently to a far corner of the greenhouse. Very gently and with a care born of genuine love, Stephen takes a cutting from a small but exquisite flowering plant.

"Hope you don't mind, Jessica. It's in a good cause and I know you'll be well-looked-after. And, by the way, Miss Nina Hughes invited me to have lunch with her. Nobody has ever… I *know*!"

On his way out, cradling the pot as others might a jewel or a tiny baby, he stops for a final word with his favourite, and perhaps appropriately named, 'Maiden's Blush'. "My eyes were closed, Rosie – I didn't even know I *was* alone." A vision of his uncle and Noreen flashes into his mind, but this time with slightly less shock and distaste. "But do you know something – I don't think I will ever be unknowingly alone again."

Stephen Gibson almost skips out of his greenhouse. He has totally forgotten to water his plants, which just goes to show you. Had you pointed this out to him, however, he would be pretty certain that his friends would forgive him.

This once.

SEVEN

Anyone here from the USA? ...Have a nice sodding day.

One of Uncle Geoffrey's favourite platitudes is 'a watched pot never boils'.

He has a string of them that he trots out at regular intervals, including 'there's nowt so queer as folk', which even his unworldly nephew fears may not be totally acceptable 'in this day and age'. In fact, his older relative's conversation, at least with Stephen, often consists of little else. Yet curiously this morning, as the familiar 'watched pot' expression plays on an insistent, noisy loop in his somewhat fevered mind, Stephen Gibson hears it in a female voice. It might be because right now the only voices he hears in that febrile space are female, particularly a certain ultra-feminine Welsh one, but part of him does wonder if it harks back to an earlier and far more nurturing time.

There are, however, no pots – at least none of the boiling variety – in his office or indeed anywhere in the entire Blooming Marvellous garden centre, save, perhaps, within the café's tiny kitchen, and even this is debatable. The words are actually roiling around his head this morning because he finds himself completely unable to desist from checking out every clock, timepiece and ornamental sundial that he can see. And he is beginning to wonder whether these very acts of relentless scrutiny are preventing noon from arriving at all.

Stephen does, of course, take a few moments off from his fervid time-checking for some vital preparatory work. Never one in the past to have been overly concerned about appearance, assuming a basic cleanliness and lack of noticeable dandruff to be quite sufficient, he now finds himself stealing furtive glances into every reflective surface, from watering cans to garden trowels to café spoons, in order to check out his presentability.

He surprises himself with this arguably vain activity yet is not totally dissatisfied with the result, despite the optical distortion. After all, he is reasonably tall, the acne has pretty much receded, without excessive scarring, and behind the thick glasses his eyes are a shade of brown you would be happy to find on a healthy chestnut. Whilst even he might admit that his clothes aren't the height of fashion, Oxfam had quite obviously cleaned and ironed them, and they wouldn't have been out there on the racks had they not previously been worn and enjoyed by someone, would they? Ergo, they are clearly wearable.

Stephen Gibson is equipped with no infallible nor indeed *any* barometer as to his level of attractiveness to the opposite sex. This has not, until now, been of primary or indeed of any importance. There was a brief encounter of a sexual nature when he was at college, but it was awkward and unsatisfactory, so he tries not to think about it. Stirrings are briskly dealt with, in order that he can get on with the more important things in life.

What Stephen does find most reassuring today, as he paces frenetically around the garden centre (because he finds it impossible to sit still in his office, despite having plenty of work to do) is to steal the odd look at Spike. He doesn't think he has ever known a man who is less physically prepossessing. The pint-sized Scot is not unlike, in his judgement, a stunted and possibly diseased tree in a forest, yet the guy doesn't appear to have much trouble in finding young women to impress. Admittedly they are mostly stupid, with an almost total ignorance of plant life – therefore hardly in Nina Hughes' league – but it's still a comforting thought.

Spike is quite aware that his colleague keeps staring at him.

"Got your bucket and spade, lover boy?" he asks finally, flashing a friendly if lopsided grin, as he passes with a set of collapsible garden chairs in his arms.

Stephen taps the duffel bag he is already carrying, although there is still some time until his assignation. The ancient bag is stocked to bursting point with equipment necessary to do the most professional job and quite a bit more stuff that he never actually uses but just might one day.

His colleague walks on, shaking his prematurely balding head and laughing to himself in a way that Stephen finds quite disconcerting. He puts it down to envy, which is the only way that Spike, whose work at Blooming Marvellous could hardly be deemed a vocation, might be considered green.

Stephen is on his way to the bathroom, to check his appearance and nose hairs just one more time, and to relieve his unusually temperamental bowels, when he is halted by a sudden, disturbing sound. It is like a succession of narrowly spaced explosions, building in volume and intensity, which seem to echo like gunshots around the centre. Inside and out.

Staff and customers freeze then spin around in alarm, as if there is an unspecified yet terrifying threat, of which they ought to be instantly aware. It is only when they realise that it is comfortingly – albeit excessively – human, that they return to whatever they were doing.

This auditory 'assault', however, has probably distracted Stephen more than most, because it has momentarily veered him off today's unusually specific trajectory. Which could be why, as he turns to confront the culprit, he makes no attempt to mask his anger.

The fact that the Wagnerian sneezer, for this is patently the source of the interruption, is a petite and red-eyed young woman in her mid-thirties, with a large, professional-looking camera around her neck and a small, rather curious-looking, rust-haired boy in tow, does not mitigate his fury in the least. She is not aided in this endeavour by addressing Stephen in a seriously nasal yet unquestionably transatlantic voice. Whilst the first element of this may, of course, be temporary, he somehow doubts the transient nature of the second.

"Hey, are you the top plant guy?" asks the interloper, between sneezes.

Stephen can't help noticing that her small, round face appears to have its own water feature, and he wishes with all his heart that he could switch it off. He decides that the best thing he can do is to turn away. Anyway, there are clocks to be watched.

"It's horticulturist, actually. Madam," he mutters, staring towards the entrance.

"Oh, excuse me!" snorts the young woman. She loosens her rather tight grip on the small boy's hand, in order to draw an already well-used handkerchief from her pocket. "Must be a linguistic thing," she mutters. "You say lift, we say elevator. You say horticulturist, we say pompous assho—"

"*Mum!*"

The young boy, whom Stephen takes in for the first time and judges to be aged about ten or eleven – although he is no expert and couldn't care less – is shaking his head. He notices that the boy is shuffling and seems unable to stand still. Stephen wonders if he needs the toilet and hopes that the child is not as wanton with bodily fluids as the parent whose behaviour he appears so anxious to moderate.

It is the boy's eyes that, for a moment, catch Stephen's attention. Or at least one of them, which is slightly but disconcertingly higher than the other. Not simply the pupil, but the whole eye itself. He finds himself wanting to ask their owner more about this, as he has never actually seen this on a face before, but he really doesn't have the time.

He does notice that both of these eyes, right now, are darting asymmetrically around the centre, as if the child is either desperately looking for something or has a psychological condition of some sort. Stephen has frequently overheard the expression 'on the spectrum' being muttered, as he has wandered past various employee conversations and, although he has been provided with no specific definition, he reckons that this might just be a case in point. There is something else about the boy, a quality that resonates within Stephen but which he can't quite specify and chooses not to examine, as he finds it strangely unsettling. (In a manner, interestingly, that the weird eye thing does not.)

"Okay," says the young woman, taking on board her child's admonishment and breathing deeply. "...And start again."

She hazards a smile, as she focuses her own increasingly reddening eyes on Stephen. He can't help observing that these same weepy eyes immediately crinkle up, as if attached on strings to the smile itself. It's quite disconcerting, watching them disappear into her face. So unlike the wide-open, green orbs of the young woman about to whisk him away. The sooner the better.

"We're lookin' for some plants." She sneezes loudly again and Stephen finds himself recoiling, as if from the blast.

"Wouldn't you be better off with some antibiotics?"

The woman sighs. "Oh, for fu... for Pete's sake! It's *you*! No offence. Well, it's this godawful place. Jesus, I hate greenery!"

This time the recoil is in Stephen's very heart and soul. It is as if someone has dashed into the Vatican and dissed Easter. Why does he find himself troubling to engage with this strange creature, when all he really wants is for her to take her curious offspring and phlegm and leave him alone? "How can you hate greenery? *Who hates greenery?* It's greenery who should hate us, after all we've done to it!"

"The plant's not for me – it's for him." The young woman points a soggy-tissued hand at her son. "He has a school project."

The boy rests some small, nail-bitten fingers on Stephen's arm, a gesture which surprises the older male and which he doesn't like one bit. But the grip is just too firm to shrug off, without possibly sending the lad flying into a nearby display or fountain. So he stands uncomfortably pestered, while the child with the strange yet mesmerising eyes, or at least one, explains.

"I want to take over the world. Using plants."

The boy stares up unblinkingly into Stephen's face, the less conventional eye appearing to ascend even higher into his head. Stephen Gibson has the strange sensation of his brain being invaded. Yet, against his better judgement, he finds himself oddly intrigued.

"That's not the project," grunts his mother, before sneezing violently again. Had the birdsong currently echoing around the centre actually represented real creatures, it would be like a scene from a Hitchcock movie by now, as they went berserk from the shock. "His class had a week of caring for things – hamsters, cactuses, cactusessii. We need to replace the cactus."

"And the hamster," adds the boy.

"So we owe the school a plant," continues the woman.

"And a hamster."

"This isn't a pet shop," snaps Stephen, realising that he hasn't examined the nearest clock for a while. To the woman's annoyance, he moves a few feet away from the irritating pair, so that he can check out the forecourt, just in case.

"I think it was a Black Lace Cactus," pipes a small voice.

Stephen turns sharply back to the boy. "But they're rather rare."

"Our teacher's wife smuggled it over. I think she's from Texas."

"What are the defining features?"

"She's very tanned and her teeth shine."

At this the young mother roars with laughter, spraying snot around the vicinity with reckless abandon. She grabs her son and gives him a sloppy cuddle tight with love. Stephen watches this display, as if observing animals at a zoo. It is clear to both mum and kid that the gawping man has absolutely no idea what they are laughing at.

The woman feels obliged to explain. "Not the wife, Nathan. The cactus! Joker!"

The boy Nathan looks at the bemused man. "It's cylindrical. Looks like a hedgehog."

"*Echinocereus.* It does actually come from the Greek word for hedgehog. Do you like plants?"

The boy thinks about this, then nods. "Mostly the dangerous ones. You know, that kill really badly."

"We showed him that TV show, *Day of the Triffids*," explains his mum. "Bit of a mistake."

"Yes, the film was far better. I saw it when I was a child," says Stephen. "My uncle has it in his DVD collection. Hated the ending. Poor Triffids."

"Yeah... heartbreaking," says the young woman. "So, horty-guy – can you help us?"

Before Stephen can respond, he hears the purposeful blast of a car horn from right outside the front entrance to the centre. Sidling away once more, he spies a smart and gleaming red sports car. Stephen has no idea of the make or model, as he has no interest in cars and can't actually drive. But he is far more clued up on the smart and gleaming driver, who is currently waving a summery arm to a happily staring Spike.

This is the woman for whom he has been waiting all of his life. Or certainly all of his morning.

"No, I can't help you," he replies, moving at some speed towards the door.

"Wow," says the woman. "Well, thanks. For the love."

Shaking her head, she grabs her confused son by the hand and makes for another, hopefully more obliging, assistant.

The final sound Stephen Gibson hears, before the automatic doors close, with him on the sunnier side, is a sneeze like a Ruislip volcano.

EIGHT

Spa hotels – what are all they about?

Nina Hughes has never really considered the etiquette that applies to being a front-seat passenger in an open-topped sports car. Yet she feels certain that staring wordlessly and apparently without blinking into the face of the driver most probably breaches a couple of the most commonly accepted rules.

It isn't that she feels particularly disconcerted. Happily, very little disconcerts Nina Hughes. She simply finds it rather bemusing. It seems almost as if this singular Mr Gibson is challenging her to break what, save for the thrum of a meticulously tuned-up engine and the constant roar of the M40 westbound, would pass as comfortable silence.

But what makes it even more curious is that she has actually attempted a few times, en route, to converse. With limited success.

"Don't talk much, do you?" she says, finally.

"Oh. I'm so sorry," he murmurs, then adds above the clamour, without diminishing the stare, "Should I be saying something, Miss Hughes?"

"It's okay, Stephen. There's no 'should'. And it's Nina."

"Like the *delphinium*."

"...Exactly." She waits, but nothing more is forthcoming. "Most of the men I meet never shut up. Bragging about their big car, their big expense account, their big..." She laughs. "... *you* know."

"Oh, well, I'm just average, I suppose. Except, of course," he adds, pointing a gloved hand, "down there, Nina." Now it's her turn to stare. "In the soil."

Nothing more is said until they arrive at their destination.

***

The outdoor pool at Magnolia International's soon-to-be-opened luxury hotel and spa, High Wycombe, is not yet filled with water. Which is no major disappointment to Stephen, as his swimming is no better than his driving.

Yet, as he examines the terrain around them, with the professionalism and expertise for which he is justly celebrated in Ruislip and beyond, he finds himself imagining how Nina Hughes might look, sitting exactly where she is now, elegantly cross-legged at a small wooden table, beside the empty kidney-shaped pool, were this same pool filled with water of a shimmering translucent blue. And a snugly fitting bathing costume filled with an equally scintillating Nina.

Stephen tries to sublimate these unexpected but hardly undesirable thoughts by staring beyond the young woman towards the splendidly multi-gabled and turreted, grey-stone Victorian mansion rising starkly out of its Chiltern landscape. This majestic yet still welcoming building has been newly refurbished by Magnolia and extended to accommodate some considerably less impressive, two-storey, off-white concrete blocks. These, with names like Magnolia Court and Garden House, are equipped with the cheaper, more basic rooms that make such properties viable and enable them to accommodate the functions and conferences, furtive liaisons and drunken behaviour that are the mainstay of the British hotel scene. The blocks appear to be in the final stages of construction, as is the state-of-the-art fitness centre attached.

On the table beside him are his pocket camera, some unrolled hotel plans and a plate of sandwiches as yet untouched by Stephen. But taking pride of place, right in the centre, covering the hole where the sun umbrella will go, is the small pot with the cutting that he has just presented to his client.

She had seemed utterly delighted – as indeed she should – which Stephen has taken as a most favourable omen. But, naturally, he must ground himself firmly into the purpose of his visit, which is to advise on the most appealing, durable and cost-effective selection of trees, flowers and shrubs. To add both congenial approaches and finishing touches to this, Magnolia's flagship hotel.

They have already explored the extensive grounds with serious, verging on anal, deliberation. Nina, who was starving, is hopeful that this late lunch, carefully prepared by the newly employed kitchen staff (in training back there in the mansion), will be the final element on the agenda.

"Quite dedicated, aren't you?" says Nina, munching ravenously on an excellent but stone-cold tuna and cheese melt ciabatta.

Stephen doesn't hear her. He is too busy sniffing the mound of earth he has assiduously trowelled up and poured into his upturned palm. As Nina is only now discovering, the senses of this horticulturist, at those times during which he is, literally, in his element, appear to contract like those of a preying animal in order that they might focus exclusively on the task in hand. Colleagues find this vaguely fascinating yet more often quite infuriating, especially when they want to close shop and have a life.

"*STEPHEN, LOOK OUT! DUTCH ELM DISEASE!*"

The man leaps up and spins around, like a Cossack dancer concluding his act. The soil spills from his hand. "What? *Where?!* I don't… elms?"

The delighted laughter tinkles in his newly alerted ears then swiftly fades as its originator takes note of the sombre face glaring back at her.

"Oh. I'm so sorry, Stephen," says Nina. "I was just trying to get your attention."

"You shouldn't joke about that, Miss Hughes. A lot of good trees died."

Nina tries to look contrite, but it's clearly a struggle. "I know. Mea culpa. Maxima. And I told you, it's Nina. I just thought we might, you know, chat." She feels him staring at her, as if she has just suggested they frolic naked in the nearest skip. "…As it is such a lovely day and I'm sure you'll agree this is a very special place. Or will be. Once you're done."

"Chat?" He rolls the word around like a lozenge. "Oh. Okay. Go ahead."

He looks at her expectantly, eyes behind the thick glasses squinting into the sun. She feels the conversational urge being drained out of her like a hotel swimming pool after a small child has thrown up.

"So. Have you finished inspecting my layout?"

"Yes. Thank you. With the soil samples, the plans and the photos, I've enough to work up a proper proposal. For the whole site."

"Great. Well, I'm impressed. Let's just hope the guys above me are too. Shall I drop you back now? Unless you want to be alone?"

Stephen Gibson's reaction to this last – and, to Nina, quite innocuous – suggestion takes the smiling executive by surprise. It isn't that she has shocked him in some unanticipated way. At least not in so far as she can judge. Rather that she appears to have touched something deep inside his soul, a sadness that clouds his face in a way she finds quite disconcerting and not at all on the day's agenda.

"Alone? *No!*" He stands up swiftly and restores his gardening tools to their snug compartments, inside his specially modified bag, like a visiting doctor completing his examination. His hands appear to be trembling. "...Miss... Nina... Hughes. Would you... would you go out?"

"Out? Out where? I am out."

He shakes his head. Is this woman dim or something? "No. *Out.* With me!" He realises that she is just staring at him, those dazzling green eyes alert, that set of immaculately white teeth now revealed behind sumptuously red lips, which are swiftly parting in what appears very much like stupefaction. "Just to eat! Somewhere. A meal. Not... you know. Well, not initially. You and I. Me. Us."

Had anyone else made such an invitation at this point, in the early stages of a still-tentative business relationship, in which tender is more usually a bargaining tool, Nina Hughes might find herself bristling and explain kindly but firmly that this was totally out of order. Yet she finds that the palpable and almost painful innocence embedding the proposal – and indeed defining the trembling offerer himself – impels her towards a far more gentle course.

"I'll be honest, Stephen," she says softly, although there is no-one else in earshot. "I've just come out of a relationship." She smiles warmly, trying really hard not to upset him, whilst pedalling back to the real world as swiftly as possible. "Can we maybe take a tiny rain check – give it, let's say, a couple of months?"

She taps his hand with genuine affection and picks up her new plant. Job smoothly done. With an economy of movement that leaves him breathless, she rises and makes her confident way towards the currently shrubless hotel forecourt, where her car is parked.

Stephen Gibson removes a small pocket diary from his bag and a pencil from his pocket. He flicks through an abundance of blank pages then pauses. Licking the pencil, he begins to write in a neat and careful hand.

"July the 28th it is."

All in all, it has been a most successful afternoon.

NINE

And where are you from, love?
...Do you wanna phone a friend?

The powerful military field-glasses are glued to her eyes.

Mrs Dave observes her protégé from her darkened glass office, at the far side of her empire, as he struggles, trusty bag on his shoulder, out of the low-slung sports car.

His exit appears to be hampered by a contorted insistence on not ever, even for a nanosecond, withdrawing his gaze from the face of his driver. The binoculared watcher tries to ascertain if this latest client (the most potentially lucrative in some bloody time) is looking gratefully appreciative or like someone who has been blitzed with so much plant-talk that she has lost the will to live. This is always a genuine possibility and Mrs Dave occasionally has to intervene with some nifty damage limitation.

Fortunately, disaster appears to have been averted and she can return to her mysterious ledgers, which she brings out in the morning and locks up in her safe every night. The staff have a strong suspicion that she has a profitable sideline of some sort, one which may involve blackmail or vast shipments of drugs from the Indian subcontinent, but, in Spike's opinion, they haven't the slightest seed of evidence for these irrational, possibly even bigoted slurs and she may simply be composing poison-pen letters to send to members of her extended family.

So, of course, she fails to notice Spike offloading a massive bag of compost onto its elderly purchaser, so that he can more easily wave to lovely Nina as she drives smartly away. The young woman's elegant, crimson-nailed hand floating in the sultry Ruislip air tells him that his effort is not unrewarded. With some reluctance, he returns to his crumpling customer and helps her shed her load into the boot of her tiny car before she expires. Finally, he turns to Stephen and catches him just as the automatic doors slowly open.

"Stephen? ...*Hello?*" He moves towards him. "Layout okay, was it?"

Stephen Gibson offers his colleague a rarely summoned and most unexpected beam. "Oh yes, Spike," he enthuses, as he strolls like a contented boulevardier back down the main aisle of the busy garden centre. "Ms Nina Hughes and I will be going out. For supper. To start with."

Spike is at his side with a speed rarely exhibited in his normal workday. "What – *you and her?* That lady? And *you*?"

Stephen gently strokes a succulent mother-in-law's tongue, which a short, middle-aged man is bearing somewhat tentatively towards the cash desk. "Bye bye, *Sansevieria*," he tells the departing plant. "They like a lot of light but not too much dampness." The man just nods behind his leaves, but Stephen is not certain that he really cares.

"Yes, Spike," he explains. "In *exactly* two months' time. I wrote the date down, although I really don't believe I shall forget."

"She blew you off."

Stephen stares at his colleague in shock. Surely the man can't mean what he thinks he means. Not on the first date.

"You wish! I meant she let you down easy, Stevie. Two months is like code for never. As in she is *never* gonna go out with you."

At first, Stephen simply shakes his head, dismissing the smaller man's total lack of faith and comprehension. Yet, as Spike continues to look up at him with something approaching sympathy, he feels the first doubtful prodding. But still his head keeps on shaking.

"Nina wouldn't lie, Spike. We have a date. She..."

To his and Spike's astonishment, Stephen suddenly begins to hyperventilate. As this has never happened to him before, he believes that his final breaths are being expelled, albeit not very successfully, and that he might be dying. When one of his plants is sick, he knows exactly what to do. Sadly, this expertise does not extend to humans, so, quite helpless and imploring, he has to look to his sceptical colleague.

Spike, who has even less idea what to do and wishes to God he had never started this, looks around wildly for something. He is not sure exactly what, but he feels pretty confident that paper bags come into it somewhere. Fortunately, he spies a large brown one on the floor under a display unit. He immediately grabs it and thrusts it over Stephen's mouth and nose. "Breathe into this," he urges with some certitude, then adds, "Or out – or both."

Stephen does as he is told and quite soon is vomiting his immaculately prepared Magnolia Spa lunch and possibly most of his breakfast into the bag. Spike is not certain whether this counts as a result or a complication, until a credible explanation occurs.

"Oh, sorry pal. Fertiliser. *Shit!*"

He pats the still vomiting horticulturist, who by this time is drawing a small crowd, rather hard on the back, which doesn't really help that much.

"What you need is a drink," prescribes the Scot, with something finally approaching confidence.

***

Stephen's hand is still shaking, as it holds the large whisky to which Spike has reluctantly treated him.

The pub, into whose embrace the smaller and less nauseous man has solicitously delivered his shattered colleague, is distinguished only by its total lack of those features which can make a neighbourhood hostelry welcoming, cosy, communal or in any way appealing. It is unremittingly rectangular, nook-free and lit like an airport runway. Fruit machines appear to dominate and there isn't a horse brass, rusting Victorian plough or collection of cracked earthenware pharmaceutical containers in sight. It does, however, have a bar, some tables and serves alcohol, so even at 5.35 on this balmy weekday evening – still some time before happy hour – it is doing a reasonable trade.

Despite his earlier, hapless ministry and the compelling nature of his current mercy mission, Spike finds his attention wandering to a small table some feet from the bar. A bar against which he and –more heavily and despondently – his charge are leaning.

Two young women are deep into conversation and, simultaneously, their phone screens. Yet they are not so totally absorbed that their flickering eyes don't occasionally scour the terrain or check the doors to see who else may venture in. It becomes increasingly apparent from their accents, the volume of which is accentuated in the cavernous room, that they are not themselves 'Slippers', as denizens of Ruislip are locally known.

They have only just locked onto Spike's personal vibrations, when a plaintive yelp from beside him echoes around the bar.

"*She recognised Ley's Whitebeam!*"

"Who the fuck are they?" asks Spike, sending a futile, he's-not-really-with-me shrug into the beery air. "Are they a band? No, of course they're not. Och, Stephen, I didn't know you were even interested in women." He senses Stephen staring at him, even though his attention is not fully on the bewildered young man. "I mean, you've never once… I thought you were…" He leaves the thought unfinished.

"What… gay?"

"No. Gay people have sex. I thought you'd been… well… pruned or something."

"*Pruned?*"

Spike realises that if this isn't exactly the whisky talking, it is certainly making whatever rubbish Stephen Gibson has to say even more strident than usual. He makes a lowering gesture with his hand, which seems to work. Although he can tell that sadness is playing its part.

"What am I going to do, Spike? I'm twenty-seven years old, shiny, erect, with strong, healthy roots. But I have yet to go on a second date." Spike downs his beer and signals for a refill. Stephen can buy his own whisky. "And this lady," continues Stephen, "I really think that she is the one."

The Scotsman lays his hand gently on his colleague's arm. "Aren't you running afore ye can walk, pal?" Stephen stares at him in confusion. "She's gorgeous, Stephen."

"*You* get gorgeous," protests Stephen. "And look at you."

Spike pauses for a moment. "…Aye. Fair enough."

As his disconsolate colleague continues to stare at him, Spike appears to come to some sort of conclusion. Stephen Gibson has no idea that what the smiling Scot is about to say will change his life and world forever. Which is probably just as well. "Then I reckon you have got to work on your technique."

"What do you mean—"

"Watch and learn."

Spike moves across to the two young women at the table, angling his body to provide Stephen with the optimum view. He also makes sure to raise his voice, so that the pupil can appreciate the full artistry of this, his introductory lesson.

"Hi, ladies!" says Spike. And even though Stephen can't quite catch the full beam of his mentor's off-white smile, he knows that the two young women are directly in its crosshairs. They look up and already their reactions to this intruder, whilst wary, are far from unfriendly. "Really sorry to interrupt. I was just wondering, you know, where you girls were from."

"We're from Sheffield," says one.

"I'm sorry," responds Spike.

The other young woman shakes her head and raises her voice. "*SHEFFIELD!*"

"Don't worry, I heard," says Spike. "I'm just sorry."

At first the girls look shocked but then begin to roar with laughter.

Spike moves back to an equally stunned Stephen, with a satisfied smile on his face and a palms-outstretched, quod erat demonstrandum posture that says everything words alone might not.

"What... what did...?" burbles Stephen, who can't take his eyes away from the young women. They are still looking amiably at Spike and chuckling, whilst possibly wondering why he has returned to his nerdy-looking friend midway into a potentially fruitful chat-up.

"A sprinkling of the funny and lassies forget what I look like. I'm not one for science, Stephen, but I think it's your wee endorphin guys that release and all they know is that talking to me makes them feel good. And then, my dear man, old Spikie proceeds from GCSE to degree level."

"And that's all you need to do?" Stephen is throwing Spike the look Einstein might have received, when he chucked $E=mc^2$ onto the table.

"GSOH!" explains his friend.

"Gussoh," says Stephen, attempting to get his tongue around this mysterious new word that his cocky colleague has just, for reasons unknown, spelled out for him. "What is it – this gussoh?"

"It's a fucking abbreviation! Jeez! GSOH! *Great Sense of Humour.* Or maybe *Good* Sense of Humour will do at a pinch. In fact, any sodding…" He pauses to watch Stephen roll the individual letters slowly around in his mouth, like a TV cookery-contest judge, until their full, underlying flavour can sing through. "All you need in this life, pal. All you need. GSOH. *Gussoh!* Don't believe me, go check the web."

Spike notices that one of the young women is glancing over at him, while the other one is smiling. "I shall leave you to your own devices. Which I assume you've brought with you." No reaction, not that he was expecting one. He nods in the direction of the young women again. "Unless you fancy your chances…?"

Stephen shakes his head. He wouldn't 'fancy' these at the best of times, and this certainly isn't one of them. Anyway, he's taken, isn't he? Or at least his heart is. As he watches the nimble Spike capitalise on his opening gambit with something equally mirth-provoking, he sips his second-ever Scotch, which he enjoys no more than its predecessor, and does some serious thinking.

The new threesome barely notices when the skinny guy at the bar suddenly slams down his empty glass and heads determinedly, if a little erratically, out of the door and into the Ruislip night.

TEN

Ever had one of those 'Eureka!' moments? You, sir, when you first realised this wasn't your flower-arranging class?

If plants really could hear what is going on around them – and there are those who swear that a flower can register the buzz of bees with scientifically measurable enthusiasm – Stephen's dearest mates would be rendered tense and sleepless by the constant, almost maniacal tapping at both keyboard and calculator on this momentous night.

Of course, if they could also read, they might have a slightly better idea as to exactly what consumes their adoring master in his moonlit greenhouse, almost to the point of frenzy. But even then it would take a pretty bright specimen to make sense of the rabid bombardment of personal ads popping up second by second, minute by minute, hour by hour on the flashing screen.

Yet perhaps they might just take on board, if only in the broadest strokes, the confused shaking of their master's head, as a new but horribly self-evident truth resonates in his disbelieving brain.

"Why does *nobody* love plants?" he moans to a previously sleeping citrus geranium.

Naturally, this isn't true. Stephen Gibson, Master of Horticulture, has incontrovertible evidence, born of years of experience, that a vast chunk of humanity absolutely worships plants. They just don't regard this affinity as the sine qua non for a suitable mate.

Finally, at about 3.30 in the morning, Stephen slams shut his laptop and gives himself a stern but encouraging pep talk. "Well, it can't be that hard, can it, Harry? Not really. Not for someone who's twice memorised *Archibald's Planta—*"

A voice that is by now quite familiar interrupts him. "You know, sometimes *I'd* talk to my plants and I could swear they'd talk back to me."

He doesn't bother turning round to Noreen – he can see her reflection all too vividly in the greenhouse glass. "Plants can't talk," he informs her. He now feels obliged to reassure his friends. "Doesn't mean you're stupid."

The nephew and the – whatever she is – share the darkened space awkwardly, neither of them exactly certain how to take the conversation forward nor convinced that they fully wish to. Finally, Stephen turns to look at her. She appears to be fully made-up, despite the hour, and is wearing a gleaming red nightie that looks like it was designed for a far smaller person. Stephen can't imagine that it's particularly comfortable but also senses that his uncle may not be over-concerned about his partner's comfort. She also reminds him of a massive Guatemalan firecracker plant.

"*Am I interrupting something, night larks?*"

Noreen sighs into Uncle Geoffrey's reflection as it closes in. She appears hugely unimpressed with the apparition to which Stephen has grown accustomed over the years. The older man is wearing frayed and greying long johns, which he must have picked up at some sort of house clearance and felt were far too precious to be resold.

"Coming to bed, heart?" he says, tapping her gently on a substantial, bare shoulder that seems to glow in the moonlight. "It's the middle of the night."

She turns to look him slowly up and down. "And you wonder why it took you so long to meet someone."

"These are vintage," he protests, which doesn't help his case enormously. "And maybe the right someone just hadn't come along." At this she snuggles into his neck, which involves her squatting slightly because of the height difference and offering Stephen a glimpse of fulsome breast he really doesn't need right now.

Yet he finds himself wondering if Noreen herself had been seduced and conquered by this same in-demand quality – the one that has been promoting itself from his computer screen like a relentlessly drummed tattoo. *Must have GSOH… GSOH a prerequisite. No GSOH no chance. GSOH! …GSOH! …GSOH squared!* Only one way to find out.

"Noreen," he asks, "where are you from?"

"Me, love? Originally? Didsbury."

"Oh, that's a shame," he responds, then notices the look of surprise on her face. "No. I mean… I'm sorry for you." If anything, the look amplifies. "You're meant to say Sheffield!" he insists. "Er… no. As you were. Just louder." This is very tiresome.

"What's Sheffield got to do with it?" asks his Uncle Geoffrey.

"I heard her," says Stephen. "I'm just very sorry."

"Well, so you should be," says the older and by now quite irascible man. He draws Noreen gently away, rolling his eyes and leaving his curious ward to whatever the hell he is up to. Although why the poor boy needs a laptop and a calculator at 3.30 in the morning is anyone's guess.

***

"*YOU'RE RIGHT!*"

Spike drops the heavy sacks of compost he has been unenthusiastically shifting and sends an almighty *Jesus!* into the scented air.

"*Och Stephen!*" he admonishes, although the damage is done. Stephen helps him to reload the bags onto a trolley, but he is far too wired to be of much assistance.

"GSOH!" he persists. "Good sense of thingy. You were absolutely *right*, Spike. It's what nearly everyone wants!"

"Every one of who?"

"Of *whom*. Ten thousand four hundred and sixty-two online profiles. On dating sites. I didn't check all of them, obviously, but somebody has kindly done some research. Exactly 94.6 per cent put 'good' or possibly even '*great* sense of humour' as a priority. GSOH! Ninety-four point six! Per cent!"

Spike nods his head towards the trolley and Stephen dutifully begins to push. Neither of them can see Mrs Dave, yet they feel certain that she is sitting in her lair, checking for on-floor deviation via the security cameras. But for Stephen – and he never dreamed that he would ever contemplate such a heresy – this percentage thing is far more important even than his gardeners' question time.

"Hang on," says Spike, as a thought strikes him. "What about the other 5.4 per cent?"

"Not sure. I think equipment was involved," says Stephen, still pushing. "Spike, I don't have it!"

"You can *buy* equipment. I can even loan you…" He shakes his head. "Oh, you mean – what we're talking about. Gussoh."

Stephen looks utterly despondent, which is rather a new look for him and not one that his colleague feels will greatly boost the young man's fortunes in pursuit of love. "I don't make people laugh," he moans.

"Aye, you do, Stephen," protests his mentor. "Just not intentionally."

They realise that there is a rather smart, middle-aged woman hovering uneasily beside them, with one hand vaguely pointing downwards, eager for assistance but unwilling to intrude on what appears to be a private conversation. Spike reluctantly decides to put her out of her misery, by turning on the charm.

"Yes, my dear?"

"Er, thank you. This stuff, on your trolley, is it any good?"

"*Any good?*" exclaims Spike. "It's like Viagra for plants. Ask my man here. It'll turn a sprout into a palm tree!"

Ignoring the puzzlement on the other man's face, the woman processes Spike's words then offers an ear-shattering hoot into the air that makes other customers glad they've never sat with her at a comedy show or, indeed, at anything. She's still chortling as she lugs one of the huge bags, like a stag she has just shot, to the check-out.

Stephen is still staring when she is half-way to her car, a journey on which Spike should by rights have been assisting. "That was *funny*?" He shakes his head in bewilderment. "It made no botanical sense."

"Don't worry about it, Stevie."

"No. You're right, Spike. I have to focus. And it's Stephen." He thumps one of the compost bags really hard in a show of determination and even the immediate pain searing his arm doesn't deter him. "All I need to do is get amusing by July 28th. Which might well be a bank holiday. Even better!"

"Could make all the difference."

"*Exactly!* As they say, I shall knock Ms Nina Hughes' socks – no, she probably doesn't wear socks, except maybe on… stockings off with my GSOH. It's just a skill, isn't it, Spike, like any other? Not anticipating too many problems. Not for someone who twice memorised *Arch—*"

"Oh, fucking spare me!" Spike shakes his head, as Stephen falls silent. Yet now, to his surprise, as he takes in the almost comically determined set of his colleague's jaw, which is about the only comical thing about him, he finds his heart going out to this helpless, deluded creature. "Okay, Stephen, tell you what…"

But this vital 'what', on the very cusp of being imparted, is immediately swallowed back and put on hold, as they both notice, with equal dread, the small yet potent force that is Mrs Dave bearing down on them like a dangerous squall.

She smacks Stephen maternally around the back of his head. "Too much chit-chat. I pay you to be lonely, sad bloody genius. I pay you to be working night and day on a brilliant Magnolia proposal."

"I was just—" partially explains Stephen.

"I don't pay you to just," says Mrs Dave. "Go to your room."

Stephen slumps dutifully off. Yet he has barely closed the door of his office and is still mired in insubordinate thought, when he hears a text coming through on his phone. Which perturbs him even more, as he rarely receives texts from anyone.

It reads: *Had an idea. Meet me after work.* This is followed by a curious graphic of a yellow, round-faced man laughing (or crying with a smile). Stephen glances out of the window into the nursery, where he sees Spike nodding in his direction, as he taps the side of his nose mysteriously with a grubby finger.

No-one has ever asked Stephen Gibson to meet him after work. Or tapped their nose mysteriously in his direction.

This is turning out to be a most peculiar week.

ELEVEN

I see we've got the usual crowd of no-hopers in tonight. Welcome to my world.

The room is above an old Tudor pub, just a few miles from where Stephen Gibson lives. Yet he has never visited this room, as he has never ventured inside this pub. In truth, he hadn't even been aware that pubs came with rooms above them – or at least ones that weren't equipped with beds or sofas or TVs.

This room, which still has the traditional oak beams (circa 1540), appears to run the length of the historic building. It has a less traditional and fairly rudimentary bar, beside which are several small, wooden tables (circa 2003) and an assortment of mismatched chairs. The people at the tables, mostly young, sit with drinks of every description, but almost uniformly alcoholic. Empty glasses are setting down and mounting up with every second that passes.

The drinkers, a fairly even split of men and women, some in couples, others in groups, are packed together quite snugly. They all face the same way, towards a makeshift stage, professionally lit for maximum visibility and effect, whilst the rest of the room buzzes in the semi-darkness. These patrons don't appear to mind the crowding, as they are all laughing their heads off at a dishevelled-looking man in his forties with the belly of a darts champion and a belligerent yet simultaneously self-deprecating manner. Even his straggly beard, into which a microphone is poking, appears angry.

Stephen, who stands at the back of the dusty, low-ceilinged room with a contentedly chortling Spike, is absolutely fascinated. Aside from the total absence of plants, which of course enhance any venue and about which he may advise the owners in due course, he cannot fault the atmosphere. People appear to be having the most wonderful time.

Except, of course, him.

He realises that he hasn't been dragged along here to enjoy himself. Or, if he has, it isn't working. Once he had begun to understand exactly where Spike has brought him – and, admittedly, it took a while, as he hadn't known that such places even existed – Stephen reasoned that this was to be treated purely as a research trip. The first, he feels certain, of many.

This is why he is clutching one of his trusty spiral notepads and freshly sharpened HB pencil, equipment he always carries on his person, jotting things down as and when the occasion demands. Which it does fairly constantly, in that he is attempting to record what makes reasonably intelligent or at least normal, functioning people laugh. It appears, from this evening's exercise, that absolutely everything does. Especially when alcohol is involved.

Admittedly, this current gentleman is engendering a better response than his predecessors, whom Stephen has understood, from the *aficionado* beside him, were fairly new to the 'circuit' and still honing their skills. So, of course, Stephen's pencil is covering even more ground this final set and the pages on his wire-bound notepad are flying.

Yet to his alarm, the student is discovering that, despite his exceptional brain, he can't quite keep up with the narrative thread. These comedians appear to be changing their subject matter simply according to how the mood takes them, although Spike has whispered to him that such seeming spontaneity is all very carefully rehearsed. But one minute they are rattling on about unruly passengers on airplanes then the next minute it's how to vomit after a dodgy curry, without the lady you're trying to impress even noticing. And then it's politics and veganism, personal hygiene or growing up Muslim in Golders Green. Or someone might pick on a member of the audience parked recklessly right at the front of the room and do a few apparently hysterical minutes on whom they've turned up with or what they do for a living.

The more the comedian insults them, the more the victim and everyone else in the place appear to fall about. It feels like the bases for human social interaction over millennia are being turned completely on their head.

Stephen finds it very confusing.

He is also rather shocked at the amount of bad language on display, especially with ladies present. Practically every other word is the f-word. And the same goes for the explicit and frequent sexual references, some relating to practises he has never heard of and can't seriously imagine being that pleasurable, even when drunk. But what surprises him most is how enormously these present ladies appear to be enjoying themselves. The absence of maidenly blushes is palpable, any reddening of faces being relatable solely to the amount of alcohol consumed. Or possibly hormones.

Stephen Gibson is not unaware that he has lived a somewhat sheltered life. But right this minute it seems as if he has just arrived from another, more genteel planet or been raised entirely by monks. He even feels, checking out the man lit up on the stage, as if he has arrived here hugely overdressed, clad as he is in his best tweed jacket, smart, Windsor-knotted RHS tie and neatly pressed cavalry twill pants. The person they're all laughing at looks like he has rummaged in his laundry basket and crawled into whatever was at the very bottom. And judging by the way his milky stomach is bulging out from beneath a fading T-shirt, at least one item of clothing has most probably shrunk over countless previous washes. Stephen is surprised that whoever looks after the man has let him go out like this.

"Stop scribbling for a second, would you?" whispers Spike. "Just soak it up."

"I'll try, Spike," says Stephen. Still scribbling.

The man on the stage, who is apparently called Tyler something (unless this is, in fact, what he does for a living) is expounding on the difference between men and women and more specifically about his girlfriend. Stephen finds that he is having trouble working out whether what the man is saying is actually a true story, which just happens to be something people find funny, or whether in truth he is lying about his relationship purely in order to make his audience laugh. He doesn't believe his fellow audience members are having any difficulty with this distinction. Or that they even care.

"Take the other night," says the man, in an accent which is not local and which Stephen reckons could be from somewhere up north, "me girlfriend says to me, all cross and hurt, like, that if a guy really likes a woman, you know, has genuine feelings, sexual feelings included, he should just bloody express them. He shouldn't keep his emotions, as they say, under a rock. But when I do exactly what she says, she stops fuckin' speaking to me! … Stops speaking to her sister as well."

To Stephen's bemusement, the audience roar at this. Despite Spike's instructions, he decides to transcribe this last joke, if indeed it was a joke, onto a fresh sheet of paper, whilst he can still remember it, the better to dissect it in the privacy of his bedroom or, better still, greenhouse and work out exactly why it is having the effect on people that it patently has. Especially on some of the younger ladies, who are gleefully nudging their pals or partners and nodding their heads.

Once done, he stares intently at this Tyler, who – to his surprise – appears to be staring with equal intensity back at him. Stephen finds this a bit disconcerting, so he decides to concentrate his attention on an as yet unsullied page in his spiral notebook.

"But I do love smart women," continues Tyler, although curiously Stephen thinks he can still feel the stare, as he writes. "Cos you're full of surprises. I dated a brilliant PhD in quantum physics" – which Stephen somehow doubts – "and one night she turned to me and said, 'Tyler, it's not enough for our bodies to meet. For a lasting relationship I need our minds to meet as well.' So I spent a whole week telling her how much I rated the theory of relativity. And it worked only too well – she went off with my brother." He even grins to himself at this. "See the synergy there? I always enjoy Ruislip audiences. You're so… handy. That's my time. I'm Tyler Watts. Goodnight!"

If the previous joke – or whatever it was that Stephen has written down – went way over his head, this closing remark was practically stratospheric. He assumes there is indeed some synergy between one story involving a sister and another a brother, but not one that bears close examination. Stephen wonders for a moment whether this whole exercise might actually prove far more complex than originally thought and if Venn diagrams would really help that much. But he mutters *Archibald* to himself several times and immediately feels a whole lot better.

"Well, watcha think of that?" asks Spike, draining his second pint.

Stephen, who is sipping a small lime and soda, pauses his horticultural mantra and nods. "Fascinating," he says, quite genuinely.

"But did you think he was funny, Mr Spock?"

"Who?" Stephen ponders for a moment. "He must have been. Everyone laughed."

"Except you."

Before he can address this, although an appropriate response doesn't spring readily to mind, a hand grabs Stephen firmly by the shoulder, painfully pressing what little flesh he has there right up against his collarbone.

"*Hoy, tosspot, what's with the fucking notes?*"

Both men turn to the newcomer, who has made his way round the side of the room without them noticing. Tyler Watts isn't looking particularly funny right now.

Realising that flattery might be his colleague's only salvation, Spike gives the comedian a hearty thumbs-up. "Great show, Tyler. Mind, I saw you before, when you were in—"

"Fashion?"

"Edinburgh," says Spike swiftly, sensing treacherous ground. "When I was back up there, you know, seeing my folks."

The larger man grunts, then turns back to Stephen, who is staring unashamedly at the comic, as if he is a rare specimen that he finds utterly fascinating but annoyingly hasn't as yet fully been able to categorise.

"So, you sneaky streak of bespectacled tweedy piss, what's with the pencil?" His voice becomes calmer. "Tell me, I'd really like to know."

Stephen warms to the sudden softening in the man's attitude. For a moment there, he had felt a tad intimidated. "Well," he responds, "I've rarely seen such a fine example of a subpar species compensating for its extensive shortcomings, in the interest of survival and even propagation."

He doesn't even see the hand before it wraps itself around his Adam's apple.

"Are you saying that us ugly, fat lads, we got to make the ladies laugh to get laid?"

Stephen is unaware of Spike's head shaking out one of his warnings, as he is too busy with his own head, nodding it in agreement with his assailant's assessment of the situation. Whilst trying not to die. Finally, the man lets him have his windpipe back.

"*Yes!*" croaks Stephen, delighted that he and this seriously unprepossessing person are finally on the same wavelength, yet disconcerted by the unwarranted bouts of aggression, which can only have been fuelled by drink. "*Just look at Spike here!* ... Well, he's not fat." He shows the man his spiral notebook. "So, I wrote it down. For further research. Not that I'm ugly *or* fat," he points out, helpfully.

While Spike waits patiently for the earth to swallow him – or, preferably, both of them – Tyler Watts wrenches the notepad away from Stephen, most probably hoping that a stray piece of wire will rip open a major artery.

"What are you, then – one of those open-spot knobs who goes around nicking other comics' material?"

"Actually, I'm a horticulturist."

"Actually, you're a shouty, joke-stealing twat. In a tie."

To further emphasise the point, Tyler rips out the pages, waves them dangerously close to Stephen's astonished mouth, then, to the surprise of onlookers, shoves them into his own mouth and begins to chew.

"Now you know how I got so fucking fat! Catch you copying my act again, petal, I'll ram those dodgy teeth of yours so far down your thieving throat, you'll need to stick a scrubbing brush up your arse to clean them... You can write that down, if you like."

Stephen turns immediately turns to a fresh sheet. "Not sure exactly when I could slip it into conversation, but—"

Spike grabs Stephen and pulls him away, before he is dealt a possibly fatal blow. "Time to go, fun-boy."

The Scot gives a final apologetic shrug to the bemused comic, who looks, perhaps for the first time in a good while, if not in his entire existence, lost for words.

As Spike leads his rattled but still fascinated pupil away from the club, they pass a green felt bulletin board right outside the gents' toilet. Pinned to one corner is a faded, shabby poster, with a graphic of a microphone standing proud in a bed of fallen chains. It is promoting 'The Killer Comedy Academy', with a strapline that proclaims: *Unlock Your Comic Potential!* Beneath this, in smaller type, are details as to the when and where of the next free introductory session.

"*Wait!*" says Stephen. Reaching into his bag, he removes his camera. Spike is too busy fitting into a corner and hoping that no-one around knows him to watch exactly what his protégé is doing.

As the flash goes off, a different flash happens in Stephen's brain. It is a fleeting but powerful image of Ms Nina Hughes, client and inamorata, laughing like a drain.

TWELVE

They laughed when I said I wanted to be a comedian.
Well, they're not laughing now.
(Bob Monkhouse)

The Killer Comedy Academy is not, as Stephen Gibson – or anyone else whose links to the real world are as fragile as a Ming flowerpot – might assume, an imposing edifice with floor after floor of sun-lit classrooms, all resonating to the sounds of humour-slanted pedagogy and unalloyed mirth.

But Stephen is still to discover this, as he sits in his Blooming Marvellous office, staring vacantly into his precious nursery, although this is not his designated staring-time. Yet again he is unable to concentrate on anything for more than five seconds at a time. Even when it is the very proposal that he is supposed to be developing for the person he wishes most to impress.

He had decided to spend some fruitful hours earlier this week researching humour via Google, so at least he now has, on the eve of his free introductory session, a working definition and the realisation that the Americans spell it without a 'u'. But beyond this, the subject has appeared far too diffuse yet at the same time oddly weighty, and he is sufficiently wise to know that he needs solid, professional guidance into this brave new world.

Stephen reasons quite astutely that this isn't like horticulture, to which he clearly has a genetic disposition and a background, however sadly truncated, of informed discussion and enthusiasm. Had he been raised, say, in a family of clowns, he would be laughing.

He tries not to think that a facility he is being obliged to develop from scratch is one that appears to come quite naturally to people of far less intelligence than himself. I mean, look at Spike, he muses. The man is lazy, uneducated, far from handsome and lacking the tiniest endosperm of ambition, yet Stephen can see him now, just outside his window, making an outwardly dissimilar female totally crack up.

In its own way, however, this is quite reassuring. How hard can it be, Stephen Gibson tells himself for the thousandth time. Especially as he is about to enrol in an academy.

And everyone knows how good *they* are.

***

Stephen can hear his stomach rumbling, as he wheels his ageing bicycle (itself an unsellable Uncle Geoffrey find) down the small, relatively undistinguished suburban street, on this equally bland weekday evening. Fortuitously, it is just a couple of miles from his own home.

He knows that he should have taken some supper and put a vital lining on his gut, but he couldn't have tolerated sitting and conversing with his uncle and Noreen, who appear no less besotted with each other than when the bewildering interloper from Oldham via Didsbury first arrived. (And shows no apparent sign of going, as most of her belongings have now joined her in the already overloaded house.)

The weirdly happy couple did still manage to fire questions at him, as to where on earth he was going at this time of night, which he knew they would, although it was only seven o'clock and perfectly light outside. Stephen is fully aware that he rarely forays further than his greenhouse or the garden. He does, however, spend a considerable amount of time in an international horticulturist chatroom, which he rather enjoys. But they can survive without his genius for a few short hours, especially as the current topic is *rhododendra americana* and he is so over that.

As he checks the address one more time, because he can't actually spot a single building on this entire road matching his image of an academic institution, he realises that it isn't only his stomach whose existence is making itself known to him. His heart is saying a big hello too and greeting him in a disturbingly percussive way. He really hopes that this will desist before he arrives at his comical destination.

If he ever does.

Finally, on a corner, he discovers a small and rather run-down, even by Stephen's standards, white stucco, 1930's semi, identical to so many of its fellows, save for a shockingly overgrown hedge and two brightly painted garden gnomes in amorous congress under the front bay window. He checks the number on the flaking blue door. This has to be the place. He doesn't want to admit to himself, at this early stage, that he is a little disappointed, because he knows well enough from the plant world that first impressions can be deceiving. Just look at the Western Skunk Cabbage.

Stephen Gibson parks his bike against the criminally ill-maintained, semi-evergreen privet. Before he can knock on the door, it swings open of its own accord, to reveal a dimly lit hallway not dissimilar to his own, save that in his uncle's house you can barely move for junk, whilst this hallway is almost totally bare. So not really that similar, he reasons, save for the vague sense of foreboding and a matching lack of interest in interior design.

"Hello…?" he says, quietly, his heart still pounding. He realises that it is not so much the nature of the course that is inducing this unaccustomed sense of panic, as his specific motive in attending. And, of course, the ultimate reward, which he feels certain is almost within his grasp. Only maybe, he worries, not quite as almost as it was. Which could be why his heart won't stop pounding.

"*Hello...?*" he repeats.

He is about to turn around and leave, or at least the thought has entered his mind, when he hears a reedy, male voice cry, "*In here!*" Stephen pushes open what he hopes is the right door.

The room into which he steps makes the hallway seem festive.

Admittedly, there is greater evidence of humanity here, but curiously the lumpy, mismatched furniture and a small row of unrelated plastic chairs render the sparsely lit room even more spartan. The only decoration comes from a sub-IKEA mirror and a set of neatly mounted, monochrome photographs on the walls.

The images are of performers, mostly male, caught standing on what look like small platforms, in varying manifestations, or perhaps even degrees, of agony. Occasionally they are captured interacting with a nearby and clearly hostile member of the audience, which only appears to add to the torment.

Had he been in any way religious – or of broader vision – Stephen might have recognised these well-taken, skilfully composed shots, in which the lighting plays sepulchrally on microphones tightly clasped or arms outstretched, as imaginatively representing the Seven Stations of the Cross. As it is, they simply appear to compound the sense of dread that is almost palpable, in this most outwardly suburban of surroundings.

There are currently three other people standing with their backs to Stephen, examining the display. They turn round in unison when he speaks.

"Is this The Killer Comedy Academy?"

One of the attendees just nods. He is a tall but slightly

stooped, olive-skinned man in his early thirties, with serious teeth and staring brown eyes. Very straight, dark hair, in need of a serious trim, frames a long, narrow nose that appears to slice his face firmly down the centre like a pizza cutter. For some reason he wears what had clearly once formed the top half of a smart if outdated dinner jacket. But he wears it over a faded yellow T-shirt, which must have borne some sort of design in an earlier life, and dark-blue, slightly ripped jeans. Stephen can't work out whether he is trying without huge success to grow a beard or has just forgotten to shave for a few days. When the concave man smiles, he reveals the full glory of his substantial mouth but also a face that suddenly appears warmer and far more welcoming.

"Evening," he says.

Stephen knows at once that this man of teeth has to be the leader of the course and begins to relax.

"You must be Mr Killer."

At this, all three of them gawp into his face and then begin to laugh. Whilst the sound of people laughing in his company, at something he himself has said, has to be a good start, he realises that knowing what might possibly be funny would probably be a better one.

The loudest and deepest laugh emanates from a rather solid yet, to Stephen, fetchingly elegant lady of mixed race, who he reckons must be at least in her forties. Dressed in a crinkly red, faux-leather jacket and charcoal denims, she sports a crisp, white T-shirt that reads '*MENOPAUSE. Been there. Done that. Got the T-shirt. Took it off. Put it on again. Took it off. Put it on…*' apparently ad infinitum. She waits patiently while the newest arrival reads her to the end, or at least to the midriff, but it makes no sense to him at all. He notices that the amused woman's be-ringed and rather beautiful hands jump around expressively all the time, almost as if they're laughing too.

The younger man standing next to her, barely into his twenties and wearing an extremely vivid, patterned jumper, the sheer exuberance of which isn't quite reflected in his manner but hurts Stephen's eyes, is clearly at least part Chinese or Japanese or Korean or – well, something from that neck of the woods. Stephen hasn't as yet developed the skills to differentiate nor the confidence to ask.

The first man doesn't respond directly to Stephen's misguided greeting but instead holds out a bony hand. "Jayson. Jayson Spliff. Just a stage name, but a good one."

As Stephen has little idea what a stage name is, he finds himself in no position to judge. "I'm Stephen. Stephen Gibson. I don't have a 'stage name'. Do I need one?"

"Lot of Stephens out there," says the only Jayson Spliff.

With unexpected velocity, the jumpered person now thrusts his hand out. "Nigel Ngo," he says, which sounds a bit like 'no' and makes Stephen wonder if this young man, with a strangely high-pitched voice, has suddenly changed his mind. He finds himself taken aback at all the introductions. Rarely – possibly never – has a crowd introduced themselves to him, one after the other. It is quite overwhelming. "It's my real name," continues Nigel Ngo. Stephen is surprised that it is anyone's real name.

Finally, the only woman present beams at him. "Hi. I'm NJ. Call me token."

"Are you new here too, Token?" asks Stephen, who feels he is really getting into the rhythm of things now.

"I'm the UK's only lesbian, black, Jewish comic. So just don't go stealing my act, you hear?"

"I don't think I could," protests Stephen, who of course has history with such accusations. "You see—"

"Er – *joke*?" explains the woman, as the others laugh. "And this guy," she continues, pointing to Jayson and doing some sort of American accent, "he ain't no killer."

Jayson smiles. His teeth remind Stephen of a squirrel's, albeit a huge one. There does seem to be a lot of smiling going on, which has to be good.

"I really don't need this," explains Jayson. "Did the course down the 'Laugh? I Nearly' last year, nailed my open spot, already booked in for a paid next year, but this guy's meant to be some sort of a guru and we all know who his funnier half-brother is, so…"

The man, this so-called Jayson, who appears to be brimming with enviable confidence, spreads out his hands in a gesture which, to the others, signifies that the rest is self-evident. Stephen, who doesn't believe he has actually understood a single word of this curious person's speech, other than perhaps 'half-brother', decides that he will devote his attention to the pictures on the wall, although, to be honest, they make no more sense to him than what he has just heard.

He spies a smaller photograph, in an alcove, which doesn't seem to be part of the same family as the others. It is of a rather podgy man, who appears to be totally naked, save for his socks, walking away from a microphone, whilst holding up a middle finger to the unseen audience behind him. Stephen decides that if this represents one of the types of comedy on offer, he may just excuse himself from that particular session. He knows from his own experience that no-one, not even him, can be master of absolutely everything, and it is hardly the type of merriment that will endear himself this summer to a sophisticate such as Ms Nina Hughes.

Stephen isn't aware of another door to the living room, until it suddenly swings open, bringing a touch more light into the dingy parlour. A large and oddly threatening figure appears in the doorway, clearly the portal to a kitchen of some sort. It is holding a half-filled mug in the shape of the Queen's head and wearing food-stained slippers and sweats. The newcomer stands silently, glaring at what the cat and his own flyers have sadly brought in.

As the unsmiling host takes in his guests, Stephen's stomach goes on a Waltzer, like that one at the annual street fair in nearby

Pinner, a ride that he was too scared to go on with the other kids as a child and couldn't quite stroll past as an adult. His racing heart reminds him of how he used to feel even looking at it. The new arrival is not, as imagined, some kindly spiritual leader ready to welcome this season's batch of eager, young, humour-seeking acolytes.

It is the angry man from the comedy club.

Stephen recognises him instantly, as you probably would if just a few days earlier that same person had grabbed you firmly by the throat. It is not quite as apparent that his former assailant has made the same connection. So Stephen prudently decides to keep his terrified head and baseball cap down, edge into a less illuminated corner and blend in with the cobwebs. (He tells himself, as he slithers swiftly backwards, that he shouldn't be quite so stunned – hadn't he spotted the flyer on the very night this man was topping the bill?)

"Hi there," says NJ to the man, with immediate warmth. "Are you...?"

The man, whom Stephen, with his extraordinary memory for names, albeit more often those of plants, recalls as Tyler Watts, raises a stubby finger to his lips. As silence falls once more, he surveys this evening's crop, one of whom appears to be wilting in the semi-darkness.

"No words. No need. You can hold your audience's attention with silence. Lesson one. Silence works."

"True enough," agree Stephen's enthusiastic colleagues. "You said it! ...Absolutely."

"So much for fucking silence," says Tyler Watts. "Okay, let's see what you know, although I probably have the answer to that one. You walk onto that stage, what do you do?"

"You introduce yourself. Hi, I'm Jayson Spliff."

"Jesus wept! *Who?* ...Okay, one school of thought. Then?"

Jayson throws his fellows a disbelieving 'who is this guy?' look. "Start telling jokes," he says. "*Obviously.*"

Stephen is a little surprised when their new teacher hurls the remaining contents of his mug into Jayson Spliff's stupefied face, whilst at the same time screaming, "*NO!*", in a voice consumed with as much despair as anger. Yet he finds this unbridled passion, in its own curious way, rather uplifting. Something in fact that he recognises in himself, although perhaps not quite so spirited.

"You want strings of jokes, puerile tricks, futile contrivances, go back to one of the shit courses you got off the world wide wanky web and get some half-ass who's never stood on a stage with just his dick in his hand spouting about the rule of three and all that." He focusses solely on Jayson now. "Unless, of course, you already tried that and it didn't work."

Jayson shrugs guiltily, as Nigel puts up his hand. Stephen finds this all quite fascinating and thinks he might find it even more revealing, were he able to emerge from his alcove and lift at least one eye from its downcast state.

"*What?*" asks Tyler. "And you don't have to raise your hand. This isn't fucking school. Even though you look like you should be back home studying for your GCSE biology. Okay – what?"

"Isn't...?" Nigel pauses, as if he wishes he hadn't put his head above the crowd. The others wait, some less patiently than others. "Isn't the rule of three really important?"

"Yes, of course it is, arsehole. Like the square on the hypotenuse is important. But it isn't *everything*! Sometimes you have to forget the rules. If it's funny, it's funny. Look at Lenny Bruce. *Monty Python*. *Groundhog Day*. You want rules, plenty of books out there."

Stephen, who rather likes rules, wishes that he had known this. He immediately takes out his notepad, writes down 'rule of three?' and 'books', then realises that maybe he shouldn't have.

"*YOU!*" says Tyler Watts. In horror. In capitals.

He moves over to Stephen, who is now pushing the peak of his cap down and scrunching as far away from available light as he is able, without crawling up the fireplace. Which is possibly not the best look for a would-be comic. Tyler Watts yanks the recessive figure's head up by the one tuft of hair that sticks out, to confirm the now all-too-recognisable face.

"Hello… again," ventures Stephen, with a smile he doesn't quite mean but has observed colleagues employ on a regular basis at his place of work.

"Well, I suppose I should be flattered," mutters Tyler Watts. "That a guy should actually have the *cojones* to come to my own class in my own home and steal stuff. But I'm not. So piss off."

Stephen has no idea whether to be shocked or offended, so rarely is he either, but he knows with some certainty that the circumstances are far too important for him simply to slope away with his tail between his legs. He also wonders what *cojones* is or are and resolves to look this up also.

"No, wait, Mr Watts. Sir. Please. I'm here to learn."

Stephen reaches into his pocket and removes a cheque already made out to The Killer Comedy Academy for the full amount. It is snatched from his yet-to-be-outstretched hand with alarming speed.

"Welcome to Killer Comedy…"

"Stephen."

"Moron."

"Gibson."

"Excuse me?" says NJ, waving her hands as if her bright red nails aren't quite dry. "Much as I'm enjoying this macho fest, what exactly *will* you be teaching us?"

Tyler removes his gaze from Stephen, into whose startled face it has been searing for some uncomfortable time, and turns back to the rest of the class.

"You. Each of you. Tell me one thing about yourself. As if I'm someone who gives a toss. And make it something you've never told anyone."

"*What?*" exclaims NJ, who hasn't been expecting anything like this and isn't certain that she wants to. The silence from the others appears to tell Tyler all that he wishes to know and everything that he was expecting to hear.

"I'll go first," he says, with a weary sigh. "I burned a house down when I was a kid. Next!"

Stephen knows that his mouth has dropped to its open position, but he finds that he has extreme difficulty in closing it or masking the shock on his face.

"Too much arson about," says Jayson Spliff, with a toothy smile, just before Tyler Watts flicks him painfully on his ear. Stephen can find no justification for this assault but interestingly Jayson appears to regard it as an acceptable and indeed expected exchange.

"*Come on!*" encourages Tyler, pointing his flicking hand at NJ. "Something that will bond us, not that I'm overly hopeful."

"I cheated on my ex. She's a rabbi. And she never knew," says NJ, in a sudden flush of honesty. She turns swiftly towards Stephen, knowing from the noisy inhalation beside her that Stephen's mouth has fallen open again. "*What?*"

"Nothing," says Stephen, who knows that these sort of things go on, but is rarely party to them. And rabbis can be *ladies*?

Tyler turns his attention to Jayson, who appears to be almost slavering for his turn. "Let me guess – something sexual with an animal." He moves on to Nigel. "You."

"I sometimes swear at my parents behind their back."

"What's wrong with that?"

"They're deaf."

"Useable," says Tyler, with a thoughtful nod. "Mine it then refine it." Finally he turns to Stephen. "And now you, sunshine. The joke thief."

Stephen stares at the man for a few seconds, rummaging. Finally he blurts it out. "I… love plants. I *really* love plants."

"Uh huh. And there we have it, ladies and gentlemen," sighs Tyler Watts. "A clear demonstration of how the cherished rule of three can end in utter fucking disappointment."

The proprietor and course leader of The Killer Comedy Academy sits on one of his stained plastic chairs and puts a chubby head in his hands.

After some uneasy moments of silence, during which Stephen has attempted to process all that has just taken place and failed miserably, Tyler Watts springs to his feet with renewed, albeit desperate, vigour.

"Okay. New tack. Last chance motel. Why are you here?"

He has addressed this to the ceiling, but this time it is NJ who decides to run with it.

"*I'm a black, Jewish lesbian!*"

Stephen still can't quite believe that all three intriguing facets, which have rarely ventured even separately into his orbit, should now be presented to him in one fetching and easily accessible package. Yet the master's take on it isn't quite so rejoicing.

"So?" says Tyler Watts.

"So – I think I have a unique view of the world," says NJ proudly.

"So – I think you have *three* unique views," grunts Tyler Watts. "Dump two and focus." Before she can respond, he turns to Nigel Ngo. "*You!* Silly jumper guy."

"I need someone to listen to me," says Nigel.

"Oh God! Audiences smell need like dogs smell arseholes." Turning to Jayson. "Okay, cocky bastard."

Jayson, clearly not fearing another assault, says firmly and with what Stephen views as commendable honesty, "I just want to make people happy." Tyler throws him a look of such scepticism, it almost makes a moan as it lands. Then he moves to hit him again. "*And get a shedload of money, so I can give up my shitty day job!*"

Tyler, hand paused in mid-flight, offers Jayson Spliff a beam of such approval that it makes the yearning man visibly swell.

Finally, the teacher stares at Stephen, clearly without a shred of hope.

Stephen Gibson, grateful that he can at last express so earnest a truth, something that emanates from his very heart and core, rises to the occasion. "There's this beautiful girl." He stops, because he can hardly breathe, awaiting the inevitable put-down or unprovoked physical assault.

"*Great!*" exults a clearly astonished Tyler Watts. "Unexpectedly so. You are here because of some beautiful girl."

As Stephen glows with a joy spiced with undisguised relief, the man opens a nearby drawer in a shabby pine dresser that even Uncle Geoffrey might turn his back on. Pulling out a black magic marker, he begins to write on a nearby wall, which turns out to be a vaguely washable surface. 'Comedy,' he scrawls, '= SEX!' He stands back then moves forward once again to write 'maybe'.

"She really likes plants!" continues Stephen.

Tyler crosses out the 'maybe' and writes 'never'.

"*So where's the conflict?*" he demands. "She likes plants, you like plants, in a way that makes me uncomfortable. What is the fucking problem?"

Stephen finds himself reacting to his tutor's raised and patently frustrated voice by responding at a higher decibel level than he feels he might ever have achieved in all his twenty-seven years, even, perhaps, in those distant, hazily recalled moments so long ago, in which he apparently yelped like a scalded puppy, before shutting right down.

"*I don't know what happens next!*"

He senses the silence in the room, as if it is washing over his entire body. Aware that everyone is staring at him, in some level of expectation, he feels obliged to explain. Perhaps in quieter, more considered tones.

"When the plant-talking stops."

Tyler Watts just shakes his head. Not dismissively this time, but in that way a person will do when they don't quite understand and require some further explanation. Stephen recognises this, as he experiences it rather frequently with customers at the garden centre, after he has bombarded them with technicalities and Latin.

"If I can make her laugh," the younger man reasons, as much to himself as to his audience, "she'll really like me. Apparently."

"You *are* joking, mate," says Jayson Spliff, not unkindly.

"Not yet, Jayson," says Stephen.

Tyler moves towards Stephen and talks directly into his face. Yet it is clear to the others that he is addressing them all.

"Comedy? What is comedy? Comedy is doubt and disaster wrapped in shit and humiliation. It will infect every aspect of your life. You will have no friends – possibly not a major issue for some of you – no family, no pensionable future, nothing but the constant desire to be in front of total strangers and proclaim a worldview that you believe to be original and amusing but is more likely to be trite and boring. And that's just the first ten years." He moves closer to Stephen and prods him in his pounding chest. "So, Mr Plantophile, is this what you signed up for?"

With a flourish, Tyler Watts lets Stephen's cheque dangle in the febrile space between them.

"Not exactly, Mr Watts. But she is simply the most incredible woman I have ever seen," says Stephen, who hasn't really gone along with much of what the extremely agitated man has been saying, especially that standing in front of total strangers bit, even though his fellows have been nodding quite enthusiastically through all the shit and humiliation.

"Good enough," says Tyler, returning Stephen's cheque to his pocket. "Okay. Freebie's over," he tells the assembled gathering. "Now get the fuck out."

"Manners!" says NJ.

"Get the fuck out, please."

THIRTEEN

Some people are just peculiar. Take you, sir, with the silly fright wig. ...Oh. Sorry.

The class stagger out of the dingy corner house onto the driveway, as doors slam shut.

Retrieving his bike from the unloved hedge, Stephen watches his three fellow – what can he call them? – students, comics, apprentices shake their heads dramatically, exhaling breath with noisy relief into the fresh evening air. It is as if they have just survived a terrifying road trip or narrowly escaped a neighbourhood mugging.

"This calls for a beer or six," says Nigel, laughing, because an experience shared, however traumatic, has its own way of bonding.

"I'm in, Nige," says NJ. "I know three places. *Obviously*."

Jayson Spliff taps Stephen gently on the shoulder. "What about you, lover boy?"

Stephen is already attaching his bicycle clips, ready to clatter off into the Eastcote night. "Oh no, thank you, Mr Spliff. I have to go home and thoroughly process what we've just been taught." He ignores their stares. "Bye, Nigel. Bye, Token."

The threesome wanders off down the road, still shaking their heads.

Stephen is too absorbed in manoeuvring his bike over the drive's shoddily uneven paving to notice the pair of arrivals just rounding the corner. A chirpy voice causes him to stop in surprise and grip the rusting handlebars.

"Hey, it's Plantman!"

It takes Stephen some seconds, reeling as he still is, to recognise the strange young boy from last week's encounter in the garden centre. Especially as the small, auburn-haired woman, standing just a few yards behind her smiling son but not smiling, looks quite different from the irritating customer he only vaguely recalls. Sensing his uncertainty, she graciously offers him a vital clue by sniffing with some force, segueing into a volcanic, albeit unprovoked, sneeze.

"Well, if it isn't Salesman of the Month!" she greets him.

Of course! He remembers now. The aversion to all things green, the snot fountain, the puzzling camera, which still dangles around her neck like a frontal hump, and the even more curious child. He nods dispassionately to the pair of them.

Nodding back with equal indifference, the young woman approaches him. And this time the sneezing comes on for real.

"Jesus, do you bathe in friggin' pollen?"

"No," denies Stephen. "Who does that? Even bees—"

"What in merry hell are you doing here? You stalking me?" As Stephen shakes his head vehemently, he notices in the dusty glow of the streetlights that the young woman's eyes are a translucent blue, almost like a Himalayan poppy, and not the blood-red of their previous encounter. He also notices that they are now extraordinarily wide open and staring at him as if in shock. "*Oh God, no!*" she gasps. "Please tell me you're not taking Tyler's course."

"I can't tell you that," says Stephen. "Are you his student too? Because I believe the session is over. He told us all to... well, to leave."

She nods, in recognition. "Yeah. No. It's okay. I live here."

"Oh," says Stephen. He's trying really hard, but he can't quite process this. "So, you live here, with…"

"Sure." She smiles now and despite the eye-crinkling it is not wholly unpleasant. Although he supposes that anything that doesn't have rivulets of phlegm flowing around it has to be an improvement. "Well, not *with* with."

This is a tricky one for Stephen, but her son (whose name, to his own surprise, he now recalls as being Nathan) seems more than happy to clarify. "She'd rather eat her own vomit for brunch than go out with another comic."

"*Nathan!*" says his mother, attempting to stem the flow, or indeed both flows, whilst throwing Stephen a smile he doesn't think she means.

"*It's what you said!*" insists the boy. He turns back to Stephen, apologising for the interruption with a tolerant shrug. "My dad's a famous stand-up. He left us for a Barbie doll."

"That sounds perverse," says Stephen, who didn't know that a person who merely stands up could in any way be celebrated.

"Metaphor," explains Nathan, with a knowing smile.

Stephen has no contact with children, had relatively little even when he was of their ilk, yet he senses that here is an example of one of the brighter, albeit stranger, ones. He finds himself wondering if the boy's schoolfellows make fun of him, because he is decidedly odd. Not simply in looks, although this would hardly help with his fitting in, but in manner. Again something resonates inside him, yet he either can't or doesn't want to go there. And he's remembering something else now – about plants that can—

"I'm Tyler Watt's sister-in-law. Well, *ex*-sister-in-law. Like you care."

"Eh?" says Stephen, returning from his thoughts. "Ah… So this – us, meeting again – it's quite a coincidence."

"Cornerstone of comedy!" laughs the woman. Alone. "Check out the manuals. And '*Coincidence is just God's way of staying anonymous*'. Know who said that? Alby Einstein! On his number one tour."

"I have absolutely no idea what you're talking about," confesses Stephen, without disguising the irritation in his voice. Or the inflection that tells her the fault is clearly her own.

"O-kay, well, you gotta excuse us," she decides, grabbing Nathan's hand. "This time we are *way* too busy to talk with you."

She brushes past him and takes out her key. For some reason Stephen finds himself incensed yet curiously unwilling to conclude the conversation.

"*You don't like greenery!*" he hurls at her, like a criminal charge. "Even dead people like greenery. Even Stalin cultivated exotic plants!"

"Great slogan. You should use it!" She puts the key in the lock.

"*I STILL WANT A CACTUS!*"

The weird child is staring up at him. Not moving.

"Wait. *What?*" says Stephen, as he now recalls more fully their earlier meeting, on that magical, Ms Nina Hughes, first sort-of-date day. "They didn't help you find one?"

"Said they didn't have none."

"Didn't have '*any*,'" corrects Stephen. "Well, I'm sorry, that is totally unacceptable. Come into the garden centre tomorrow, please, Nathan, and we shall definitely do something about it."

"No shit!" says Nathan, excitedly.

"*Excuse me?*" chides his mum. "Anyway Nathan, we can't tomorrow."

As if struck by a sudden bolt of lightning, from an otherwise tranquil nighttime sky, Nathan immediately prostrates himself on the gravel path, a small, nail-bitten hand clasped to his forehead, and begins to roll around, screaming several drawn-out 'NO-OOOO's into the Eastcote air.

Stephen is devastated. "Oh no. Please. Nathan! Don't do that." He looks to the boy's callously indifferent mother. "Can't you see? He's hyperventilating. Oh my God! The child will have a seizure. *Do something!*"

"Okay, kid," says his carer, "show's over."

Nathan instantly hops up, dusts himself off and shrugs at a bemused Stephen. His mother begins to chuckle. The laughter has a raw, throaty quality – so unlike the gracious tinkling of Welsh chords.

"His father used to do that," she explains. "Made me laugh every time, the bastard."

"I thought he'd swallowed his tongue," protests Stephen.

"I wish!" She stares up at a shocked Stephen, as though examining him, her small head to one side and a single, shiny auburn lock falling over an eye. "Hey, this course – maybe better you should ease your way in. Y'know – start with 'Smiling 101.'"

As she opens the door, Stephen stares at the young boy. "I'm sure that was meant to be amusing, Nathan," he says, with some sympathy. "But I actually believe your mother is a rather peculiar person. And you're quite possibly heading in the same direction. Just keep your eyes open. And I don't mean because one of them is a bit wonky. Well, more than a bit. We've all got blemishes. Even me, believe it or not. I've got a green—"

With a glare reminiscent of their earlier encounter, albeit less fluid, the woman yanks her child away and into the bleakness of the Killer Comedy Academy, shaking her head.

Leaving Stephen alone with his bike and that appalling hedge.

FOURTEEN

Last night a fella shouted out, 'Be funny!"
Well, I don't normally do requests.

The great advantage of The Killer Comedy Academy for Stephen Gibson is that the lessons are bunched very closely together. So he has already been through half a dozen in the first fortnight, each one more baffling than its predecessor. Which this most committed of students assumes is simply par for the course.

Tyler Watts justifies the deliberate 'intensity' as being essential for the maintenance of comedic momentum. Jayson Spliff has informed Stephen that it is purely for the benefit of Tyler Watts, so that he can arrange his gigs and fit in as many students as possible. And also, as even the master himself admits, to ensure that he can see the back of this bunch of no-hopers in record time. (Nigel has explained to Stephen that this is a type of reverse psychology – a challenge to the class, from the expert, to prove him wrong. NJ thinks that he's a misanthropic arsehole.)

Stephen informed his classmates, at the first proper lesson of their course, which took place a mere twenty-four hours after induction, that he has absolutely no problem with this fast-tracking, as he has an immovable deadline. He really does need to be pretty funny pretty fast. In fact by July 28th or even a couple of days before, for safety. His fellow wannabes did appear to appreciate the urgency, if not the feasibility.

Aside from Tyler setting fire to Stephen's new, eco-friendly notepad with a disposable cigarette lighter fifteen minutes into that first session, the least experienced but possibly most focussed pupil feels that things are actually going far better than expected.

Module 1 was all about the basic mechanics of humour and what makes something funny, so it had a quasi-scientific underpinning that rather appealed to Stephen. He didn't actually understand the jokes or why the others were laughing, but he kept reminding himself that these are people who are all working – or almost working/would kill to be working – comedians ('stand-ups', as he must now bewilderingly term them) and he, of course, is a devout horticulturist. And, as such, has absolutely no intention nor desire to make a career out of comedy. Who in their right mind would? He just wants to acquire, in the swiftest possible way, the most basic of those particular skills with which life has hitherto omitted to endow him. Much the same, he tells himself, as if he were learning to drive. Or knit. Even Tyler Watts, apparently quoting a dead Frenchman called Voltaire but in English, says that it is necessary to cultivate our own garden, although NJ mutters that the wanker was just showing off.

Whilst their instructor is dead set against his pupils being in any way derivative and is urging them almost at knife point – or at least magic-marker point – to develop their own individual style, he does also encourage them to watch and learn from the masters. To facilitate this, he kindly provided them in Module 2 with a verbal list of exactly who, in his incontestable opinion, these masters are.

No longer having notepaper to hand and his brand-new HB pencil rendered pointless when Tyler stabbed him with it in the thigh, Stephen was obliged to memorise the unfamiliar names.

Seinfeld? Pryor? Izzard? *Rock?* Nigel Ngo, however, recognising his fellow student's difficulties, had promised that he would email the list over to him as soon as he returned home that evening. Which, to Stephen's surprise, the young man actually did.

This small but significant gesture has exemplified for Stephen a totally unexpected by-product of being part of a compact yet quite disparate group. People are being really kind.

Well, not Tyler, obviously, but anyone who torched a house as a child clearly has serious problems. The others, however, appear genuinely to appreciate the nobility of Stephen's quest, so he understands and indeed values their honesty in expressing some natural scepticism.

Interestingly, it is Jayson who really seems to get it. Stephen Gibson won't forget in a hurry the grinning man's stirring call to arms, during that early seminal lesson. *Dream on, sunshine* will be his watchwords and his mantra from now on.

What has surprised Stephen most of all, however, has been the reappearance of Tyler Watts' peculiar sister-in-law, who is apparently called Kerry, which Stephen doesn't believe is even a real name. Despite being clearly and overarchingly American, he concludes that she was perhaps conceived in a certain apparently picturesque county in Ireland, renowned, of course, for the Greater Butterwort, and for some reason her parents wished to celebrate this fact.

This causes him to ponder that there are even more curious names – he recalls that at college their tutor had told them of a woman he encountered who had called her new daughter Chlamydia, because she had presumed it was a flower. Despite the accompanying chuckles from his instructor, Stephen was quite shocked when he looked it up after the lecture. Perhaps, he thought, she had meant Clematis, although that's not much of a name either. He wonders now if this is in fact oddly amusing, that someone should be named after a sexually transmitted disease, and whether it is something that he might share with

Ms Nina Hughes, should the appropriate moment arise. He somehow doubts it, but you never know.

This Kerry person is not involved with Killer Comedy in any way, yet irritatingly she does keep popping in throughout the sessions, on the pretext of taking photographs, with the rather large and battered camera she appears never to be without. Her motives have not as yet been explained to Stephen and he wonders if she is responsible for the particularly unattractive and disturbing images on the wall. He wouldn't be at all surprised, yet he supposes that he can't begrudge a young woman her hobby, however bizarre, and the others don't appear to have any objections.

Tyler once vaguely explained that, in the highly unlikely event of any of them becoming professional stand-ups, they will need decent photographs to help them with their publicity. Stephen doesn't actually think the photos he has seen are particularly decent but acknowledges that he is possibly no expert. The course leader has also instructed his foreign ex-relative not to spend too much time on Stephen, advice which she appears to be following all too readily.

At least, thinks Stephen, as he mulls over this first block of sessions back home in his greenhouse, the amateur photographer doesn't appear to be quite as misanthropic as her English landlord. In fact, he has noticed that she laughs an inordinate amount for a human being. And jokes quite a lot too. Or tries to. Rather too much, in his opinion, as it tends to interrupt the comedy class.

Kerry doesn't joke with him, obviously, but happily does so with the others, who don't appear to share his frustration. She even jokes with Tyler Watts himself, who – despite being a comedian and running the course – rarely seems able to raise a smile across his own miserable face. If Stephen were asked to sum up his tutor in a word, he would probably say angry. Or – if permitted two words – really angry.

The young woman never seems to be around at the end of a session, at which celebratory point his fellow comedians generally request Stephen's company, for a drink and what they call a post-mortem, which he doesn't think sounds particularly comedic. He admits to feeling slightly torn but has to explain gently yet firmly each evening that they simply don't have the time pressures that are weighing upon him so heavily. He must cycle straight home after each lesson to continue with his studies and swiftly jot down everything he has recalled about being funny but isn't permitted to record in situ. And when he explains again about Archibald's classic tome, they nod with what he knows is genuine understanding.

"Dream on, sunshine," he calls to them, as he goes. Although his back may be turned, he knows somehow that his new friends are smiling.

FIFTEEN

Is it just me or has the world gone raving mad?
...Yeah, okay.

Were Stephen's Uncle Geoffrey to list those elements in his life that might impede him from making love, late on a weekday evening, with a woman to whom he has only recently lost his rusty heart, an adult, plant-infatuated nephew would probably not figure that prominently. Yet it is exactly this that is cramping his barely perfected style tonight, in his only recently decluttered bedroom.

No-one could accuse his current squeeze – and, indeed, his only squeeze for some considerable time – for not squeezing hard enough. Noreen is doing everything in her not-inconsiderable power to make her dealer-in-old-things more interested in things considerably newer and finer. But the sounds from the adjacent bedroom, sounds that have been emanating for some nights now, are way too distracting for a middle-aged man who needs his attention to be focussed firmly on the job in hand.

Geoffrey can't actually hear what his nephew is saying, which probably makes it all the more disconcerting. The noises-off aren't at all of the usual variety. Indeed, there *is* no usual variety, as he doesn't believe his only living relative even snores. If the older man had to describe the off-putting sounds that have been insinuating themselves through the thin Ruislip walls, he would probably refer to them as mutterings. Yet it is almost as if the occupant is essaying several different styles of mutter, perhaps trying them on for size. When, finally, it gets too much for any man to bear, Geoffrey quits what he is doing – or failing to do – and lumbers disgruntledly out of bed, pulling his brand-new boxer shorts up and over his disappointment.

"Honeymoon done already?" says Noreen.

"Sorry, love. Worried about the boy."

"If you're not back in ten, I'm starting without you."

Geoffrey nods, as he makes for his bedroom door through the darkness. He notices yet again how reduced are the obstacles around which he has to manoeuvre, now that this Noreen has begun to make over his home and his life. He reckons that she is the best thing he has picked up in some years and yet another acquisition with which he would feel painfully loathe to part.

"Knock, knock," he says, as he thumps gently but firmly on his nephew's door.

"Who's there?" comes from the voice from within.

"It's me," says his Uncle Geoffrey, entering the room. The only light comes from the old laptop propped on Stephen's leafy-duveted knees and the only sounds those of curiously muted laughter from whatever is going on inside the computer.

"Me who?" says Stephen, as the remnants of an obscure and long-forgotten childhood joke seep back in.

"Me – me, for pity's sake. Is everything alright, lad?"

"That's not how the joke works."

Stephen doesn't notice his uncle's confusion, as he is already back on his laptop. Geoffrey can hear a man talking, in what he discerns could be quick-fire American, but beyond that he is mystified. A state he senses might continue for some while.

"Okay, check this out," says Stephen, before launching into an accent which bears no resemblance to anything or anyone his uncle has ever heard in his life. "*What's up, motherfuckers?*" asks

Stephen. "*Woke up this morning in a ambulance. And it wasn't nothing but white people staring at me. I said, 'Ain't this a bitch—'*"

"Stephen!" interrupts Uncle Geoffrey, for the sake of his sanity. And possibly not just his own.

The young man is immediately apologetic. "Oh, sorry. Er... my bad. I was forgetting Tyler Watts' Golden Rule Number Four. Tailor your material to your audience." He looks like he could kick himself. "Could you ask Noreen to come in, please?"

Geoffrey just shakes his head and turns back to the door. "Think I've got an old set of headphones in one of my boxes, if Noreen hasn't dumped it yet. I'll find them in the morning. Now just switch that off, lad, whatever the hell it is, and get some ruddy sleep."

"Heckler," mutters Stephen, although he is not a hundred per cent sure what this means.

***

The following morning, Stephen Gibson is feeling rather sleepy.

Which is hardly surprising, after another unremitting night of classic stand-up comedy. He had finally managed to unearth some earphones from a defunct yet still treasured mobile phone and, to his great satisfaction, has now acquainted himself with every name on Nigel Ngo's kindly-provided list. Plus a few he has discovered for himself. The sound of Mrs Dave, however, having a good scream outside his door, even before she steams into his poky office, is sufficient to rouse him into at least a semblance of alertness.

"*What in the bloody hell have you been doing?*" she rants, slamming the door into a perturbed customer's face.

"Whassup, Mrs Dave?" he asks the irate woman, as he taps randomly on his computer.

"What is up? I will tell you what is up, Stephen. Ms Nina Hughes of Magnolia Head HQ is most definitely bloody up. She called me personally herself this morning. She hasn't heard one bloody word from you about the presentation."

"Well… I'm nearly there, Mrs Dave," says Stephen, a fraction weakly, even in his own estimation. "No point in giving her only half a proposal." He realises that he has rather taken his eye off the ball since those first magical encounters but reassures himself that it is all for the greater good and he can certainly make up the time necessary to – well, to do what he's actually paid for.

"You are not 'nearly there', Stephen," persists the irate employer. "Any more than… any more than Delhi is nearly Madras, just because they are both in India."

"Is Madras a place as well as a curry?" He has seen the name scribbled on the takeaways that his uncle regularly orders but which he himself can never stomach.

"I would like to remind you that the presentation is on Monday not Christmas. *Or* Passover. Where has your head been these days, boy?"

Stephen looks unjustifiably offended. "I've been broadening my skill set."

"Are you trying to be funny?"

How did she know? "As a matter of fact—"

She sits down on the only available chair and appears to be settling into normal conversation. Her voice softens, which doesn't usually reassure Stephen, but this time, after being in The Comedy Store, the O2 Arena, Carnegie Hall and similar heaving venues most of the past few nights, any reduction in volume is to be welcomed.

"This is our golden ticket to join the big leagues, Stephen. I say 'our', but of course I mean 'my'. I have a dream, my young friend. An entire bloody luxury hotel and spa chain! With our highly-prized Blooming Marvellous trees, plants and shrubs right there on display, everywhere you bloody look. Hmm? Not just one spa hotel – *all of them.* What do you say to that?"

Stephen feels his heart pound and swell, as the adrenaline floods back into his veins. It always seems to do this when Mrs Dave rallies her troops. He experiences that unmistakeable surge of excitement, spiced with abject, bladder-loosening fear.

"I won't let you down, Mrs Dave."

She reaches a small hand across the table and taps his special thumb. Which is today, unusually, quite unsheathed.

"Oh, Stephen, dear." She smiles, kindly. "It isn't me you'll be letting down. Tell me, where will your own self-esteem be, when you're summarily dismissed with appalling references and no back pay?"

She watches Stephen nod in accord with the obvious wisdom of this, but then his eyes wander over her tiny head and Mrs Dave realises that her chastened employee has noticed something behind her in the garden centre. She turns to see a distinguished-looking Indian gentleman in a smart suit gazing around, as if seeking someone.

"Ah, and here is my beloved husband and minority shareholder. Now you get back to your work, Stephen, dear. And remember our catchphrase – nobody is irreplaceable."

For reasons he might genuinely find hard to explain, although overwhelming fatigue and industrial quantities of stress perhaps play their part, Stephen rises with his employer and joins her to meet Mr Dave in the body of the garden centre.

Their paths cross at the striking water feature in the very centre of the room, a giant, stainless-steel sphere with clear liquid trickling noisily over its entire reflective surface onto a bed of whitish rocks.

"Hello, Mr Dave," greets Stephen.

"Good morn—"

The smiling gentleman doesn't manage to complete his response, as his breath is quite removed by the sudden, unprompted nudge he receives from his wife's young and apparently gifted employee, which sends him skittering towards the giant sphere. The poor man's panic is wonderfully reflected in the huge ball's dripping surface, as his arms glide helplessly, wetly over it and his legs gently buckle before leaving the ground.

Stephen can see Spike and the other members of the Blooming Marvellous staff, along with several customers, stare in mystified horror at the floundering man, as his unprovoked assailant strolls blithely away from the incident.

Although the newly aberrant horticulturist is talking only to himself, Stephen hopes in his elation that Spike isn't close enough to hear his humorous colleague say, "Module Number 6: visual comedy. 'The secret is all in the surprise.' Nailed it!" as he calmly makes for the door.

PART TWO

The Build

SIXTEEN

...and a woman walks right up to him, bold as bloody brass!

The studio is a converted double garage at the rear of the property. It can be accessed uneasily by manoeuvring round the side of the semi-detached house, through dense and occasionally thorny shrubbery and down an ever-narrowing path.

Kerry has offered to have the way cleared or even to do it herself, but Tyler Watts is adamant that he prefers the security of what looks to anyone like tricky if not impossible access. Added to which, it apparently keeps Kerry's costly photographic equipment safe from opportunistic burglars from Ruislip or beyond.

It doesn't, however, smooth the passage of customers wishing to avail themselves of Kerry's professional services. Especially those with small children in tow. Yet Kerry can't really put her young subject's current inability to stay still for one God-almighty frigging second down to the fact that the little girl has just been dragged through a hedge backwards.

Dressed in a hot-pink camisole ballet tutu, the petite blonde nine-year-old, whose mother has fled back through the undergrowth for some precious shopping relief, is frantically pirouetting on the concrete floor. It is as if someone has threatened that should she stop, even for a nanosecond, she will never dance again. Which frenzy, of course, would be perfect for a heart-nourishing and strictly family video but not particularly helpful for this harassed photographer, attempting to immortalise the action in one single, captivating image.

"Sweetie, can you please not do that?" asks Kerry, with admirable restraint, as she sashays around the busy child, moving closer and closer with her lens, in the vain hope of picking up the shot she so desperately needs. Or, at least, knocking a nearby lamp onto the ever-bobbing head and capturing her supple little body as it gracefully crumples onto the floor.

The walls around Kerry bear witness to the fact that she *can* actually achieve some modicum of artistic success with children and their families, as well as glamour models, stand-up comics and, incongruously, the odd chastening shot of men in combat. But right now these all seem relics of a distant and majorly yearned-for past.

"Honey, if I shoot you like this, your folks are just gonna think I was drunk or got the shakes… Again." The manic pirouettes, far from slowing down, like that ballerina on an old-fashioned music box Kerry suddenly recalls her parents back home owning and eventually weaponising, appears to speed up with renewed vigour. She wonders if perhaps the little girl actually has ADHD and that she should be more sympathetic, but happily the feeling doesn't last too long.

"Hey," suggests Kerry, with the inspiration of the desperate, "why don't we… play a game… of you standing very, very still or I superglue both your teeny-weeny feet to that floor."

"*If you do that, she could quite easily fall and break her ankles.*"

Kerry spins round to identify the new and overloud mystery voice, although she believes that she would know it anywhere.

Stephen Gibson stands in the doorway, thorns in his hair and on his tweedy jacket, holding a large Blooming Marvellous gift bag in both hands.

"Oh! It's... Stephen, isn't it? Well, that was just me... using a bit of, y'know... *hyperbole*?"

Stephen grabs at this, like a zoo tiger being offered a skinned rabbit. "Exaggeration employed to *increase* the power of a joke exponentially!" He looks at her, almost as if he is expecting a pat on the head, then happily amplifies. "As in, 'I would not say that my wife – or husband, if you're a heterosexual woman – is a really fat or indeed morbidly obese person, BUT SHE – *OR* HE – DOES IN FACT HAVE A POSTCODE THAT IS ENTIRELY HER/HIS VERY OWN!'" There is still no reaction from Kerry, other than perhaps a slight nod. "Because they are so fat. Or clinically obese. See?"

"Uh huh," says Kerry, because she really can't think of anything else to say.

The soundscape around them has changed – or they've become more acutely aware of the silence. As one, they both turn slowly round to look at the little girl. Scared shitless by the woman's recent threat, she has cracked her last nut and is frozen in pose, one dainty foot still very slightly raised, like a prisoner about to climb the scaffold.

Kerry immediately hoists her camera, goes down on one knee and, in a series of rapid clicks, appears to secure the shot she needs.

"Okay, Tilly," she smiles, warming to the child again, "bravo, hon, you did good. Now why don't you pirouette back into the house and hang out with Nathan for a few minutes?"

"*NATHAN?*" protests the little girl.

Kerry and Stephen stare at her, as a look of disgust swallows her adorable face. Turning to Kerry, the man notices, with some surprise, how a light appears quite swiftly to dim in her eyes, almost like one of those nearby lamps being turned down, as she absorbs the child's reaction.

With a flounce of extra-soft cotton lace blending, the little girl moves unwillingly towards the door. She can't resist a final, tiny entrechat, but it's clear that her heart isn't in it.

Kerry sighs then immediately shakes her head and perks back up again, strangely embarrassed that this oddly irritating man might have spotted a vulnerability. Although, from what she has witnessed of him so far, the odds on this are small.

She now recalls why he has turned up yet finds herself far less certain as to what the large bag is about. Unless, of course, he has decided to include a plant in his mugshot. Which isn't wholly off the table.

"Sorry, Stephen. I'm running late. And out of patience." She smiles, which of course is met with a blank nod. "Take a seat, why don't you, and we'll get those headshots you bafflingly want done." Still game, she adds, "If you can bear to sit for a plant-Nazi like me."

Stephen shrugs in what he hopes is a magnanimous, grown-up way. Still holding the bag in both hands, slim head slightly bowed, as if weighed down with responsibilities, he wanders around the studio/garage, clearly fascinated by this strange, arcane world he has rather reluctantly entered. But needs must and he does believe that a good photo can do no harm. Indeed he has been thinking quite seriously that on some future happy occasion, perhaps framed and with a signature or even brief message appended, it might make a suitable gift. Provided Kerry allows him to leave his clothes on and not look like he is about to be shot.

There do appear to be lamps everywhere, ground-level to towering, and an assortment of disparate objects, such as sun umbrellas, artificial flowers and mechanical toys, children's scooters, and fancy-dress items, which he believes you might find in any all-purpose, domestic garage, but not usually in such good condition or laid out so deliberately.

Against a plain white wall is a screen made of some sort of material, hanging down from a huge roller. The purpose of this eludes him. In fact the only things he can get his brain around are the photos on the opposite wall, and even some of these are causing him to wrinkle his brow and subject to closer scrutiny, through his thick lenses. Of course, he isn't too surprised that this rather brash and perpetually snotty foreign woman should work in such a peculiar environment, as she is patently far from normal herself.

He can sense her staring at him.

"You have an... unusual work space," he tells her, opening a large wicker basket with his shoe, to reveal a long, coiled, plastic snake.

"Yeah." She shrugs, almost apologetically. "Bit of a car crash, actually."

Stephen doesn't answer for a moment. He gazes around, like someone slowly beginning to realise that he has arrived at the wrong address and is completely and utterly lost. Finally, he looks at her.

He has never considered, at least not consciously, how a person's appearance can telegraph their innermost qualities, yet the notion of complete and almost terrifying honesty instantly enters his head. Which Stephen finds quite perturbing, especially as experience has led him to believe he is not perhaps the best at 'reading' people. Yet he feels certain that whilst he might be disconcerted by this perceived quality in the young woman, he isn't mistaken.

"So what do I do here, er... Kerry?"

"Didn't your folks ever drag you to 'get your picture took'?"

"'Taken'. No."

"Well," she smiles, raising a lamp to adult height, "it's never too late."

"They're dead."

He switches a wall light on then off again, repeating the process as if fascinated by the miracle of electricity. Kerry watches him in some sadness.

"Oh, Stephen, I'm so sorry. But I didn't mean having your picture took – taken – *with* them. How did they... how did they pass? Illness?"

"Car crash."

"*Shit!* Now I'm really sorry."

"That's alright." He appears almost to be talking to himself now. "It was twenty-three years and seven months ago. In Bolivia. They were famous botanists. World famous. Apparently, Kerry, as we can't know this for certain, their attention was diverted by an extremely rare, low-growing Poke-Me-Boy shrub, *Acacia anegadensis* – well, whose wouldn't be? – and they smashed right into a far less rare Twisted Acacia – *Vachellia...*"

Kerry gently touches his arm, but he flinches and sidles swiftly away. Picking up his uneasiness, which is hardly nuanced, she decides to move on. "Why don't you just sit down, Stephen?"

Stephen pauses for a moment, as if efforts have been demanded of him way beyond his current competence, then looks around for a chair. He finds an old wooden stool a few feet from where the little girl was dancing and plonks himself down. Kerry mulls for a moment whether to ask him to shift centre-stage, then decides it will probably be far simpler to heft the lamps.

"Could you maybe lose the bag?" she suggests. She might have realised this would confound him. "I don't mean 'lose', like put it in some place none of us will ever find it the rest of our lives. Sorry – my fault – technical term. Just put it—"

To her surprise, he thrusts it out towards her. "It's for Nathan."

She takes it with a mounting dread, tear-ducts at the ready. Inside she sees the weirdest cactus on the planet and instinctively finds herself recoiling.

"It's alright, Kerry," he assures her. "Succulents are pollen-free. I don't think anyone is allergic to cacti."

"Good to know," says Kerry, examining it, gingerly. "Kid'll think all his birthdays came at once. New hamster will probably hang himself."

"I get a staff discount."

"Even so. Thank you, Stephen. Hey, you know something, you're a really lucky guy – sit up straight, please – I mean, doing something you love. *Straight, not rigor mortis!*"

She moves towards him. He is now sitting quite rigid, almost as if a spike has shot up through the centre of the stool. Wondering for a moment whether he might resist even being 'professionally' touched, then ignoring her concerns as time is getting on and she needs her supper, she simply rearranges his limbs like a puppet.

"Let's loosen you up a bit," she suggests.

For reasons best known to himself, or perhaps because he is trying desperately to comply with this strange woman's even stranger demands and get her off his case, Stephen immediately buckles his legs and causes his entire body to become floppy. A floppiness she has hitherto only encountered in very small babies and very drunk comics. When she shakes her head, out of pure amazement rather than simple frustration, he reverts to rigid mode. Whatever the posture, it is becoming perfectly apparent that he would prefer to avoid physical contact of any sort. And so, throwing in the towel, she returns to her lighting.

"Don't *you* love doing this?" he asks.

By this time, Kerry has almost forgotten her previous comment and has to struggle to retrieve the context for his question. "Oh. This? It pays the bills. I preferred my old job." She pauses for a moment or six. "Which was, now you ask, working freelance for Associated Press, covering conflicts."

"Wasn't that dangerous?"

"I'll say. Drop one of those camera boxes on your foot – Jesus!"

Stephen shakes his head. Is this woman a total idiot? "*No!* I meant bullets and bombs – why would anyone go to a war zone?"

"*Why would anyone love a cactus!*" she retorts. Kerry watches the anger rise on his face, blending seamlessly with utter mystification, so she decides she won't go there. "Guess it's a lot to do with my dad being in the army. Gulf War One?" She laughs but for once doesn't appear amused. "Feels like I was always involved in some sort of conflict. My mom and I would catch the 'friendly fire.'"

"At least it wasn't Vietnam," says Stephen, to which Kerry nods, in muted agreement. "All that vegetation destroyed by Agent Orange."

She switches on a lamp that beams right into his face, like the first stage in a brutal interrogation. Or, indeed, a comedy gig.

"What about *people*, Stephen? People die in wars."

"People die in all sorts of places," he retorts. "The vegetation didn't grow back for years in Vietnam."

"Apocalyptus Now," says Kerry, but would find it hard to say why.

"I'm sorry?" He frowns. "Oh. Was that a joke?"

"Look at *you*, kiddo, you're learning."

She walks over to the screen behind him and, after a moment's deliberation, unrolls a backdrop of greenery. It makes her smile.

"You need to relax, Steve."

"Stephen."

"Okay." She gazes into her camera and her face brightens, as if in vain hope that it might be catching. "Just think of something that makes you smile… Stephen."

She looks up to see her subject thinking very hard indeed. All it would take to complete the pose, she reckons, would be a clenched fist burrowing into his narrow chin and, of course, a few less clothes. "Surely *something* makes you smile."

It might only be a matter of seconds, yet Kerry feels it is time lost that she can never retrieve. She can't quite believe that she is being hired to take a publicity shot for a painfully misguided and congenitally hopeless wannabe funnyman. It feels like putting a shot of your dead granny on Tinder and hoping to get some hits.

"...Stephen...?"

"*Nina!*"

"Eh? Oh. Okay. Nina makes you smile? So what about the Pinta and the Santa Maria?"

"No, just Nina," insists Stephen. "Nina Hughes. She's a beautiful woman, Kerry. Beautiful like a – like a *nelumbo lucifera.* You know, Indian Lotus. Not that she's... Nina's the reason I'm learning to be funny!"

"She is? Well, good luck with that! Seriously. So – you're a romantic at heart, Stephen. That's cool. Okay, now smile."

And this time he actually does. Apparently.

Although to an outsider it might appear as if the man has ingested a lethal dose of poison and it is just beginning to take effect.

Kerry shakes her head. "Got another idea. Take a deep breath."

Stephen does as asked. If nothing else, he has a serious respect for skilled professionals, especially those adept in fields where he would graciously admit to a certain lack of ability or knowledge. Which is practically every field known to man, other than his own.

"Okay, now hold it. Hold it, Stephen."

He can feel the strain on every muscle in his face and body, like a wet towel being wrung out, but is resolute in sticking to the task in hand. The woman clearly knows her stuff. He recalls her instructions just now to that little ballet girl.

His chest is beginning to hurt.

"Okay, keep holding, kiddo. Just a bit more. *More.*"

Stephen is really struggling now. The pain in his body is verging on the intense and he is turning a delicate shade of blue. But he is not going to surrender. At least not yet.

Just as he believes he is about to pass out...

"*And – let it go.*"

As her subject explodes, she takes her shot.

"Perfect comedy headshot!" she exults. "Well done, Stephen. Come take a peek?"

Had he bothered to think about it, Stephen Gibson, joker-in-waiting, might have had a reasonably accurate idea as to how a photo of him expelling air contained in his slim frame to virtual bursting point would conceivably look. Yet he is totally shocked to be confronted with the image on Kerry's clearly expensive digital camera.

"*This is funny?*" he hurls. "Me, suffocating? Me, nearly dying!"

Kerry has to nod. What else can she do, in all honesty?

Stephen stares at the young woman as if she is a particularly unattractive, yet still somehow fascinating, species hitherto not encountered by man.

"You do this a lot, don't you, Kerry?" he says, seriously. "Make jokes."

The young woman thinks about this. "And you wonder why I'm single!"

"No," says Stephen Gibson.

SEVENTEEN

So who should come through that door but…

It is during his eighth intensive-training session, the one for which they've all had to pay a suddenly increased fee, that course leader Tyler Watts introduces a new and unexpected element into the mix.

He has spent the majority of course time, since that first introductory meeting, attempting mercilessly to deconstruct, reshape and brutally hone the rough and in some cases barely credible stand-up routines that his class have brought with them into the room. With occasionally flagging and generally dispirited energy, he has been working with them on structure, content and, of course, technique.

This instructor is firmly of the opinion that he can best nourish his raw recruits by building on what they already are, rather than trying vainly and perhaps arrogantly to turn them into something they clearly are not. Which, although he wouldn't say it to their faces more than three or four times per session, is gifted.

Stephen, of course, is the exception, in that he has brought absolutely nothing with him into the room, save for pollen and a singular absence of any sense of humour whatsoever. Which, despite palpable frustration and an ill-disguised hostility, Tyler Watts would have to admit he finds strangely fascinating.

All that he has been able to do, without upping the tally of violence from merely spasmodic, is to instruct Stephen to watch his fellows diligently, learn by their mistakes and benefit from their almost infinitesimal improvements. Whilst, of course, spending every waking moment beyond these dingy walls rigorously imbibing the humour of those blessed few who have somehow made it into the stratosphere of this cruel and bloody profession.

Despite the plant-loving weirdo's protestations that this is indeed what he has been doing twenty-four seven and that he is pretty sure he is on his way to becoming absolutely hilarious, Tyler encourages him to plough that furrow just a tiny bit deeper. He has every certainty that this particular field is fallow or that the mine is full of fool's gold, but if it keeps joke-nicking, miracle-seeking Stephen Gibson both quiet and paying up (the teacher also runs a healthy sideline in overpriced and often pirated DVDs), then Tyler Watt's job is done.

Right now Stephen and his fellow students are once again waiting patiently for Tyler to slump out of his mysterious and strictly off-limits kitchen, from which lukewarm coffee very occasionally emerges but into which no aspiring comic dares venture. Unusually they can hear him this evening chatting to someone 'offstage'. Someone who doesn't sound remotely like his sister-in-law.

The quartet spend this time, as they regularly do, swapping notes and attempting to outdo each other in their funniness. Yet, amidst the banter, they also listen attentively and with some degree of empathy to each other's fears, hopes and dreams. Including those more targeted but less realisable ones of Stephen Gibson himself.

Stephen also listens carefully.

To his surprise, he finds himself rather touched by the

unanticipated mix of ego and selflessness present in the dingy room. This is something even he realises that he has never before encountered. Not in school, where he was a rather dorkish loner and swot, the designated class oddity who thankfully was never bullied, or at least not too enthusiastically, but about whom nobody really bothered or cared. Nor at college, where he was equally regarded or disregarded and where his 'sadness' confined him to his studies and his plants. Which actually suited him perfectly well and was happily reflected in his academic attainments.

At work, of course, there is Spike and Mrs Dave, but he doesn't think that either of them are the best of listeners, not like this gang, and wasn't Mrs Dave singularly unamused by his inspired water-feature 'shtick' with her husband? In fact, he is on his first warning, although he has no idea how many one actually gets, as the clear indication was that one is too many.

His three Killer colleagues are actually laughing together at a joke that Stephen really believes he practically almost nearly gets, when Tyler emerges from the kitchen, drink in hand. At which point the laughter immediately stops, which even Stephen thinks may not be the ideal prescription for a comedy course. But he accepts that his fellows, despite their bravado, could well be nervous, which he quite understands. Although, of course, he isn't experiencing this to the same degree. Why would he? After all, it isn't like he wants to switch professions and become a comedian full-time. Or even part-time. Or at all, actually.

As Jayson Spliff says, "We get it, Stephen. Really. You're learning a new skill, with a fixed and very narrow objective – like the guys on 9/11." An analogy which Stephen can understand yet still makes him slightly uncomfortable. (Although those men, whilst malign, did achieve exactly what they set out to do.)

"Got a surprise tonight for you sorry wannabes," announces Tyler, with an actual smile. "A special guest who's going to make you all famous. For at least fifteen minutes. And who absolutely needs no introduction. So say hello to Suzie V!"

From the kitchen, yet it could just as easily be out of the wings and into the spotlight, appears a very tall, sultry, Goth-like person, with short, carefully styled raven hair that frames and perhaps deliberately accentuates its wearer's overly bulging blue-grey eyes. Large hands sport almost equally large, incarnadine nails and there's an impressive cleavage on show, of which she seems extremely proud, as if it is something she just found on eBay and can't wait to see if the supplier merits its five stars. For reasons yet to be explained, she wears a high-end, GoPro camera on her head.

Stephen has never seen anything or anyone like her in his life. He can only compare her to an *Aristolochia grandiflora*, and you can't get more exotic than that.

If he is taken aback by this unexpected new arrival's appearance and the way she manages totally to dominate the room – whilst still exuding a palpable generosity of spirit to which he finds himself instantly warming, even as he is vaguely disturbed – it is her voice that both throws and captivates him. The accent, he thinks, is from somewhere way up North, a region of the country, like the East, West and most of the South, into which he has rarely ventured. But it is its surprising depth and resonance, emanating from somewhere way down inside the statuesque frame of this marvellous, slightly scary creature, which holds him in unsettling thrall.

"Hello, aspiring Killer comics! Poor bastards." She gives a laugh as rasping as her words.

Stephen gazes around at his fellow students, who are staring open-mouthed at this stranger. A person who, it is becoming increasingly clear, is strange to Stephen Gibson alone.

"*Oh my God!*" exclaims Jayson Spliff, who is quite beside himself. "It's you! It's THE Suzie V!"

Stephen appears equally amazed, but for slightly different

reasons. "You mean there's more than one? Now that *is* a humorous coincidence. As Alby Einstein would say."

Suzie V instantly propels her head, and the camera mounted thereon, directly towards Stephen. Now that he has worked out that this isn't a particular type of feminine accessorising, with which he would naturally be unfamiliar, he begins to feel a little self-conscious.

"And that would be... funny?" he hazards, less certain of his ground.

Suzie V turns her focus back onto Tyler, who is shaking his head sadly. "Comedically challenged," he explains. "But he knows people won't laugh at him here."

At which people understandably do laugh, save, of course, for Stephen.

The newly arrived celebrity grabs a spare plastic chair and sits down, long, oxford-grey trousered legs stretched out in front of her like aggressive tree roots.

"So. Here's the deal," she explains, to the enthralled, stand-up throng. "Lovely Tyler here writes for my show, one of the best. Not a fan of cameras himself – since he chose to offer his best side to an unappreciative TV audience." She points over Stephen's head to that blurry rear view of the almost naked man flipping a double-bird to the camera with his upraised hands. The others simply nod, as if this is not new information. Stephen is absolutely fascinated.

Tyler shrugs at this, although he appears not totally displeased. "Yeah, anyway," he says, "Suzie has this insane notion. She wants to film you sad shower for what will be, in due course if it's any good – *big* if – a running segment of her webcast."

His friends turn instinctively to Stephen, knowing in their hearts that their friend will be struggling with 'running', 'segment' and 'webcast'.

"*Suzie V on the Verge!*" yelps an elated Jayson. "Never miss it. You are so gonna get picked up any day."

"Are you a fan or a cop?" Suzie V laughs. "Okay – I'm gonna call it, oh, I dunno – '*Gagging for it*.' Whaddaya think?"

This is clearly Stephen's opportunity to shine. "I believe that gagging is a reflex that helps prevent choking, Miss Vee. Not sure it would be quite appropriate."

Suzie offers him a look of pure, are-you-for-real fascination.

NJ, who has been relatively restrained until now, bursts noisily from her chair. "Whoa!" she cries. "Stop there, girlfriend. Will this be one of those meshuggener, cleverly edited shows, where we have absolutely no control over what's put out there?"

"And the camera will be permanently on the whole time," adds Nigel.

"Yeah," chirps Jayson, peering around NJ. "And we don't get paid a sodding bean! Even if it goes viral."

Suzie V and Tyler Watts exchange a look. "Well, yeah," says Suzie.

Jayson, NJ and Nigel check soundlessly with each other.

"We're in," says NJ.

In the true spirit of democracy and with a silent prayer that he won't fuck things up for everyone, they look to Stephen for his answer. He is still trying to get his head around the question, when his phone informs him that a text has just arrived. Two in less than two weeks! He checks and discover that it is a photo. An angry face, a raised fist and another tiny hand strangling Benjamin, his prize *ficus*.

"I'm not in. I'm… out," says Stephen, to the consternation of all. "Excuse me."

Without another word, he is through the door.

"Elvis has left the building," says Suzie V.

***

The conversation with Mrs Dave doesn't last long. In fact, if you deleted the 'bloody's, it would take no time at all. Especially as

Stephen has precious little space to say anything, other than the occasional 'sorry', 'really sorry' and 'I truly will, Mrs Dave. Sorry'.

What he would like to tell his increasingly incandescent employer is something he now realises he has been formulating and finessing in his mind for the past fortnight. That he is in fact spending all of his leisure time – and quite a sizeable proportion of his non-leisure time – perfecting those skills that can turn a good presentation into an exceptional one. And, naturally, win him the woman of his dreams in the process, although he would never mention that bit.

But, of course, the ladies in his life will learn all of this soon enough.

Meantime, he resolves, he had better push on with the horticultural side. Let's face it, after seven-and-a-half rigorous modules and so much extra-curricular study, the comedy side is quite comfortably looking after itself.

EIGHTEEN

So she said, "Talk dirty to me"…

Anyone passing Uncle Geoffrey's house this particular Thursday evening, a couple of days after his nephew's first encounter with the weird camera lady, might be forgiven for thinking a disembowelment is taking place within its creaking, junk-ridden walls.

They would, of course, be entirely correct.

It is only paused – and this quite reluctantly – when the doorbell rings.

Uncle Geoffrey, snuggling up to Noreen on his favourite, moth-ridden Victorian chaise-longue, turns to her in the manner of someone whose doorbell only rings at night when it's tiny trick-or-treaters or the Jehovah's Witnesses. (One memorable Halloween they all arrived together, right in the middle of a grim little masterpiece called *Stigmata*. Geoffrey considered it quite serendipitous, so he allowed them all in to watch and took abuse from parents and elders for several weeks thereafter.)

"Wonder who that is," he grumbles.

Noreen, whose love of carnage is, by the happiest twist of fate, a match for his own – a match made in hell, as they themselves have remarked – resists the obvious and merely shrugs.

The path to Uncle Geoffrey's doorway is far less hazardous these days, now that his new houseguest has instituted her own brand of decluttering. This consists predominantly of stacking almost to the ceiling myriad disparate items which were former sole occupants of any given dusty space. Despite looking like weird formations from some national park in Utah, nothing too drastic has happened and the occasional avalanche has been regarded as a small price to pay.

As he wrenches the door open, a diminutive person whom Uncle Geoffrey has never seen in his life smiles up at him. Rather a sweet smile, he can't help but notice, yet he's not sure that it's worth pausing a good movie for.

"*Hello?*" says Uncle Geoffrey. "Got the wrong house, dear?" As it's not Halloween and she isn't holding a pamphlet, this is the only other possible explanation.

"No. Well, I hope not. I'm a friend of Stephen's. My name's Kerry."

"Good name. Evocative of hills and butter." He shouts back into the house of horror. "Did you hear that, Noreen? A *friend*. Stephen has a friend and it's female."

"*Well, let her in!*" calls Noreen, striding into the hallway to join him, her arms and smile open wide. Clearly, assesses Kerry, this new and unexpectedly junoesque arrival is the more hospitable of the two. The tall woman, however, begins to do a lot of stuff with her eyes, mouth and shoulders, which Kerry immediately understands as a non-verbal enquiry as to whether she and Stephen are more than just friends. Kerry, for reasons best known to herself, decides to perform a rather elaborate mime of her own that signals you must be bloody joking. So that's that one taken care of.

"So, how can we help you… Kerry?" asks Uncle Geoffrey.

Kerry would have thought it was obvious, but she doesn't want to be rude. She has no idea who this gentleman is, but she knows, at least, that he isn't Stephen's father. She guesses, however, that he must be a relative, presuming that whilst a certain weirdness does clearly run in some families, it most probably stampedes in this one.

"I just need a moment, please, with Stephen."

"All it takes for some," says this Noreen, cryptically.

Uncle Geoffrey turns on his heels, which Kerry takes as a signal to follow him into the living room.

Weaving a precarious path through the junk obelisks, she suddenly pauses, as she glimpses the image newly frozen on the huge TV screen. A limb, resembling a leg, has clearly just been sawn off. Whoever has performed the amputation, most probably without resort to anaesthetic or sterile equipment, as this is outside a log cabin in the woods at night and the leg is still in its trouser, is waving it in front of the naturally apprehensive person who is clearly next on his waiting list.

"Advise you to make it quick," says Geoffrey, unmoved by the sudden pallor clouding this perky young foreigner's face. "Lad's rather up against it, dear. Got a big presentation in the offing. But," he smiles, kindly, "as my old pa used to say, 'Aardvark never killed anyone!'"

Noreen, who is clearly of a more sensitive disposition, notices the effect the onscreen grotesquerie is having on their visitor. "*Severance Pay 3: Return of the Liquidator*," she explains, helpfully. "Geoffrey says it's seminal, which sounds a bit rude to me." When her laughter, which does go on for a while, has subsided, she points towards the garden. "Our kid's in his greenhouse. Where else! Would you like to—"

To the older woman's surprise, Kerry recoils even more at this suggestion than she did to the image on the screen. "*NO!* Er, thank you. Could you just… tell him I'm here?"

"STEPHEN! GOT AN AMERICAN HERE!" announces his uncle. "JUST A LITTLE ONE."

Noreen offers Kerry an indulgent smile and presses the 'play' button. Kerry stares hard at anywhere else, but it doesn't stop the sounds of carnage. She tells herself that she has been in war zones, for pity's sake, and wonders if years of suburban living might have unduly softened her.

Eventually, Stephen emerges from the greenhouse.

Kerry notices that the young man's hair seems bedraggled, if a clearly self-administered short back and sides can edge in that direction. He looks as if he hasn't slept, changed or possibly even washed for some time. The unusually thin face appears even more pale and drawn; the boyish, almost rabid, enthusiasm she has regularly observed in the stand-up sessions, whilst totally aberrant and unjustified, is currently nowhere to be seen.

"Oh, hello, Kerry," he says, in a dull monotone, conveying little surprise and even less delight.

"Hi, Stephen. Am I disturbing you?"

"Yes."

"No, she's not," cries Noreen, multitasking above the noise.

"Yes. She is, Noreen," insists Stephen, ignoring the new set of amputations. "I was working on my presentation, now I'm not. So yes, I'm disturbed."

"O-kay," says Kerry. She points towards the door, not that she can actually see one, because of the endless towers of tat. "Can we—"

"Stand in the front garden?" says Stephen. "If you want."

"Or go for a nice walk?" suggests Noreen, who is finding this even more painful than the movie. "Maybe."

Stephen shrugs dismissively, as if this is the last thing he would ever wish to do. Kerry can't think why she has bothered to come, when she could be at home with her son, but she is determined, for reasons she herself might find hard to explain, to see this mission through. She makes for the door, in the uncertain hope that Stephen could pick up the hint and follow. Which finally, after a good few moments, he does.

"Bye, guys," Noreen waves, "take your time." Kerry has no idea whether this is a kindly remark or simply self-serving, because the woman really doesn't want to be interrupted again mid-sever.

"Oh, and lad," calls Uncle Geoffrey, just as Stephen is disappearing behind one of Noreen's columns, "if you see anything, on your travels..."

Kerry has no idea what this means and has a feeling she really doesn't want to.

***

As they walk slowly and aimlessly through the crisp Ruislip night, Stephen's mind appears to be elsewhere. Yet Kerry notices that this doesn't prevent him from examining and naming, at his usual unhelpful volume, every blessed bush and tree en route.

He reminds her of a mutt she once had back home, except that the dog probably made more sense. But it also makes her think of Nathan, when he was a little boy and his eyes were closer to the ground. He would spot and pick up minuscule items almost invisible and certainly uninteresting to the adult eye – a dropped bead, a discarded sweet wrapper, a piece of solidified poo – and treasure it as if he were Howard Carter stumbling upon the tomb of boy-King Tutankhamen. A walk to the local shops could take a morning, by which time she would have forgotten why she was there and it would be time to go home for lunch.

When she has had all the shrubbery a person can take and is on the point of garrotting her companion, Kerry decides to break what she might laughingly call the silence. "They seem nice. Your folks."

"Noreen isn't folks. My uncle is, I suppose. A folk. They're in love. Like the briar and the rose."

"Kinda romantic," she ventures. "Opposites finding each other." She's not sure quite how opposite they are, but it makes for conversation.

Stephen, however, picks it up like Nathan and the poo and runs with it. "*Like me and Nina!*" he yelps. "Although, of course, we both love plants, so we're really more peas in a pod. Or *pisum sativum.*" He senses her staring at him. "Was he injured?" he asks.

"Was who injured?"

"Your father. In the Gulf?"

"*What?* No! Well, yes. If you include the mind. And the spirit. Which I do, actually." How did they get on to that? She'd almost forgotten the conversation in her studio.

This isn't what she turned up for.

"Why did you come here, Kerry? To my home."

It hasn't occurred to Kerry, until now, what an unusual situation this might be for the man. Pondering on the last time he might have had any sort of visitor, she would like to feel that she is doing him a kindness. Yet he doesn't appear anything other than put out by her turning up unannounced.

"We were worried about you," she says.

He stares at her as if she has recklessly slotted a totally new concept into his brain. Finally, he believes he understands. "I won't be asking for a refund."

"Well, that's good. Because you won't be getting one. Stephen—"

"I should have phoned Tyler. About rushing off, I mean. And missing an essential module with my fellow comics. They've all been texting, which is very kind and unexpected. I was… it was… *Leylandii*!" He is pointing into a garden now and shaking his head. "Spreads like—"

"Herpes?"

"Leylandii."

They walk in silence for several minutes.

It has always fascinated Kerry that one person can be totally at ease in circumstances that another would find excruciating. She has perpetually regarded silence as something to be immediately filled and reconstituted, like a cold bath that needs constantly heating up. A Swedish colleague, a fellow photographer, once told her that his countrymen would find her particularly annoying. She has made a point of never going there.

"Tyler thought it might have been Suzie V," she explains, when she can stand it no longer. "Y'know, who put you off. With the camera. And the webcast?"

Stephen ponders this for a while. He picks a leaf from a hedge and gently sniffs it. "No. I think I'm alright with that. If my friends are. It's very important to chart progress. I do it all the time at work." He turns to her. "She is a man, isn't she?"

Kerry nods. "Yeah, but not for long."

"The Four-Wing Saltbush does the same thing. Without a scalpel."

"Uh huh. This big presentation – I'm guessing it's something to do with gardening."

"It's something to do with Nina."

He moves to ease back an errant branch that is hanging too low over the pavement.

"*Can you stop with the friggin' foliage!*"

"Someone might poke their—"

"Let 'em. This Nina person—"

"The beautiful, clever young lady who loves plants and will very soon love me."

"Yeah. That Nina. Stephen—"

He doesn't allow her to finish.

She watches as a sudden heady excitement lights up his face with disturbing intensity, even as the night grows dark. Yet there is apprehension here, discernible in the way his lanky frame tenses and his usually assured voice, albeit monotone and overloud, develops just the slightest tremor. This is something she hasn't noticed before, certainly not at those times when she has popped in and out of Tyler's classes and caught the young horticulturist being almost preternaturally unfunny, whilst appearing to make voluminous notes in his head.

"I have to present to Ms Nina Hughes and her bosses on Monday," he explains. "At Kew Gardens, no less, Kerry! They're very famous gardens. In Kew."

"Who knew? Well, wow, Stephen. *Big time!* Hey, you know your stuff, don't you?"

He stares at her and shakes his head, as if he can't quite believe what this woman just said. Has she not been paying attention? "I don't want to impress her with my 'stuff', Kerry."

"What then – your body?"

"Not initially. My wit."

Kerry finds it rather hard to look at him. "Your what?" When he doesn't answer, she turns to him.

He isn't there.

Stephen Gibson has completely disappeared.

Kerry feels confused but also strangely responsible, as if it is she who must now return to his house alone and inform the resident uncle that she has lost or at least misplaced his nephew.

"Stephen?" she calls, but not too loudly, because for some reason she fears it might panic him. "Er… Stephen?"

"*In here!*" pipes a voice, in which she hears rather more elation than fear, with a touch of where-else-would-I-be, which she actually finds slightly irritating.

She looks around but all she can see is a massive skip in someone's driveway. It is almost overflowing with domestic rubbish and detritus and – oh, shit! – Stephen. He has managed to find an unfilled corner, in which he can just about stand. His bespectacled head on its lanky frame is peeping out like a discarded angle-poise lamp.

"What the fu… what in hell's name are you doing?

"Searching," he continues, in that tiresome, what-do-you-think tone. "For Uncle Geoffrey."

"But we only just left him." She shakes her head. "Oh, you mean…"

Stephen's bony arm, its sleeve ruffled up to the elbow, emerges like Excalibur from the lake, with a huge and garish, cracked vase (circa 1975) grasped firmly and lovingly.

"You'd be amazed at what people throw away, Kerry. But the man is a genius at repairing things."

"Did he put you back together again?"

Stephen simply looks at her, as if her words make no sense, or at least none to which he might wish to be party. Then he dives right back in. Yet within seconds his bobbing head is up again and he is staring across at the bemused young woman apologetically.

"Oh, I'm so sorry, Kerry. How rude of me. Would you care to come in?"

"Er, no."

She finds the man gazing at her, with such sadness in his glassy eyes, as if he has been mysteriously snubbed and is wondering exactly what his faux pas could have been.

Kerry glances around, in the hope that no-one is watching. Or perhaps simply to reassure herself that she hasn't been teleported to an alternate universe, one in which such invitations are prized beyond rubies. With a huge sigh for such a compact frame, she hitches up her second-best pair of denims, which she anticipates will very shortly plummet down the closet league table, and clambers uneasily into the beckoning container.

The invitee can't quite believe that somewhere within her befuddled brain she is still thinking that the experience of visiting a crap-laden and filthy builder's skip, on a suburban Ruislip driveway, as night is falling, might actually be so much more wondrous and incredible than she could possibly have imagined. She tells herself this is from watching too much *Doctor Who*. In reality the sensation is as she might have expected, which is exactly like sinking into a messy, manky dumpster in somebody's drive late on a summer Friday. It's stacked, spiky and dark, with only the streetlights to point up the more noticeably dangerous obstacles.

Kerry tries to wade towards him, as if his company might offer some small protection from rough-edged planks with rusty nails sticking out and shards of smashed-up furniture.

"I hope you don't think I'm one of those gals a guy takes her somewhere classy and she immediately puts out for him," she says, although she does wonder why she bothers.

"Sometimes I have no idea what you're talking about," says Stephen, but in a way that signals the fault is not of his making. "You really are a bit strange, do you know that?"

There are so many ways a person could respond to this, that she fails to select even one before he is off again.

"*Look at this!*"

He fishes out a battered, brass bedpan and holds it up to her, like it's one up from the Turin Shroud.

"Whoa!" exclaims Kerry. "Way to go!"

She tries to grab his attention, which is not so easy, as he has suddenly turned into a huge, mutated rodent, his body trapped but his arms busily burrowing and scavenging. Yet she knows that she must persist, because something in a hitherto untapped region is telling her that she has to help this young guy from planet weird, as it doesn't look like he's doing too much in the way of helping himself. Except, of course, to discarded and worthless bric-a-brac.

"Stephen, about this presentation—"

Stephen hands her a particularly ugly lampshade, just as lights go on all over the adjacent terraced house, in whose garbage they're currently mired. They hear an upstairs window bang open.

"HOY!! WHAT THE FUCK DO YOU THINK *YOU'RE* DOING?"

They both freeze, which doesn't actually look so different from the way they were before, save for the alarm spreading over their faces.

"Oh dear," says Stephen. "I think we had better go."

"You reckon?"

The householder, whose question was clearly more of a statement, is not waiting patiently for an answer. "You want something for the weekend?" he continues. "Sodding try this!"

The man disappears for a matter of seconds then returns fully armed with more crockery and vases, which he hurls with some accuracy towards the skip-raiders. Much of the bombardment bounces off the junk already there, but hard as they try, they can't escape every teacup and dessert dish. A chamber pot glances off Stephen's shoulder, as they hear another, more questioning voice.

"*Andrew?*" says the woman, in the tone of someone who has vaguely wondered what all the noise was and discovers it is her husband going slightly insane. Possibly with old wedding presents or valued heirlooms.

Stephen finally manages to hoist himself out of the skip. It might have been less of a struggle, had he surrendered the large, oak-framed mirror he is currently holding in both hands. He turns to look for Kerry, who is still laden with Stephen's 'finds' and is attempting to effect her own escape, without a Royal Doulton-related injury.

"Come on, Kerry! *Quickly.* If we break this, it's seven years' bad luck." Always polite, he manages to send a swift 'THANK YOU, SIR' back up to where it rightly belongs. But the family china keeps on descending.

Amidst the crashing, they hear the woman's voice, noticeably more brittle and anxious now, as she watches the man in her life, whom Kerry has swiftly assessed as having serious anger issues, dispose of the contents of their home. Perfume bottles, paperbacks and, confusingly, dolls from all nations, come hailing down.

"Have you stopped taking your Prozac?"

Kerry barely has time to log this nugget, and admire her own perception, when they hear a further and deeply concerning plea. "Andrew, no! *NOT ERIC!*"

Kerry and Stephen can only stare at each other in dread, as they await the imminent defenestration of a third household member.

It is almost a relief when a small, black cat flies at some speed out of the window. The animal, presumably Eric (and, mercifully, not a small child with an unfashionable forename) offers an understandable screech as it lands in the skip. He then lightly pads over the debris, hops down past the real culprits, his rigid tail brushing their faces, and trots off into a hopefully safer world.

The upstairs window is firmly slammed.

Stephen and Kerry shuffle off at some speed with their loot, in order to avoid whoever is presumably even now hurtling down the stairs. In pursuit of them or Eric.

They are on the safer side of a nearby corner, when Stephen hears it.

Being some steps ahead of Kerry, he spins round in alarm to check out the source of the new and chilling noise, which he rightly worries could involve his fellow forager.

He finds her standing doubled over on the pavement, the night's valuable booty set aside on a low wall. The curious sounds, which definitely emanate from Kerry, grow louder by the second.

"*Kerry!*" he says with genuine concern. "Are you alright? Are you in pain?"

She just nods. But the squeals, rapidly building to a higher pitch, continue unabated.

"Tell me where it hurts."

By now Kerry is crossing her second-best denimed legs, which he notices for the first time sport those ugly rips that certain people these days consider fashionable. How come he missed these before?

She shakes her head. Balanced precariously, on one small trainered foot, she is unable to talk. In fact, she is unable to do much of anything. Except shake. Her whole body is quivering, as if she is having some kind of fit.

Suddenly, Stephen recognises the sound. It shocks him to his marrow. "*What on earth is so funny?*"

"Ooohhhh!" she responds, unhelpfully.

Realising that she is not, in fact, in pain – or, if she is, that it is totally self-inflicted – he walks on with his seriously distressed mirror. He can discern from the pace and volume of the snorts behind him that she is attempting to catch up but must clearly be finding it tricky if her legs are still crossed (for reasons he is at some loss to comprehend).

Finally, she reaches him. She still has trouble allowing her words to escape beyond the tremors in her twisted body. "*You! The skip. The guy. Eric...!*" She looks up at him, her eyes watering. "*Didn't you find any of that at all funny, Stephen?*"

He stares at her with bemused curiosity – as if she has suddenly decided, for no apparent reason, to spend the rest of her life talking in a language neither of them speak. Turning back, he catches his own and far longer face in the scratched mirror. Kerry watches him as he gazes thoughtfully at his sober reflection, then swiftly flashes himself what he must consider one of his best and toothiest smiles.

Stephen Gibson begins to laugh into the cool Ruislip air.

"Yeah," he chortles. "The skip – ha! The guy – ho! *Eric* – hee hee!" To Kerry's consternation, he segues for some inexplicable reason into what she assumes has to be his impression of the late, great Tommy Cooper. "Just like that – ha ha ha!" But, of course, she is only guessing, as it sounds nothing like him.

When he finally dials down his particular brand of laughter, with its less than passing kinship to true mirth, the face with which he is left looks so lost and helpless, as if a mask has been brusquely ripped aside, that Kerry can only watch in compassionate fascination.

"Yeah. Okay," she says.

She can think of nothing more to add, certainly nothing encouraging, until she recalls the real reason that she has actually walked over in person to see him, rather than simply making a call. Handing him the cracked vase and the battered bedpan, she moves under the light of a street lamp and burrows in her shoulder bag.

"Oh – got something for you."

Stephen shows considerably more surprise than she could have imagined this relatively neutral announcement might warrant. What was he expecting – a writ? It is only now she realises that perhaps no-one ever hands him anything at all. Kerry finds herself hoping that he isn't too disappointed.

Finally, she fishes out a small, white envelope. On it, in what appears to be a child's handwriting, is Stephen's name. He stares at it and then at her. She nods, as if giving him permission to open what is patently his. He does so and removes a single sheet of paper, in the same scrawly hand. He starts to read.

"It's from Nathan," she explains.

"His spelling is lamentable."

"*He's not asking you to fucking mark it!*" As Stephen recoils, Kerry finds herself shrugging almost apologetically. "He's got plenty enough people at school making fun of him." He notices a sadness that he doesn't recall picking up before. Until he remembers the little ballet dancer in Kerry's studio and her disdain for the young boy.

"Oh, I wouldn't," he protests. "Not ever. I know how it can be, when…" He doesn't finish. "He didn't need to say thank you. Well, 'thenk' you."

"Yeah, he did. For the cactus. And for listening. So, if there's anything I or he can, y'know, ever do for you—"

"Are you free on Monday morning?"

"Jesus! That was swift," says Kerry.

NINETEEN

Now this pretty girl walks right over to him,
laughing her bloody head off...

Stephen is quietly (well, for him) rehearsing his presentation in an uncultivated corner of the Blooming Marvellous nursery. His delivery is a tad breathless, as he is simultaneously lifting heavy bags of compost from a sack-truck to their storage base beside a massively overpriced garden shed.

As a highly qualified and respected horticulturist, it is in no way part of his job description to heft weighty garden materials from anywhere to anywhere, but he is under serious and, most probably, binoculary scrutiny from Mrs Dave. He knows that if she asked him to pop round to her house and clip her toenails with a pair of anvil secateurs, he would be on his bike to her place in seconds.

He can vaguely hear someone muttering his name, but he is in mid-speech and it is going extremely well, so he ignores it and continues humping.

"*NINA'S HERE!*"

Stephen immediately drops the bag he's carrying onto the gravel path, where it bursts open with a messy whoomph. He turns to see Spike smiling at him.

"*Where?*" says Stephen, running a hand under his sweat-soaked baseball cap and through his hair, hoping that his teeth look brushed. He swiftly shakes the compost off his shoes. By now Spike has replaced his smiles with delighted laughter, so Stephen replaces his excitement with a sigh. "Oh. Joke. Spike, as you know, I'm really good at jokes now, but I *am* a little wrapped up."

"How come you're suddenly good at jokes?" asks the sceptical Scot, but he doesn't wait for an answer. Not that Stephen feels a lot like providing one. "Hey, I never asked you about old Mr Dave and that water feature. Looked hysterical, but mebbe not in a good way." Spike stares straight into his colleague's innocent face. "Stephen – what the fuck are you up to?"

"Nothing, Spike. Nothing at all." He raises his eyebrows and tries to appear both mysterious and cunning, although it simply looks like he is pulling a face for no apparent reason. "But just you wait until Monday." He suddenly grabs Spike's arm. "You *will* be there, won't you, Spike?" he asks, urgently.

"At Kew? Yeah. Course. Mrs Dave has asked me personally to help set things up in the room. Hey, not like you to be nervous, Stevie. Shit, man, you know your stuff – you can do these things in your sleep."

"Monday… is going to be different."

"Ah. Okay." Spike nods, like the man of the world he is. Aware, however, that this could be taken by his less worldly pal as endorsement or even complicity, he adds, "You're not still lustin' for yon Welsh rarebit, are you?"

Stephen just shrugs. He feels that the word 'lust' truly sullies whatever is roiling around inside him, yet can't help wondering what lust could be like, if it doesn't indeed comprise most of what he is currently feeling. He has been experiencing more stirrings than he knows what to do with, and what he does do with them doesn't seem to help.

Spike puts an arm around Stephen's shoulder, remaining careful not to step in the compost, as he is aware that it's not a good look. "My man, you are more than a little stressed out. It's called puberty, pal. Comes to some of us just a wee bit later than others."

Stephen nods. "Like the *Amorphophallus titanum*!"

"Took the Latin right out of my mouth. And Uncle Spike has an idea of *exactly* what his wee buddy needs."

Ignoring the spurious claim to kinship, Stephen says, "You have?"

"I have indeed. A relaxing evening. A rare chance to unwind. I know just the lady."

"*Lady?* Spike, I've got a lady!" insists Stephen. "Well, I will have, come July, end of. Especially," he smiles enigmatically/weirdly, "after Kew Gardens."

"Aye. I've no doubt you'll knock her pretty Welsh clogs off. But let's look at it practically, my friend. You go home of an evening, rehearse your big speech to your poor plants all fucking night, none of you gets any sleep, and Monday morning the foliage all hold up wee white flags and you die on your arse at Kew."

On thinking this over, Stephen realises that, for once, his colleague is making perfect sense. And what better than a trial run, like one of those mocks he did for his A levels? Yet suspicion adds more lines to his already weary face. "This person – she's not a lady of the night, is she?"

"No more than we're still living in 1863. That is offensive, Mr Gibson – and expensive. She's a friend. Nothing more. Are you in?"

Stephen nods. After all, what does he have to lose?

A massive, amplified beep suddenly echoes around the busy nursery. Startled customers gaze about them, as a familiar voice booms into the heavily scented air. "*Stop the chitter-chatter, brush up that compost and get back to your bloody presentation! All climbing plants today – ten per cent off.*"

***

There is a fine selection of cars outside The Five Balls this pleasant, early-summer evening, but not a single bicycle.

Arriving at the old Tudor pub on his sturdy Raleigh, Stephen finds this rather odd, as he has heard that cycling is on the rise. But he supposes that whilst a car can transport a clutch of willing drinkers and one sober or at least less drunken driver, the range of options for the clubbable cyclist is considerably more limited. For probably the first time in his life, he wishes that he could in fact drive. Or, better still, have friends who would happily convey him, as he finds himself experiencing a rather rare urge this evening to go just a notch over the limit.

So much has been happening to him over the past few weeks, so many experiences that have been new and different and in their own way rather scary, that this desire to lose himself, or at least to uncoil a bit, doesn't surprise him as much as it might otherwise have done. He has found himself struggling for a botanic equivalent, in order to make sense of all the conflicting emotions, but even on chatting to his own plants, who really should know about these things, he has failed to unearth a single, satisfactory example.

"I'm not a common poppy," he eventually told them, in language they might more easily comprehend. "I'm not self-seeding!" Which he realised, as the words came out of his mouth and into an attentive sunflower, was actually sort of a joke. Well, naturally, it was. He's a man of humour, for pity's sake. Or soon will be. Reaping material from his own life, which isn't the bottomless pit he might have wished but not without its depths.

Module Number 3: observation. Job done.

Stephen recalls, of course, that he had noticeably failed to laugh during the entire skip incident with Kerry, something she was only too keen at the time to point out. Yet he truly believes that he knows pretty much everything about comedy now, having listened to, watched and annotated Tyler and his fellow students, not to mention absorbing literally days' worth of apparently class

'A' stand-ups on stream and DVD. Quite sufficient, in fact, to be convinced that a disturbed man on medication, launching an innocent domestic animal out of a window, at people who were, if Stephen is to be brutally honest, stealing from said man's front garden, is by no stretch of the imagination even mildly amusing.

Mulling it over on his way home that awkward evening, he had realised that the whole scene was actually rather sad. Kerry had exhibited an unattractive streak of cruelty, which quite surprised him. Although perhaps it shouldn't have done. A woman who makes jokes about absolutely everything and everyone on the planet quite possibly lacks the compassion to realise that the world is, in fact, a really serious and often very cruel place.

And yet, of course, when she spoke about her son…

It is all very confusing.

Stephen wonders, for a moment, what exactly it is that people are seeking, when they specify GSOH as one of their prime requisites for workable romance. Surely not this.

As he walks through the forecourt and into the darkened, oak-beamed bar, removing his bicycle clips with practised grace, he realises that everyone from the car park must be in the south-facing beer garden at the rear of the pub. The only patrons remaining indoors, in the low-ceilinged fug, appear to be old barflies determined not to allow Saturday sunshine or a poncy all-day menu to put them off the serious business of emptying pint glasses down their mottled throats.

Stephen staunchly resists a temptation to discuss the miracle of the hop, or *Humulus lupulus*, with these ruddy-faced and slightly crumpled regulars of The Five Balls (or the Two-and-a-Half Men, as Spike confusingly called it), and walks instead towards a light that is almost blinding in its contrast.

He realises, at the threshold, that perhaps he ought to order his drink before he settles down. Abandoning all restraints, he asks the rather portly gentleman behind the bar for a half-pint of low-alcohol shandy for himself, then adds a glass of white wine for his imminent guest, because this is what Spike has told him ladies most usually drink.

Stephen is sitting at a slatted wooden table for two, sipping his brew and hoping that the white wine remains chilled, when he notices a warmly attractive and extremely smiley brunette glancing around from the doorway.

Their eyes meet, hers pleasantly inquisitive, his suddenly intimidated.

As she approaches, he rises politely, banging his knees with a thud on the table, which he now discovers is firmly attached to the bench on which he is sitting. Realising that this might give the impression that he is either offering the newcomer a courtly bow or that his back has spasmed, he sits sharply down again and uses his best handkerchief to mop up any drink that has overflowed. He is not sure now whether simply to say her name or accompany it with an outstretched hand. Or, as he has seen people do, even some at neighbouring tables, offer her a kiss. But this would mean he'd have to stand up again, risking more spillage and discomfort, so he decides not to go there.

"Stephen?" greets the young woman. She is now quite certain, from the hitherto questionable description Spike has provided, that this has to be her man.

"*HELLO?*" booms Stephen, then worries that this has sounded like a response one gives to the surprise arrival of an unwanted stranger, rather than the reaction to someone with whom you have arranged, albeit via a third party, to meet. So he tries again, sounding slightly more cordial. "Yes. Stephen. That's me… *Hell-o.*"

Holding out a small, multi-ringed hand, the young woman says, "Hell-o. I'm Clova, with an 'a'. Spike's friend. Nice to meet you."

"If it was with an 'e-r'," responds Stephen, with a slight smile, "I'd ask you if you were of the genus *Trifolium.*" To his delight, she smiles gently at this and sits herself down opposite him. As he hasn't taken her hand and it's just lolling there, she withdraws it and runs her finger over the cool-ish wine glass. She wonders if this drink was actually bought for her or simply left unquaffed by the table's previous occupant.

"That's for you. It's white wine," he explains. "And I'm Stephen. With a 'p-h.'"

As Clova sits down, taking in the view, which includes couples and groups of friends happily enjoying a summer's evening in this most English of surroundings, just beside the M40 and under the flight path to and from Heathrow, Stephen tries out a smile on her.

"Hello. Clov-a."

To his delight, she returns the smile, with only one hundred per cent more spontaneity. "Hello. Ste-*ph*-en."

This particular conversational seam appearing to have run dry, Clova – still smiling sweetly – generously attempts to seek more fertile terrain. "So – you work with Spike? Isn't he the funniest man?"

Stephen finds himself delighted at the new turn that this fine little discussion is taking. Smack bang into his very own home territory. "Actually, Clov-a," he informs her, "in a recent survey, a Mr Will Ferrell came out as the funniest man." The young woman just nods, clearly interested. "But Mrs Dave did say that if the Blooming Marvellous Garden Centre and Nursery in Ruislip were a circus, Spike would be the bloody head clown." He pauses, then adds, "Sorry. The 'bloody' is what *she* says. Rather a lot."

Stephen Gibson isn't certain exactly what reaction he expects from reporting a somewhat irate work discussion. Yet he is quite positive that what Clova does next would rate as highly unexpected.

Without the slightest warning, the young woman lets out what anyone in earshot could only describe as an unearthly honk of potentially glass-shattering mirth. People at nearby and even far off tables swivel around in shock, beer is spilled en route and lovers clasp each other for support. Stephen wouldn't be too surprised if passing traffic suddenly veered off course.

The manufacturer of such a seismic reaction, however, appears blissfully oblivious. "Oh, that is hilarious, Stephen," she yelps. "You're right, he would be the 'bloody' head clown! That is priceless. Ha!"

Stephen is initially so thrown and, were he to be completely honest, so unsettled by his exuberant guest, that he can barely respond in any intelligible manner whatsoever. He is completely unaware that chatter has subsided all around the garden, and that he and his partner are being observed with both fascination and concern. Yet, as this roaring woman gradually tails off, he finds himself staring at her and experiencing a sensation he has seldom, if ever, felt.

That of vague yet definite encouragement.

"And Mrs Dave," he continues, with mounting enthusiasm, "well, she'd be... she'd be the ringmaster!" He can hardly believe his sudden inventiveness. "No! No, Miss Clov-a, she would be the lion-tamer! No, forget that. *Elephant Woman!* ...Because she's from the Indian subcontinent. Where they have elephants. Indian ones. With the smaller ears."

By this time Clova is beside herself, clutching her stomach and hooting like an angry trucker on the adjacent M40. Nearby drinkers are wondering whether she might be having a seizure, which could be interesting.

Stephen, who knows enough about the rules of comedy to realise that it is often possible to top a good laugh with a bigger one – although admittedly, in Clova's case, this might prove problematic and even downright dangerous – decides to seize the moment and go for broke. "And I would be... I would be..." Pause for effect. Wait for it. "...*the plant-juggler*!"

Clova's lukewarm wine, of which she has foolishly snatched a sip, comes shooting out of her incredibly wide-open mouth, between two sets of gleaming white teeth. It splatters Stephen's face, a face already so drenched with elation that a splash of cheap projectile Chardonnay is really of no consequence.

For the first time in his life, Stephen Gibson has – intentionally – made someone laugh.

***

Before Stephen and his new greatest fan finally roll into a hastily summoned minicab, their audience – including the old drinkers, who for once have ventured beyond the darkness – are treated, alongside an enraptured Clova, to her new acquaintance's entire repertoire.

This includes jokes, or what pass for jokes on Galaxy Gibson, stand-up routines (for which Stephen does indeed precariously stand up), impressions, mime, mangled versions of other, infinitely more accomplished people's best stuff and a touch of slapstick for luck. By this point, Clova is smacking him so hard, in her incredibly loud and utterly uncontrollable paroxysms, that he knows he will see bruises in the morning.

It has to be worth it.

Tonight has been the most sublime of evenings, even if Stephen has drunk considerably more than intended. This was partly, he justifies to himself, in order to lubricate his larynx, which instrument this magical interlude appears to be working overtime. His gleeful guest, who has kindly treated him to as many top-ups and alcoholic variations as he has in turn offered her, is giving every indication that the evening has not yet drawn to a close.

As soon as the cab pulls up outside her small, terraced home in nearby Ickenham, Clova yanks Stephen out onto the pavement with an extraordinarily strong right arm (especially considering the languid floppiness of the rest of her) and instructs the driver to be on his way. An instruction the man appears only too willing to obey, as his ears already ache from the unusually painful assault to which they've just been subjected. Stephen has mere seconds to extricate his bicycle from the car's expansive boot, before it zooms gratefully off.

Once inside Clova's neat but sadly plant-deprived little house – a desolation Stephen resolves to alleviate first thing after Kew – his hostess plonks another drink into his hand and immediately disappears off somewhere.

He sits contentedly, if slightly blearily, on the cosy, oatmeal DFS sofa, musing that he has never actually been in a woman's house before – except for elderly neighbours and Mrs Dave, and this was only because she had left a lipstick in her office. He tries to make sense of the Bridget Riley reproduction on the wall, but it is causing him to feel rather sick, so he decides to look away and concentrate on that which he has discovered this evening he clearly does best. Being funny. Or perhaps second best, as naturally nothing will replace *Archibald* and the sublime safety of the horticultural world. Yet still more than satisfactory, and a good omen for things to come.

Things to come happen rather fast.

Stephen hardly has time to down his drink, the exact constituents of which he is not entirely certain, when Clova reappears dressed in considerably less than when he last saw her. He can't help noticing, despite the weird things his eyes and brain are doing, that beneath whatever the dark, floaty garment is that she is wearing, she has a rather lovely figure. Not perfect, certainly not Nina-perfect, so far as he can recall, although it has been some weeks since their last encounter. (His fragrant client has generously left him quite alone in the meantime, which he takes as trust rather than indifference. And a laudable hesitancy to rush things.)

Yet the smile on Clova's face as she joins him on the sofa, and the scent that accompanies her nice-but-not-quite-Nina-nice body, are causing sensations in Stephen's own body with which he is regrettably not over-familiar.

Although over-familiar is exactly the effect Clova appears to be going for right now.

"Hi, plant-juggler StePHen," she purrs, tapping him lightly on his hand. If she notices the green thumb, she has the courtesy not to allude to it.

"Hello, four-leaf ClovA," he responds, with a wit that surprises even him.

Stephen is rewarded with an industrial-scale shriek that he imagines must be piercing the thinnish walls on either side of this tiny, terraced house. He hopes that there aren't any small children or insomniacs within range. Or dogs. Yet at the same time he feels rather proud of his effect on women, at least on this particular woman, although pride is swiftly overtaken by more basic emotions, as his smiling young hostess slithers breast-nudgingly close to him.

"Now be honest, Steve, do you laugh all your lady friends into bed?"

"It's Stephen. And tonight, Clova, you didn't even get all of my best stuff. You should hear my Miss Joan Rivers. I do, of course, realise that she's a lady and I'm not, nor am I of the Jewish faith, unlike NJ (or at least half of her) but as the great Tyler Watts himself says, 'Forget the rules, you wankers, funny is funny.' And wait till I tell you about my water feature!"

Clova roars all over again.

Stephen can't help but notice that this causes major vibrations in her body, distinctive tremors of which he wasn't as aware earlier in the proceedings and to which he has never actually been party on anyone else. He processes what he believes but can't as yet quite believe she has just said.

"*Bed?*"

Hands flailing, she thumps him violently one more time, before settling down to gentler, more exploratory pursuits.

Stephen has the disquieting sensation that he is watching this encounter from up an available tree, a sessile oak, perhaps, or even an aspen, whilst still experiencing it in all its unbelievable earthiness right here at ground – or just slightly above ground – level.

This will be, as the saying apparently goes, something to tell his grandchildren.

TWENTY

Anyway, so I gets myself over to Kew, where the aforementioned Gardens are… is.

The small Kew Gardens' meeting room that Mrs Dave has hired for the Magnolia Group presentation, at ill-concealed great bloody expense, isn't amongst the grandest or most impressive of those available in West London's botanical wonderland. The views from its floor-to-ceiling windows, however, of the large lake and Treetop Walkway, with the day's fortuitous sunshine enhancing a glassily magnificent Victorian Temperate House just glimpse-able beyond, are hopefully sufficient to impress even the most hardened business prospects.

And, of course, who could resist a huge banner that proclaims, in confident day-glo red and green, '*Blooming Marvellous hugely welcomes lovely Magnolia Hotels people!*'? It is these small details, Mrs Dave tells anyone who will listen, that single out the professionals from the barrow boys.

"Isn't this glorious, Stephen?" says Mrs Dave, as she brutally scours the Victorian oak presentation table just one more time, using cleaning materials she has brought from her own home, because you can't leave anything to chance or cleaners.

Stephen just nods, as he continues to check his notes, because he knows that this isn't one of those many hundreds of questions she has been firing at him since six-thirty this morning, to which an immediate answer is expected.

He spies Spike lumbering in with yet another plant from the nursery's liveried van, although an uninformed observer might have thought that Kew would have one or two half-decent plants of its own. But these, of course, are actual living examples of what Stephen and the team are proposing for the brand-new Magnolia Hotel he only recently visited.

"The atmosphere…" continues Mrs Dave excitedly, listing the attributes on her small, immaculately manicured fingers, "the refinement… the *prestige*! Oh, Stephen dear, everything feels so right. Screw this up and I will slash your bicycle tyres and then your bloody throat."

Mrs Dave completes her scouring and turns immediately to setting out an array of tempting Indian snacks on a long side table, one that she has also treated to an unforgiving retread for the occasion. These sweetmeats have been kindly supplied by her brother-in-law, the caterer, business cards available. Delicacies, as she has informed her employees on more the one occasion, unlike anything rival horticultural concerns could possibly offer. Even Kew Gardens itself. Spike would indeed vouch for this, as he has not been above snaffling a few as he works. Stephen remains untempted, being uncomfortable with foods that are foreign and don't have 'sandwich' and 'tuna' somewhere in the description.

Turning to face Mrs Dave, Stephen realises that, since he and Spike first arrived this morning in the van, he has consistently avoided doing so. He notices that she is wearing a most striking sari of clearly significant green. The vermilion dot on her forehead appears to glow with augmented luminescence. Stephen finds himself wondering whether there are varying intensities, depending on how the particular person feels or what she wishes to express. There is so much about other cultures and customs – and indeed other people in general – about which he has absolutely no idea. Something that has never truly bothered him, yet curiously is just beginning to now. Perhaps, he muses, he is finally becoming what they call 'a man of the world'.

"Don't you worry about a thing, Mrs Dave," he assures her, with growing confidence. Adding, with more than a hint of ambiguity, "You and I are *both* going to get what we want today."

"I want George bloody Clooney," says his employer with a rare smile, or at least a rare unprofessional one, "but I'll settle for the entire Magnolia Hotels and Spas account."

They hear Spike land one of the heavier shrubs down onto the floor with a thump. "*The entire account, Mrs D?*" he asks, in some consternation. "I thought we were only after yon brand-new hotel that Stevie here went to."

"That is why you are a plant-shifter, Spike, and I am a business tycoon. I think big."

"But my presentation is only on the one hotel, Mrs Dave," exclaims Stephen, the colour leaving his face – not that there was much there to start with.

"I didn't want to stress you out, Stephen," she insists, tapping his gloved hand. "So please don't worry or have a trouser incident. You won't have to talk about the other hotels – when they see our wonderful plans for their new High Wycombe flagship, they will put us top of their list for all the rest, new, refurbished and yet to be even bloody thought of. Right at the very top of their list!" She is almost physically swelling with the sheer scale of it all and Stephen feels certain that he has caught the forehead dot on the cusp of a beam.

He finds himself feeling a bit shaky. Admittedly, he has had bouts of this light-headedness on and off since Saturday night, with its overwhelming and still almost unbelievable Clova experience. Did that really happen? Was he really there! Did she *really…*?

Stephen Gibson realises that he had never fully appreciated the true allure of comedy until that night – but now, of course, he recalls all those dating websites. The internet doesn't lie. And, come on, you only have to look at the almost criminally unprepossessing Tyler Watts and Spike. GSOH rules, OK!

It was in the early hours of Sunday morning that he had finally staggered home from Clova's little house. He is still not totally certain how he was able to remain on his bike, or at least not fall off it so badly or so often that he did himself any serious, permanent injury. He managed to barricade himself in his greenhouse for the remainder of the day, trying to remember and then finesse his presentation for Kew, whilst nursing his first-ever hangover and avoiding the weird looks Uncle Geoffrey and Noreen kept hurling at him through the glass. Not just looks but grins, outright smiles and bizarre double thumbs-up gestures.

At one point, Uncle Geoffrey had even begun to parade mysteriously around the house, brandishing a faded and fraying American flag, one that had been rolled up in an elephant's foot umbrella stand for as long as Stephen could remember. What was all that about?

He begins to make for the meeting-room door.

"*And where do you think you are going to?*"

Stephen shakes his head but doesn't look round. "I just need some air, Mrs Dave. To clear my head."

He can still hear her voice as he is walking down the path towards the lake. "What do you need air for? You're not a dolphin. We've got bloody air here. It comes with the rental."

A pair of ducks flies off to somewhere more peaceful.

***

"'*Good morning, everyone. How you doing?*'"

Fortunate visitors to these lush and celebrated gardens, on this gloriously sunny morning, might well discover themselves observing with some curiosity a rather formally dressed, thickly bespectacled young man, waving a pair of skinny, garden-gloved arms around and talking at some volume to himself, as he strides purposefully between the towering trees.

"Point to front row, look straight into her eyes. No blinking unless from sun. Okay… '*And what's YOUR name? …Nina? Nina who? Oh, Nina Hughes. Well, welcome Nina Hughes. You got in okay? I hope there wasn't too much of a KEW!*' Wait just a beat. '*…Gardens.*' Now leave a few more seconds, until the laughter just starts to tail off, then hit them with, '*It's a great pleasure to Mag-*KNOW-*lia!*' Boom boom! Don't have to say 'boom boom!' Just think 'boom boom!'"

It is as if he is trying out some manner of one-man performance, a work in progress, complete with smiles that resemble grimaces and the imagined laughter of an invisible crowd. Being British, however, or simply following the example of those who are, these same visitors would be far too polite even to acknowledge such a rehearsal. (Aside from perhaps affording the man a slightly wider berth than one might normally do.)

Rather appropriately, Stephen Gibson finds himself strolling down Princes Walk towards the magnolias. It is, of course, too late in the season to encounter the deciduous varieties in full bloom, but he is delighted to see that the *Magnolia grandiflora* are still putting on a more than respectable show this year.

By the time he has completed what has to be his final run-through, Stephen finds that he has walked straight past the *wollemi* pine, which he usually adores and in whose arboreal company he has over the years passed many precious quality hours. Right now, however, even these giants among trees haven't been sufficient to entice him off course. He is already at the beautiful, eighteenth-century Orangery, with its grand, arched windows and apparently excellent cheddar, chutney and pickle sandwiches.

When, finally, he has made his bows and graciously accepted whatever plaudits his enraptured 'audience' feels obliged to bestow – "*Thank you. Oh, thank you. You're very kind. That's me, Stephen Gibson*" – he is approaching Elizabeth Gate itself, one of the three main Kew Garden entrances.

As he doesn't actually want to exit the venue, although he has to admit to an unfamiliar, nervous churning in his stomach, which he knows is all about seeing his special someone again ('butterflies' his uncle once called it, but, of course, they'd be dead in seconds), he swivels over-dramatically on his ruthlessly polished and never-quite-in-fashion, black leather shoes.

It is as he is retracing his steps some yards further on, heavily into the process of deciding whether to return via Gingko Lane or to dare take the longer route through his beloved climbers and creepers, that he hears it.

A massive sneeze. Followed instantly by the screech of a peacock.

Stephen has no idea of the identity or whereabouts of the peacock, but he is pretty certain that he recognises the source of its alarm. Especially when that source is now shouting, '*Shit – shit – shit!*' at almost exactly the same volume.

He has to admit that Kerry looks absolutely dreadful.

It is a look he had almost forgotten but now recalls with some clarity. The red eyes, the streaming nose, the mounting fury. He shouldn't really be surprised and this time he actually feels some sympathy for her. Especially as she has arrived with her son, for some unexpected but not unwelcome reason, and it can't be easy for a young boy to watch his mother suffering. For a moment it occurs to Stephen that this must be something that falls on so many sons in time and that this, at least, has been spared him.

"Oh, you *did* come!" says Stephen. "With your allergies."

"Never leave home without 'em. Didn't I say I'd be here?" she responds, through the sniffles, but he doesn't hear, so she repeats it with more force and sputum.

"Yes, but I find people don't always keep… and Nathan, I didn't expect *you* too!"

The boy is wearing an unusually vivid T-shirt, sporting a graphic of a disturbing plant, with the words '*Day of the Triffids*' emblazoned beneath. Stephen had no idea that such items were available and briefly wonders if one in a larger size might enhance his own 'stage' persona.

"Man gives me a cactus," says Nathan, "least I can do is come watch him screw—" A sharp nudge from Kerry and he holds that thought. "And it's half-term. None of the boys in my class could make a play date."

Stephen notices that the boy doesn't seem upset by this. His posture appears rather to signal a world-weary resignation. It is Kerry's eyes that show the sadness, but this may, of course, be because tears are streaming anyway.

Stephen Gibson has himself had the odd play date in the past, although he doesn't believe that this is what they were called back then. His memory is that they were never very satisfactory, because little boys are confusingly far more interested in cars and football and games than they are in the care and propagation of plants. He would probably have enjoyed a play date with a child like Nathan, but recalling the boy's particular sphere of obsession, his play partner could well have killed him.

"Oh, well," he says, in an attempt to cheer them both up. "Prepare to be amazed. And – of course – amused!" This was rather neat, he thinks, but then something far more wonderful draws his enraptured gaze. He points to a massive tree, its girth unrivalled, the distant, uppermost branches almost lost in the soft morning sunlight. "And this beauty," he exclaims proudly, head upturned, "is a Sequoia. *Sequoia sempervirens.*" He smiles at Nathan. "Your mum will know all about them."

"Coming from Queens." Kerry sniffs. She begins to shuffle uncomfortably. "Can we get away from…?"

"Pollen? No. It's a garden."

Kerry nods in weary resignation, yet her eyes still seek vainly for some sort of plant-free haven, which has to be like living in a high-security prison and hoping to keep your distance from criminals. She reasons, after yet more uncomfortably futile walking, that she will simply have to sniff and bear it.

"You'll be pleased to know, Stephen Gibson, that Nathan here actually said he *wanted* to come with me today. He checked this place out online. Go figure."

"Gotta have someone here to tell you when the snot comes out your ears," says Nathan, with a smile. He gives Stephen a conspiratorial wink, with his good eye, which confounds the older man, as no-one ever winks at him with eyes of any efficacy.

"So, mister horticulturist," says Kerry, "do you have all the facts in your head? Y'know – for your presentation."

"*Of course!*" insists Stephen. As if he wouldn't.

"Then why the hell do you have to be 'amusing'? And why did you ask us – well, me – to come hear you?"

"As my audience, silly!" He shakes his head. Does the woman know nothing about comedy? Wasn't her own husband – well, ex-husband – a big-time comic, for pity's sake? Perhaps he still is. "Mr Watts said to us very clearly – I had it down in my last notebook, before he added my pages to the stew that was simmering on his hob – 'Laughter is infectious.'"

"Well, something sure as shit is." She sneezes again and tree birds scatter. A personal best.

"*Bless you!*"

The voice isn't Stephen's. It isn't that of any sort of male. Nor is it redolent of London or the outer suburbs. Before Kerry can look around, she catches his face. Stephen has transformed into a cartoon character – eyes bulging, mouth dropping open, words failing. She can almost sense his knees begin to buckle, at what he has glimpsed just behind her, which she doesn't think is a talking shrub.

When she finally turns, Kerry almost wishes she hadn't.

If sunlight can enhance the already magnificent Sequoia tree, it does much the same for this vision in front of her teary eyes. Even the look of vague repulsion on the young and far taller woman's face does little to diminish her beauty. Indeed, one could almost believe that other women, on witnessing this reaction, would themselves endeavour to adopt the 'visceral recoil' and make it part of their own alluring repertoire.

Nina, who really doesn't wish to be impolite, makes an effort to smile. It is a smile of some radiance, which Kerry attempts and fails miserably to return. She swiftly runs a hand across her face, to harvest some of the errant snot, then unthinkingly offers same hand up to the newcomer. Until she hears Nathan groaning beside her.

"Hi, sorry about the… I'm Kerry." She tries wildly to hoover whatever is coming down right back up again, whilst digging into her bag for a tissue. She can sense a bemused Nina looking over her shoulder at Stephen, either for clarification or to escort her the hell out. And she can also feel the man's besotted eyes whizzing between herself and this other woman, as if he's playing one of those 'spot the difference' games and scoring double figures.

"Nina," says the vision. "Hello, Stephen. Good to see you. Team Magnolia and I got here a little early, so I thought I'd enjoy the glorious flowers. So glad I did." She smiles at Kerry, simply to include her in the conversation. The smile Kerry returns is brimming, but not with warmth, so Nina moves on. "How's it all going?"

"Splendidly, Nina," enthuses Stephen, his heart beating so violently it feels like it's about to shoot right up and out of his larynx and become a pulsating mass in the scented West London air. "Prepare to be overwhelmed."

"*Ladies' room!*"

Nina points behind her, with some authority. Stephen isn't exactly certain what kind of disaster is imminent or in progress but can see Kerry apparently torn between leaving her son with this pair of flower people or dragging him with her.

"Look after Nathan," she yells. "Nathan, *stay*!" They watch her scoot uncomfortably but purposefully away.

Whilst clearly bemused, Nina Hughes of Magnolia Inc doesn't want to waste valuable work time on an explanation about which she really couldn't care less.

"Hope this hasn't been too much for you, Stephen. When Mrs Dave suggested that you present for *all* our UK business..." She sees his face. "You *did* know this?" Stephen nods vigorously, like a sapling in a storm. Of course he knew! "Well, I didn't honestly think it was necessary. You're the key, Mr G. Which rhymes – ha! As I've told everyone, when it comes to the green stuff, Steve Gibson is our go-to guy..." She gives him the most delightfully warm and trusting smile. "I'm sure you've got something *very* special up your sleeve for me."

Before there's time to ramp-up the nods he has already been doing with such intensity throughout her comments, the power of speech having apparently deserted him, Nina lays a gentle hand on his shoulder. He turns, in a manner he believes quite casual, to stare at it. Those elegant, long fingers, so exquisitely manicured, nails the colour of his favourite *Astilbe chinensis* (how did she know!). And he does believe his own hypersensitive nostrils are detecting what has to be highly expensive lotion on her smooth, lily-white, Welsh skin. Could this dear lady be any more gorgeous? Hasn't his already sound judgement been even more categorically vindicated this crisp summer's morning?

Finally, the words return. At an increased volume, even for him. "Oh YES. I do. Have something special, Nina. VERY. Thank you."

"Well, that's tidy. Because, as you know, Stephen, this finishing touch, this 'perception of perfection', as we say, is so very important to our corporate ethos. Our unique Magnolia bloom." She takes on an almost corporate glow, as she moves a fraction closer towards him. Stephen can hardly breathe. He thinks he may just vomit but will try very hard not to. "And I'll let you into a little secret, Mr Gibson. Our two major shareholders, a sweet couple from Atlanta, Georgia—"

"Home of the *Magnolia macrophylla* or Bigleaf Magnolia—"

"If you say so. Well, as luck will have it, they happen to be in town – they adore London. And they told my boss they might just pop in. So, do what you do best, Mr Green-fingers, and—"

"Just the one," says Stephen Gibson, proudly removing his glove and holding up a thumb.

"*Jesus shitting Christ, what is that?!*"

"My green finger. Well, thumb. Sorry Nina, I interrupted. Do what I do best…?"

"How did I not notice that?" says Nina, totally thrown but gamely getting back on the horse. "Er, yeah. Do… what you do best. And make me look good."

"You always look good," gushes Stephen.

"You're very sweet, Stephen." She begins to wander off. "I'll just enjoy a bit more Kew. See you in the meeting room."

Stephen nods and watches her go.

He finds himself riveted by the way she walks, casual yet purposeful, head held high, hips swaying with a bold but unswaggering confidence that he can only imagine she was born with, like some lioness or other noble beast, as no-one could feign or develop this. It does increase his apprehension just observing her, but he smiles briefly to himself, knowing that he now has the tools to do the job. Especially after—

"*Where's Nathan?!*"

He turns reluctantly to see Kerry, who has somehow arrived behind him. The panic on her cleaned-up face can't totally mask the blame hurtling his way. Along with yet another massive sneeze.

"I don't know! He was just—"

"I know he was friggin' just – while you were mooning over Wonder Woman. Well, he clearly *isn't* now. You gotta help me find him."

"I can't. I have my pres—"

"He's an eleven-year-old kid. Obsessed with killer plants!"

"Well, he's chosen the right day," says Stephen, helpfully. "They're doing a '*Deadly and Disgusting Plants Trail*'. I imagine it's for that half-term thing."

"The little devil!" says Kerry. "He must have found it on the website. No wonder he was so keen to join me."

Stephen can't help looking a touch disappointed but can't quite work out why.

"So you gonna help me find him or just stand there lookin' disappointed?"

Stephen extracts a printed map from the spiral notepad bulging his inside pocket and points out to her exactly where the trail would be. "It'll be ever so interesting for him. There'll be *Strychnos nux-vomica,* you know – the strychnine tree—"

She is grabbing his sleeve now and pulling, although she has no idea where to head. "*Strychnine!*"

"It'll be perfectly safe. There's sure to be *Ricinus communis* too – that's castor beans."

"OMG – *castor beans!* ...I have no idea what they are. Come on, Stephen."

"You're pulling me in the wrong direction." He stands firm, like a Sequoia. "Kerry, please don't worry. He won't get anywhere near them. This isn't India, where strychnine actually comes from. Or even South East Asia. This is Kew."

"*And he's Nathan!* This is no ordinary kid. Wile E. Coyote I call him. I'm scared, Stephen." She stares at him, but he's looking back at her blankly, as if he is suddenly lost in an alien world. She shakes her head in disbelief. "Forget it. I'll find him on my own."

Stephen can just make out Nina, in the distance, walking towards the meeting room. He looks down at Kerry, who is frantically studying the map. He has no idea what to do.

"I'll call," he says. Finally.

"You'll call. You'll *call*! What are you – friggin' Tarzan?"

"No. I meant a telephone call. I know some people here. For my research. They'll find him and keep him for you. I mean, he's not exactly hard to spot, is he, what with that..." He notices her glaring at him, for some reason. "Can you tell me your phone number, please?"

"Can't you just come with me and fetch him? This is your, y'know, hood."

He doesn't respond. So, with a meaningful sigh, she gives him the number. He makes the phone call, while she stands there, listening, offering information and trying not to throttle him.

"They'll bring him to the gift shop," says Stephen, closing his phone.

"Dead or alive?"

"They didn't say."

He pelts off to catch up with Nina and his meeting. Yet he can't help feeling he may have said something wrong.

TWENTY-ONE

So this guy says to me – I suppose you think that's funny! …Er – yeah.

Stephen has to admit that Mrs Dave and Spike have done a wonderful job with the room.

The view, of course, was splendid anyway. Especially in the morning sunlight. But now, with an expansive selection of Blooming Marvellous plants festooning and only slightly overwhelming the smartly chosen venue, an antique table buffed to within an inch of its life and sporting an array of tempting, heavily discounted Indian snacks, everything indeed offers a 'perception of perfection'. At least to Stephen.

Just a few minutes earlier, as he was striding briskly back into the room in order to assist Nina through the foliage, he had heard Spike mutter something under his breath that had to do with Newcastle and sodding coals, which Stephen didn't quite understand. He wasn't able to gain further clarification, as his bouncy co-worker was suddenly right next to their attractive guest, happily and manually delivering her to a vacant seat amidst her colleagues. Even within this tiny window, Stephen had noticed that Spike was able to make Nina chuckle trillingly.

He reminds himself that he really must thank the little Scotsman after the event. An MC's job is, apparently, very important, as indeed is the first 'warm-up' act. Which would obviously be Mrs Dave, although she is in no-one's estimation a natural comedian.

Right now this important lady has a smile on her face that looks as painted-on as the dot on her forehead. Her dark eyes move across the front row like minnows in a tank, taking in smartly suited Magnolia executives of both genders, who sit, laptops and minds open, awaiting whatever she has to say.

Stephen also stares, with perhaps a touch more blinking, as he attempts to size up his audience. Yet he finds his eyes constantly returning to that chair exactly in the centre, wherein sits Ms Nina Hughes, utterly composed in a cream blouse of pure silk, legs encased in finely tailored slate-grey trousers (why do so many of the ladies in his life wear grey, without looking grey in the least?) and so elegantly crossed at ankles of disarming slimness. She is looking expectantly up at him with the most trusting and fragrant of smiles.

He won't let her down.

As the clock above the meeting-room door hits eleven, Mrs Dave begins to speak. She knows how important time management is to very top, high-level executives and she wants them to know that she knows.

"*Eleven o'clock!* On the button. Okay, team?" She turns and nods to Stephen, her main speaker, and to Spike, the technical genius, who will be working the PowerPoint. They both nod in return. All systems go. If adrenaline had a scent, the room would be saturated.

"Welcome, welcome. Thank you so much, very kind Magnolia people, for attending our little – but incredibly important – presentation," she begins, striking what she believes is the correct balance between humility and knocking them sideways. "As you know, Blooming Marvellous of Ruislip, Middlesex, the garden of England, has a reputation for stocking and sourcing the finest product in the entire civilised world. As to what kind of top-quality shrubs, plants and trees and suchlike are bloody perfect for you, with your famous reputation and fussiness, let me present Mr Stephen Gibson, my protégé and our resident horticultural genius. And I have to say, almost a son to me. Although I have a proper son, Deepak, who is studying medicine at Kings College, London. Second year. Time flies. … Stephen, dear…?"

Stephen moves to join his proud boss. "Thank you, Mrs Dave. I've got it from here."

As she moves aside, towards the table with the snacks, she taps her protégé almost maternally on the cheek. "Bugger this up and you're compost," she whispers.

Stephen nods, happy to observe that his confidence is actually growing rather than receding. Perhaps his unscheduled encounter with Nina today was a really good omen. They're almost old friends by now, and his pointing out and naming every single specimen on their stroll back to the meeting room, including grass, weeds and the occasional passing horticulturist, appeared to go down really well. But, of course, she has no idea what else he has up his green sleeve.

"Our Mrs Dave, ladies and gentlemen! One Indian about whom I don't have any reservations." He waits for a reaction to this long-crafted yet seemingly effortless wordplay, but none is forthcoming. Early days. Tyler Watts himself has said that an audience, even of the friendliest kind, takes a while to warm up. Don't rush them and for God's sake don't lose your nerve. One battle is not the war.

"Okay. Well. Good morning, everyone. I see you all made it in this morning. But this is especially for *you*, Nina Hughes." Stephen stares straight at her. Nina stares warily back and wonders why he is holding a long, metal pointer just in front of his chin, as if he is expecting it to provide some sort of amplification. Perhaps it's a confidence thing; she totally gets that.

"How you doing, alright? I hope there wasn't too much of a KEW at the entrance! …To Kew Gardens. Victoria *or* Elizabeth Gates… Well, I just want to say, to all our visitors – really good to Mag-*KNOW*-lia!" He waits this time for the inevitable laugh, yet suddenly it doesn't seem quite so inevitable. Still, early-ish days.

Stephen picks up some movement by the sunlit doorway. He manages to shift his gaze just fractionally away from Nina to spot Kerry and Nathan, arrived at the very back of the room, each wearing a look of some concern. Nathan also appears to be wearing a new layer of soil. Kerry, who is gripping her son's arm with knuckles of white, nods to Stephen, her face still stern. Nose still red. He doesn't return the nod.

"They say when it comes to choosing a horticulturist," he continues, gamely, "you should beware of imitations. But not today, Magnolia ladies and gentlemen. Not today."

To the surprise of his audience, not that they are exactly suffering a dearth of the unexpected, this young man with the stick adopts a new voice, which sounds like that of a much older gentleman, or rather like a young man attempting not altogether successfully to sound like an older one. "'*Morning Stephen! Get your brolly out. Looks like rain again.*'" He smiles at Nina but conscientiously remembers to take in her colleagues. "That was an imitation of my next-door neighbour, old Mr Crossley. And it's… uncanny. If you knew him, Nina, which one day you very well might. Unless he does finally die from his cirrhosis of the liver. Drinks like a fish. Brandy, mostly."

The faces of the executives have segued from vague bemusement into what can only be described as mounting concern. Feelings mirrored on the faces of Spike and Mrs Dave, with a slight tint of homicide colouring the latter.

It is Nina, however, about whom Stephen is most troubled. He senses that he hasn't entirely drawn her in. By unfurling a corner of his best Oxfam-tweed jacket with his free hand, he manages to grab a swift and he hopes surreptitious glance at the handwritten notes sticking out of his inside pocket. Wherein the magic lurks.

"Fine. So. Okay. I've been working really hard to outline and source just the right plants for your hotels and spas." He even chances a smile. "To maintain your reputation for excellence and that trademark Magnolia 'perception of perfection.'"

The look of relief on the faces of everyone in the room is palpable, including the out-of-place faces of Kerry and Nathan. Mrs Dave can't quite understand why a small, sniffly woman and a strange-looking, mud-stained child, whom the former appears to be holding prisoner, are attending her presentation, but as they could be something to do with Magnolia or even Kew itself, she isn't going to make a fuss just yet.

"Although, as my Uncle Geoffrey always says," continues the smiling speaker, "'*Aardvark never killed anyone!*' But let's hope there are no aardvarks here, just to be on the safe side. Ha!"

As the relieved looks disappear almost instantaneously from the faces of everyone around, to be replaced with audible sighs, Mrs Dave's being the most unfettered, Spike edges discreetly up to his troubling colleague.

"I really don't think so, Nina," continues Stephen, undaunted, "because to my knowledge they're indigenous to Africa, and anyway, this is a garden and not a zoo. Although I gather there is a very nasty oak processionary moth around these days, that can get all the way up your nose and, if you have asthma, then woe..."

The Magnolia people have begun exchanging 'is he on drugs?' looks. But not of the class or category they might themselves wish to enjoy in their precious, out-of-hours moments. Spike is now standing next to him, smiling warmly towards Nina, whilst urgently whispering out of the corner of his mouth.

"Word of advice, pal. *Lose* the funny."

Stephen, who by now has spotted the looks of pure astonishment on the faces of everyone else in the room, including most of the plants, begins to shake his head. "No, no, Spike," he whispers, clearly mystified. "I *am* funny. I'm hysterical. Clova said!"

Spike's look of justifiable concern turns immediately into one of palpable shock. Tinged, it has to be said, with an unfamiliar trace of guilt. But there's no way he can speak. Yet even before Stephen can process what's going on with his mercurial colleague, that same pasty Caledonian face transmutes yet again, like some sort of desperate actor at an audition, into one of outright terror.

Stephen follows his gaze. The perturbed Scot has clearly noticed, along with his already rattled fellows from Blooming Marvellous, the pair of new arrivals just walking in.

Nina, inevitably, notes that attentions have suddenly strayed and glances behind her for the source. She smiles slightly nervously, as she watches the elderly and rather statesman-like gentleman of colour lead his equally dignified wife, who is walking with a hand-carved wooden stick, slowly towards them.

The newcomer nods graciously to everyone as he proceeds through the shrubbery. Reaching the seats directly behind Nina, the charming and clearly important man from Atlanta makes his apologies. He tells Stephen, in a comfortingly deep, Southern drawl, to please carry on, sir, apologies for the late interruption, as he gently helps his wife to sit.

Stephen smiles back to them, as if it's his birthday.

"*What's up, muthafuckers?*" he says, cheerfully.

Ignoring their stares, he continues. "Woke up this morning in a ambulance. And it wasn't nothing but white people staring at me. I said, 'Ain't this a bitch. I done died and wound up in the wrong muthafuckin heaven!'"

Even Stephen Gibson can't help feeling that he might have slightly misread the room. These things can happen, he reminds himself amidst the silence. But the secret is flexibility. You must simply adjust your material accordingly and ignore the row of open mouths, the soiled, eleven-year-old child with his head in his hands, the red-eyed woman wildly waving her arms, a handkerchief over her lower face.

Or the small, Indian lady making movements one might use when strangling a live chicken to music.

He can't, of course, ignore Nina, who has her own lovely mouth wide open and is staring at him with those huge green eyes, like he's one of Nathan's triffids and the room is locked from the outside.

"Now. As to your immediate horticultural needs..." says Stephen. Moving seamlessly on.

TWENTY-TWO

It's all going terribly well, isn't it?

There was a time when nothing would have given Stephen Gibson more pleasure than simply to occupy a clean wooden bench at his very special Kew Gardens, in the shade of a favourite tree, watching visitors admiring the flora and helpfully calling out the full Latin names, countries of origin and potential diseases.

This is not one of those times.

Spike is the first from the already infamous presentation to approach him. The others are still huddling outside the venue, conducting a post-mortem, exchanging apologies and keeping their distance.

"Tough crowd, pal."

"I don't understand it, Spike." He looks up into his colleague's bemused but not entirely hostile face. "I *killed* on Saturday night. Clova could not stop laughing!" He shivers slightly at a memory. "Even when she was—"

"Aye, she's a good wee laugher, right enough," agrees Spike. "She'd laugh at soup, actually." He finds himself at a bit of a loss. "Stevie, she was just meant to relax you – y'know, boost your confidence a bit. Not make you think you were God's gift to fucking comedy!"

Stephen looks suddenly suspicious. "What did you say to her…? Spike?"

"Just that – *nothing*. Not a thing. She was too busy laughing."

Stephen's face sags. He seems appalled. "My chances of happiness with Nina, gone. The big contract with Magnolia Hotels – who knows? And as for my… my bloody job…! This is all *your* fault."

The outrage on Spike's face is like nothing Stephen has ever seen. Even the smaller man's backside appears offended, as he stomps off, muttering, "Try to help a friend and this is what I get? Not funny, pal. Not funny at all."

"Sorry, Spike," he murmurs, but he doesn't think the man hears him.

A solid object now appears to be dimming his light, not that pure despondency isn't dimming it anyway. He turns to look up at Nina, sturdy as an oak, with the sunlight behind her. To his surprise, Stephen finds that he can't bear to talk to her. What could he say? He has heard the expression 'beautiful when angry', and this clearly applies to the woman glowering down at him, as she clenches the slick presentation document he had lovingly prepared.

"Well, that was… unexpected Duw!. What in hell's name were you thinking, Stephen?"

"I don't understand, Nina. It worked for the late Richard Pryor. And 'funny is—'"

"*Excuse me?* Jesus!" She appears not to be able to stop shaking her head. "I had to bullshit that poor, sweet couple that it was a British thing – we always like to welcome our visiting foreigners with an edgy joke from their culture. To break the ice. But you were the effing Titanic. I also told them you were, you know… special."

"Thank you."

She just stares at him some more, then shakes her head. "Doubt they believed me for a nanosecond, except for that last bit, but hopefully the rest of what you did, when you went back on piste and stuck to shrubs and Latin, was enough to paper over the wisecracks." She flicks her by now mangled Blooming Marvellous document. He takes in the rapid click of her nails on the shiny surface, with unabashed fascination.

"So I didn't ruin my chance with you, did I?"

She has stopped shaking and is just staring. "Chance for what?"

"*You* know," he tells the patently mystified woman. "Our date. July 28th. I wrote it down." He takes out his diary and shows her the evidence. He doesn't notice that Kerry is hovering nearby, close enough to hear.

"Oh. Our 'date,'" repeats Nina, patently having not the slightest memory of any such scheduling. "Tell you what. I'll call you. Meantime, I need to look over these costings." She smiles tentatively at him and taps his hand with the document. "I'm sure we can get to a figure that works for all of us."

"Your figure works for all of us," says Stephen, employing a felicity with words of which he thinks his fellow comics and even Tyler himself would approve. He feels quite relieved that he's still got it, even under pressure.

Nina just nods, as if she really hopes she didn't hear that and moves swiftly away.

Barely a second later, he hears a familiar sniffing. He turns to find Kerry and Nathan, hovering as if they are at a funeral and that it's their turn in the condolence queue.

"I'm so sorry, Stephen," says Kerry.

"For what, Kerry?" he asks her, in some confusion. "I know some of the jokes didn't go down that well. Well, quite a few of them. But it can happen, apparently. Ask your ex-brother-in-law. Tomorrow's crowd could be totally different."

"What tomorrow's crowd? That was a one-night stand, kiddo. And I reckon you just lost your audience."

"That's what you think. Nina said she'll call me. She said I was special!"

Kerry turns to her son, who is hovering beside her, clearly fascinated. "Nathan, can you back off just a little?"

"If we can go find the malevolent plants."

"I promise. Deadliest nightshade in town."

Nathan moves away and starts checking his phone.

Kerry sits beside Stephen on the bench, causing him to shuffle up until he is parked almost on the arm. When she has finished the latest bout of sneezing, and he has identified exactly what genera of pollen-producing trees and grasses might be around at this precise location and time of the year, she tries gently to shut him the fuck up and explain.

"Stephen, when a woman says she'll call you—"

"Yes?" He finds himself curiously fascinated by the trickle running inexorably down towards her rather expressive mouth.

"Means they're not gonna call you. Ever. In this lifetime. On this planet."

Stephen doesn't say anything for a moment. Through her hay-fevery tears, the woman watches this unfathomable man's face gradually harden. Behind his thick spectacles his eyes, usually rather kind, become cold and glassy. "You're *JEALOUS*!" he tells her, at one of his higher decibels. "I don't believe this, Kerry. You're just… jealous."

"Excuse me? I'm *jealous*! Of what, exactly?"

"Of 'whom'. Of *Nina*, obviously." He looks up at the tree, as if it symbolises so perfectly his own spiritual heights. "Because she's beautiful. And successful and tall. And allergen-free. And… Welsh."

"*Welsh?*" shouts Kerry, ignoring the stares of bewilderment from passing garden-lovers. "I'm *jealous* because she's *Welsh*? Nathan, back up some more, you've moved in again. Well, here's news for you, dickhead. Your precious 'perception of perfection' craps just like the rest of us!"

"I can still hear you," calls Nathan.

"*Then put some sounds on!* And I'm sorry, Stephen, you are acting like… like an eleven-year-old who just discovered his pee-pee."

"Been there," says Nathan, which doesn't really help.

"Can't you see? Jeez! She was *using* you, Stephen."

Stephen suddenly stands up and towers over her. He can't ever recall feeling as angry as he does right now, although he senses somewhere that this snotty little person has been curiously central to almost every one of his recent bouts. "You… you don't want me to be happy." He nods, almost in satisfaction. "Oh yes, I get it now. Just because your own marriage to a funny guy failed so miserably."

"Okay, that's it!" says Kerry, standing up at exactly the moment another sneeze lets rip. She expels the latest consignment onto his chest, but this time he is too rigid even to flinch.

"Bless you," he says.

"Thank you. C'mon, Nathan. Let's go find something less toxic. Like hemlock."

The small couple rumble off, without glancing back, leaving Stephen alone, confused and muttering *Conium maculatum* into her uncaring wake. He wonders how anyone can be so bitter. Especially someone who he had genuinely believed might become a friend, of sorts. Perhaps his first, at least of the opposite sex. (Although he has to admit that NJ is also stepping up to the plate rather well and doesn't sneeze so much.)

From his bower he watches Mrs Dave making her farewells and hopefully her peace with the sweet but shaken couple from Atlanta and the remaining Magnolia executives. Every so often he catches one of the looks she throws at him, none of which are cocooned in warmth.

When the small crowd has thinned and Mrs Dave, aided somewhat listlessly by Spike, commences to remove every trace of Blooming Marvellous from the room, unconsumed Indian snacks and all, Stephen decides that he had better be of some assistance. He is in no doubt that he is about to receive one of Mrs Dave's legendary hard times but is unsure, as yet, about the degree.

"You look terrible, Stephen," she says, as he attempts somewhat nervously to tear down the day-glo banner.

"I am *so* sorry, Mrs Dave," he ventures, gliding in first.

"It is okay, dear. You let your animal lust for this woman get in the way of business. It can happen to any one of us. After all, we are only human."

Stephen feels the tension gush from his unusually rigid body. He wouldn't be surprised to find a pool of discarded stress bubbling around him, steamy and throbbing, so palpable is the release.

"But she's not going to want you much now, is she? When you don't have a job or the least bloody prospect of one. Ever. Grab a delicious chapatti then help Spike load up the van."

The steamy pool shoots back inside him, as if it had never left in the first place.

TWENTY-THREE

Nothing ever goes according to plan, eh? You're nodding, madam, or is it just the Botox weighing your head down?

The hot light is drilling straight through the thick spectacle glass into Stephen Gibson's tormented eyes and, he can quite believe, poaching his brain. He can just about make out figures moving softly some way in the distance, but his focus is on the unremitting beam and the strident voice coming at him through the darkness.

"*Describe it to me, Stephen!*"

"Well... I had a plan. I'd tried all my lines. I'd worked them. *Kew*. Mag-*know*-lia. *Aardvark*. Okay, 'muthafucker' was thinking on my feet. But I blew it. Apparently. Not only that, it has cost me my beautiful job, my reputation and, quite possibly, the one love of my life. Even my sunflowers are turning away from me. Especially Rosamund. The one thing I have left in the world is this class, and that's only because I paid for all my sessions in advance. And what with all the really pricey DVDs—"

"*CUT!*"

The light beside the video camera suddenly goes off. Dazed, Stephen removes his glasses and wipes the moisture from his eyes. He notices that his hands are shaking.

As his vision normalises to a myopic blur, leaving his mind still frazzled, he can just make out his classmates staring down at him. Restoring his spectacles, he finds a disturbing composite of pity and disbelief etched on their faces, with more than a shading of there-but-for-the-grace-of-God. Even that strange person or mixture of persons Suzie V is gazing gently down on him, very nearly concealing her professional excitement at what manner of clown (or non-clown) good fortune has delivered her way.

Only Tyler Watts is examining him without any trace of compassion. It is as if nothing has happened to Stephen or the others that he hasn't been expecting all along.

"Camera's off, Stevie. Well played, mate. Now shut it."

The maestro gazes around, at Jayson Spliff, Nigel and NJ, each of whom looks suitably horrified. Especially when the big man smiles.

"All of you, look at what you just witnessed. Really look. This – humiliation, degradation, this total and utter failure. At a *gardening* talk, for fuck's sake. To a captive audience! *Who hadn't even paid to come in!*" He moves in close to Stephen's face. His victim can smell the cheap beer, coffee and sheer contempt on the teacher's unfailingly rank breath. "You are not the artist you thought you were, Stephen Gibson. You are nothing. No, less than nothing. You are comedy plankton."

"Do you know Mrs Dave?" asks Stephen, who recognises the tone.

"He's one of *you*, guys," says Tyler, pointing at Stephen, but glaring around the room. They can hear the camera being quietly switched back on. "It will happen to each joker here, maybe once, probably forever. And it will be worse. Much worse." Tyler looks at the group and sees the defiant, almost smug looks. "Okay, maybe I'm wrong, maybe it will *never* happen to you guys. Maybe you're totally unique."

"Don't need the 'totally'."

"I said shut it! Now just listen, all of you. Tomorrow night, I've invited a random selection of people to check out your acts. Here, in this room. You get ten minutes each. On camera. Then they piss off back to the pub, so that their evening hasn't been a complete wash-out and you get to watch yourselves on playback. What fun, eh?"

"I'm cool with that," says Jayson Spliff. "I've played in bigger rooms."

"I live in a bigger room," says NJ, which gets a smile she appreciates.

"I think I'll just watch for now," says Stephen, whose despondency is growing by the minute.

Nigel, wearing yet another mind-alteringly fluorescent pullover, as if it's always Christmas in his torso, lays a bobbly arm around his classmate. As Stephen has no memory of anyone ever putting an arm around him, neither male nor female, bobbly or sheer, he discovers, to his own surprise, that he can't prevent himself from nuzzling his head deep into the rich wool and polyester mix. Nigel finds this a tiny bit disconcerting, yet he doesn't move away. Instead he hugs the distraught man even tighter, until he feels it is time to have his jersey back.

***

Stephen Gibson has quite possibly watched more recorded stand-up performances, in a shorter space of time and with a greater injection of concentrated intensity, than anyone in history. And, most probably, to far less effect. Yet nothing has prepared him for the video on which he is currently focussing, in the living room of his belligerent comedy tutor, the evening after his own wrenching 'debrief'.

His colleagues had politely beseeched him not to sit amongst the night's small but select audience, at this first Killer Comedy 'public' session, as his miserable face and total lack of comprehension would have been seriously off-putting. Especially with Suzie V's camera and lights at full blast.

As it turns out, Stephen's misery could well have been subsumed into that of the wider public.

He has to admit that Jayson Spliff starts well and has the requisite confidence when greeting his audience and saying his name. It is in the humour department that he appears to let himself down.

"*Yeah, Jayson Spliff ain't my real name. I was adopted. But I'd like to have kids of my own one day. The kids in the basement aren't mine.*"

There are one or two polite chuckles, but to Stephen this is clearly not a joke, as there's no reason why any man, adopted or not, should have children who aren't his own in a basement. How did they get in there and why would their parents let them go into someone else's house? Yet this would appear to be Jayson's signature gag, which is quite a mystery.

NJ fares no better in Stephen's eyes.

"*A black girl, a Jew and a lesbian walk into a bar and the barman says, 'Hello, NJ, is this some kind of joke?'*"

Well, this of course makes no sense whatsoever, as it is far from clear which one of the three customers NJ is supposed to represent, and why can't the other two go out for a drink, without the man behind the bar singling them out for ridicule? Clearly the audience felt the same, as Stephen discerns precious little laughter on the soundtrack.

Sadly, it doesn't get a lot better.

Stephen is rather looking forward to seeing Nigel on the small screen, as the young man has been so kind to him. So his disappointment is at its height when the would-be comic signally fails to light up the room.

"*The good thing about having deaf parents is that they can't tell you're so drunk you're slurring all your words. The bad thing is they can smell the drink on your breath before you've left the pub.*"

Stephen doesn't find this at all credible, as no-one has such a powerful sense of smell. Poor Nigel – he had such hopes for his friend.

As far as he can ascertain from the video, Stephen's opinion appears to have been endorsed by this evening's 'crowd', without demur. His critical faculties must still, he reckons, be at their peak – although it does vaguely perturb him that he has made the same sort of incisive comments to himself whilst watching the professional DVDs, on whose soundtracks he could patently hear infinitely larger audiences laughing themselves silly.

He does, however, find it curious that when he turns away from the onscreen carnage for just a moment, he catches Suzie V and Tyler Watts exchanging clearly satisfied thumbs-ups, almost as if they're delighted by the abject failure and public humiliation of their class. But he supposes, in this strange new world, that he might be misreading the signals. It wouldn't be the first time.

Finally, the recording completes its grim playback and Tyler switches off the TV. As he tries to lose the smile on his face and revert to the gloom that has infected the rest of the room, Suzie V zealously resumes her filming.

"So, what did I tell you?" he tells them. "Comedy is a hard taskmaster. Comedy is a cruel mistress. Comedy is an unforgiving whore. And when you fail, you bunch of abject losers, you fail big." This is greeted with accepting nods. "I'm not knocking the material. Some of it was almost average. But did you learn *nothing* about what I've been trying manfully to drum into you? Structure. Delivery. Build. Momentum. Truth. And Timing – timing – timing."

"I learned all that," insists Stephen. Suzie V immediately swings round to him.

"Yeah, but you got to be funny too," says Tyler.

Stephen writes this down in a brand new spiral-pad. Good note.

Suzie stops filming and smiles at her subjects with genuine kindness. "Hey, don't get too down, guys," she says, in a voice that appears to be growing deeper by the minute. "You made a good start. Seriously. If you'd peaked on your first outing, our future show here would be dead from the get-go. Maybe they were just a tricky crowd. Handpicked but tricky." She looks at Tyler as she says this and is greeted with a knowing smirk. "Bad shit makes great television. The audience wants to see the knocks, course they do. But they also want to watch you get better. Stronger. *Funnier!*" She suddenly swivels on her huge high-heels to Stephen. "What about you, Stephen Gibson – are you ready to come on the journey?"

Stephen looks confused. Journey – what journey?

Tyler moves across to him and speaks quite gently. Well, for him, gently. "Hey, plant guy. Remember, matey, when we first met – at the club when you were nicking my jokes?"

"I wasn't actually—"

"I'm talking. Remember you watched me with the ladies and you got your first taste of the awesome sexual potency of the comedic form?"

"I'd observed Spike first, but yes, it confirmed for me that truly unprepossessing men such as yourself can do inordinately well, if—"

"Yeah, okay." Tyler smiles, not entirely in comfort. "And so?"

"And so?" repeats Stephen, who isn't quite there yet.

"And so, Stephen Gibson, are you ready to work? Are you up for tapping the comedic potential deep inside of you? Way way deep. In your case, fucking subterranean. And just maybe, finally, possibly, winning over gorgeous, pouting plant-girl?"

"*Nina?*"

"Whoever."

"But I lost my job."

"Who's talking about your poxy job?"

"I'm sorry?" Stephen can sense the entire room simply staring at him. As it finally, stupefyingly dawns. "So you're talking about…?"

Tyler nods. "Making you into a pukka, genuine, fully fledged, stand-up comic! Yeah. God help me. Pygmalion with real pyg!"

Stephen stares at the larger man, as the full force of his extraordinary challenge registers. They all wait, his fellows and teachers, in dubious yet respectful silence. Until, finally, "I'm in your hands, Tyler. Do with me as you will."

Tyler winks at Suzie V. "Oh I will, Steve-o. I will."

"*From Dire to On Fire!*" cries Suzie V, inspired.

"*From – Jesus! to Caesar's*," adds Jayson.

"*From total schmuck to holy fuck!*" says NJ, getting into it.

"*From grass-kicker to ass-kicker!*" contributes Nigel.

"*From Finchley Road to Ruislip Manor, changing at Rayners Lane!*" screams a revitalised Stephen Gibson.

The others just shake their heads, as Suzie V switches the video camera back on.

PART THREE

Playing The Audience

TWENTY-FOUR

I'm not great with hecklers. Last time a guy heckled,
could I think of a witty comeback?
So I stabbed him.

Stephen Gibson is working out his notice with the same selfless diligence that he brought to his original employment. For which the middle-aged Indian gentleman, recently poached from a rival garden centre in Wembley, to 'step into his gardening gloves', will be eternally grateful.

"No job is for life," said Mrs Dave, with an uncharacteristic economy of words, as she introduced the new to the old. A pronouncement which Stephen, of course, accepted as simply the brutal confirmation of a rather obvious status quo, whilst the new guy took on board that he had better step up to the plate from day one. "Even for second cousins, once removed," she added, which Stephen didn't quite understand.

Stephen has had no further contact with Nina Hughes.

After the Kew debacle, Mrs Dave immediately took over any dealings with Magnolia HQ, having deemed the comprehensive and indeed highly imaginative proposal which Stephen had finally put together quite bloody sufficient for that lot to be getting on with. To his chagrin, the young woman herself has made no further effort to stay in contact with him. He has a feeling that late July, whilst still in the future, may well be a dream of the past.

Stephen can't help thinking, if he is being brutally honest with himself, that Kerry might have been correct in her feminine assessment of the situation, but this is hardly something to make him feel more grateful or favourably disposed towards her. As he himself has been told on more than one occasion, nobody loves a know-all.

He does, however, explain to a sweetly sympathetic Spike, over a lunchtime tuna sandwich, in a corner of his cherished and soon to be forsaken nursery, that hope is not entirely lost.

"*A STAND-UP? A fucking stand-up!*" yelps Spike, who even Stephen can discern is seriously impressed.

"I'm taking lessons," he finally confesses. "I didn't get to this level on my own."

"I'd sue the teacher," says Spike, which Stephen puts down to sheer envy on the part of his colleague.

"I do realise I'm not quite there yet," admits Stephen. "I'm not stupid, Spike." Without waiting for Spike's response, as it wasn't a question, he continues. "The class has been doing some intensive – and rather expensive – training, every night of the week, and weekends too. There's this lady, who used to be a man, who's filming us for something or other that she's hoping to put on."

"*Not Suzie V!*" exclaims Spike, suddenly excited.

"Indeed. But not just any Suzie V. *The* Suzie V."

"Well, shag me for Christmas!" Spike suddenly looks serious, plummeting back to earth from heady, webcast heights. "Aye, well, that's great, Stevie, awesome, but what about a new job?"

"Spike," says Stephen, with a sincerity that takes on an almost religious fervour, "this could *be* my new job."

The young man, who still has an old job, finds himself unusually lost for words. After a few moments of blink-free staring, he shakes his head and walks silently back into the garden centre.

Stephen isn't fazed. He has been told by none less than Tyler Watts himself to be prepared for people walking out on him. So he offers up, perhaps a trifle over-theatrically, "*I must try to remember what that last gag was – I shall use it on my wife.*" Which confuses an old lady, who only wants to buy some petunias for her window box.

Actually, it confuses Stephen too, because he is still working more from regurgitation than inspiration.

***

The small community theatre, situated not far from where Stephen lives, is accustomed to amateur theatricals. So Tyler and Suzie feel that it is ideal for their purposes this drizzly Sunday afternoon.

They have to work around the set currently in place, which is for the Slippers Amateur Dramatic Society's ambitious production of Stephen Sondheim's *Follies*. The company have recently been stung by less than flattering comments overheard in the foyer, concerning the production itself, which is centred around a reunion of once-glamorous ladies from a fictional equivalent of the Ziegfeld Follies. In fact, when these featured ladies – local mums, businesswomen and stalwart Slippers regulars – gamely strode down the huge, curving staircase in their finery, to the heralding strains of '*Beautiful Girls*', there had apparently been uncontrolled laughter from the audience.

No such luck here, thinks Tyler, as he stands in the front of the auditorium, staring up at this same impressive staircase on the otherwise empty stage. The microphone stand is in place; the lights are up. Suzie V hovers to one side of him, with her cameraman poised and ready for anything.

Behind her, spread out amongst the front rows, are Jayson, NJ and Nigel, although there is no particular reason why they should not be sitting together. Perhaps they sense that by selecting this initially puzzling arrangement, they are affording whoever appears on stage some semblance of an audience. In the meantime, they can't help silently thinking that this could also reflect the audience they themselves are likely to face in due course, only possibly not as warmly disposed.

"Okay, let's get this shit-storm over with," says Tyler, in the time-honoured tradition of dedicated pedagogues everywhere. "Stephen, shift your arse out here."

Stephen Gibson walks slowly out from the darkened wings onto the stage. Staring around the functional, totally characterless auditorium, he tries hard to ignore the majestic but wobbly staircase just a few feet away. Although the house lights are still fully on, he blinks wildly through his thick lenses. When, at a click of the fingers from Tyler, this illumination is suddenly dimmed and the theatrical lighting takes over, the man onstage jolts as if electricity has quit its original application only to shoot right up his body. As the quivering subsides, he remains rooted to the spot, like one of his sturdier plants.

"*Fucking walk to the mic!*" encourages the teacher. "The mic!" Tyler can tell without asking that his pupil is looking around wildly for someone who might conceivably be called Mike. "Sorry. My mistake. Using such ridiculously arcane jargon so early on. The microphone? The thing on a stick that isn't a liquorice-flavoured ice-cream cone."

Stephen walks over to the object in question, like an astronaut approaching an alien life form that may or may not be friendly.

"Now, take it out of its stand, please." Tyler is sufficiently aware of his own operational mode to know that he is talking in a highly patronising manner, as if addressing a particularly backward child. He really doesn't care.

Of course, Stephen is struggling to remove the mic from its well-designed and user-friendly stand. Why wouldn't he be? Tyler turns to Suzie, who is watching the performance, or lack of it, as if there is a God.

When, finally, Stephen succeeds, the microphone is ejected from its lodging with such force that it flies out of his hands and lands some yards away, on the first step of the staircase.

"That was great, Stephen!" says Tyler, who even knows how to clap sarcastically. "Thank you so much. Now the class knows how to fail before the first fucking joke."

Stephen picks up the mic, taps it and, when it makes the appropriate sound, stares down at it intently and with genuine fascination.

"Is this thing on?" he asks, almost to himself. "Yes, I think it is. Indeed, it does sound on. *Hello…?*"

"Christ, get off the stage! Go!" says Tyler, who genuinely feels he has the patience of a saint. He turns to Suzie. "Is it the lighting or does our twat really have a green thumb?"

Obedient as ever, Stephen walks back the way he came, into the wings. They can hear his footsteps continue, as if he is strolling back home. Tyler has to shout in order for Stephen to hear him.

"You gotta walk onto the stage like you own the place. Is he still there? *GIBSON!*"

After a few seconds they hear footsteps, building in both speed and volume. Finally Stephen arrives onstage once more and peers out into the stalls, still clearly hesitant.

"What are you, a Japanese sodding tourist? *Again!*"

This may be the first 'again' Tyler shouts in Stephen's direction, but it isn't the last. Whilst confidence does perhaps increase in minuscule increments over the following few attempts, microphone technique still has some way to go. Stephen walks back into the wings then doggedly returns into the unforgiving limelight.

"How did you ever survive childhood, matey?" asks Tyler, with a curiosity that, whilst possibly less than helpful, is genuine in its sense of wonder. When he swivels his nicotine-stained finger in the air, Stephen simply returns the gesture, as if it is some kind of comedic greeting, rather than an instruction to repeat. "Fucking AGAIN, you pillock! Confidence!"

Finally, Stephen strides out from the wings, this time with his glasses inexplicably peeping out of his pocket. He evidences an assuredness of which none of the great comics of today or the hallowed past would be ashamed. Ripping the microphone smartly from its stand, with an impressive level of concentration, he delivers it firmly and unwaveringly into his eye.

"Perfect!" whoops Tyler Watts. "Now the other eye. Blind comics are cleaning up right now." He points the same imperious finger straight at him. "Okay. Let's take that bit as read, for the time being. Just stay there. Don't move a single, retarded corpuscle."

Stephen remains onstage, holding the mic and peering out at his bemused fellow comics, spread thinly around the large auditorium.

"Right, so let's just say for now that you succeed in reaching centre-stage, without maiming or electrocuting yourself. You say hello or good evening, which you can probably just about manage, if you put in the hours, then you start talking, okay? Maybe you tell a joke you've memorised out a book but clearly don't for a moment understand. And two minutes later – *this* begins."

To Stephen's consternation, Tyler turns his back on him and signals to the other would-be comics in the audience.

Nigel is the first to shout. "You're shit, get off!"

Stephen looks like a deer caught in the headlights. He puts his glasses back on and stares at his extravagantly pullovered friend, with a mixture of such shock and sadness that it cuts the guilty heckler to the bone.

Then NJ stands up and yells at him. "My nan tells better jokes than you and she's dead. *Olvashalom*."

Finally, Jayson joins in the fun. "There used to be a pool table where you are that was funnier."

Suzie V keeps her camera trained on the stunned victim, as the taunts keep coming. She mutters into her own microphone, "Each well-aimed heckle hits poor Stephen like Ivan Drago pummelling Rocky."

Now the entire audience is standing up.

"Your mother wears combat boots," yells NJ.

"My mother's…" Stephen doesn't finish, because he notices Kerry slipping in through the door at the rear of the theatre. This reminds him of something, but he is in too much pain to recall exactly what.

"Who writes your gags – Goebbels?" shouts Nigel, bobbing up for his second shot.

"Nigel, I don't even speak German."

"You're not real – you're a plant," adds Jayson, with a smirk.

"Isn't it time you joined your jokes in the morgue!"

Stephen stares out at them all, a man bereft, as they jeer and heckle mercilessly, each barb crueller and more pointed than the one before. Gradually, he crumples into a foetal position on the floor of the stage.

Tyler moves towards him, showing no mercy. "This is it, Gibson! This is the life you're asking for. You ready to quit now?"

"No!" murmurs Stephen.

"It can only get worse, you talentless little crumb. Say the word and you can walk out of this crappy theatre, safe from lonely nights, ridicule, oblivion and fast food. But without your cheques, obviously."

"I can't quit!" says Stephen quietly.

"Why the fuck not?"

"BECAUSE THIS – YOU – IT'S ALL I'VE GOT!"

In a theatre accustomed to dramatic silences, and not just because a Slipper has forgotten his or her lines and the prompter's asleep, the quality of silence experienced right now by everyone present is of a particularly potent and poignant order. It is only broken when a familiar voice chimes from the very back of the hall.

"*You're an idiot!*" screams Kerry.

Stephen looks out at her from the floor, the hurt in his eyes apparent to everyone there. He scrambles to his feet and stumbles almost blindly into the wings.

"Jesus, Kerry," says Tyler, "that was a bit harsh."

TWENTY-FIVE

And if there's any critics in tonight, I've been Jerry Seinfeld.

There is a gently flowing stream that runs behind the small community theatre, into which the entire cast of a Slippers' production traditionally jump on opening night, before the evening show, in order to bring them luck. Photos of dripping thespians plaster the lobby, alongside a tribute to one of the founder members, who sadly died of pneumonia shortly after a particularly haunting Blithe Spirit, although the two events are not believed to be connected.

Kerry finds Stephen sitting by the bank, staring into the water, as if he wishes it might carry him away.

"Hey," she says.

"I'm not an idiot, you know," he says, without turning round.

"You're a bit of an idiot," says Kerry, sitting down beside him.

"I'm sorry I said you were jealous of Nina." She simply nods. "It's like me being jealous of… Steve Martin."

"…Yeah. It's exactly like that," she says. "Well, you were right. She is an amazing-looking, tall, non-sneezing Welshwoman." She turns to him. "Friends again?"

She offers him a fist to bump. He stares at it as if she is about to punch him, so she lowers her hand once more.

"I just want to MAKE her LAUGH, Kerry," he yells, without meaning to, "because 94.6 per cent of all the ads—"

"Yes. I got that. Do you like her?"

He stares at her. "*Do I like her?!*" She nods again, although she wants to tell him that this isn't the most complex of enquiries. Yet perhaps it is. "You saw her, Kerry. She's *incredible.* She loves plants. And you said yourself she's—"

"Not what I asked you."

Stephen takes a moment to consider this, then launches himself up from his perch at a speed so unexpected that it quite unsettles his companion. "I have to get back inside. Do you know, I believe they were trying their very best to put me off this morning? Which was kind of them, in a way. But right now I'm not sure that anything could."

"All this, Stephen. The abuse. The humiliation. *For a woman?*"

Yet suddenly, despite herself, Kerry understands.

The look of sheer determination that rises like a wash over the face of this peculiar young man is telling her, in a way she is certain that the man himself could not, how he has managed to survive all these years. She almost finds herself envying the narrow but deep seam of resolve within him, a seam that he doggedly keeps mining, however misguidedly, to attain what he needs. Or believes that he needs, which probably amounts to much the same thing.

"Think about it, Kerry. If women like men with a GSOH, they have to love them a whole lot more when they can make an entire room laugh!" He shakes his head. "You don't plant just one bulb when you can have the whole bed! Look at your awful ex-brother-in-law, even though he's not apparently as funny as he thinks he is. And, I imagine, your former husband with the Barbie doll." He stares at her, his jaw rigid. "I have never left a job unfinished, Kerry. *Never!* Not even the Hanging Gardens of Tesco Hillingdon, when the supply of zonal pelargoniums completely dried up. Okay, there's Magnolia Hotels and Spas, but the groundwork has been laid and the rest of what happened wasn't entirely my fault. Although, it mostly was. So… yes. In answer to your question."

She tries really hard once again to recall what this question was. Are his conversations always like this? Ah, right. Okay. "You do know she doesn't deserve you?"

Watching the confusion spread on his pale, slim face makes her want instantly to change the subject. Fortunately, she has a new one to hand, with a lot more hope in it. "Anyway… Nathan's twelfth birthday party is this Sunday. He wants you to join us."

The seconds pass slowly once more, as he processes these last words and tries to convince himself that he has actually heard what he thinks he has. He then proceeds to gawp at her, mouth hanging open, as if she has just offered him a headline spot in Las Vegas.

"Me? To come to…? Nathan wants *me*?" He shakes his head at the wonder of it. "Nobody has ever…"

She finds what he is telling her, or nearly telling her, almost unbearable, but is not totally certain whether her sadness is for this man or for the smaller one she has left at home. It could be a painful mixture of both.

For reasons best known to himself, he now adopts what she has come to recognise as his comedy face. Which is no more amusing than any other face he might exhibit but is clearly more purposeful. "Saturday… Hmm… Now let me just check the old calendar." With a well-honed lack of any apparent skill, he hums and haws, ponders, mulls and chews things over. Then blurts out, at twice the volume, "*OF COURSE I CAN COME!*" He beams at her. First one of the day. "That was a timing example. And I don't even *have* a calendar. Good, eh…?"

"Consummate," agrees Kerry, as Tyler emerges onto the backlot, with a beckoning fist.

Ruislip's newest stand-up strolls back to the auditorium, a marked spring in his step, for his next lesson in the cruel and debasing world of professional comedy.

"See you at the 'bash,'" he calls back, although she hasn't, as yet, told him where or what time it will be.

***

At Suzie V's small flat in Camden Town, after a massive takeaway pizza and a bottle of cheap Rioja, she and Tyler Watts settle down to watch something.

"Okay, I did a little editing," she says, as she presses the 'play' button.

Five minutes later, Tyler Watts, who – despite being a comedian – seldom laughs at anything other than someone else's misfortune, is curled up in pain on Suzie V's kilim-strewn sofa.

She strokes his hair and wonders if this time he will stay the night.

TWENTY-SIX

You got kids, sir? No? What do you do for aggravation?

Uncle Geoffrey and Noreen from Oldham aren't so wrapped up in themselves that they fail to notice there is definitely something different about the nephew these days. But they are sufficiently absorbed in each other not to bother the younger man over-zealously about it.

Both are, of course, somewhat mystified that he is working out his notice at Blooming Marvellous, which Uncle Geoffrey had always assumed was a job for life. They take some comfort in the knowledge that he has those skills in abundance that would make him a delicious prospect for any enterprising horticultural concern. And at least the boy isn't strapped for cash, as he rarely buys anything and dutifully makes his agreed contribution to the household expenses.

Were someone to inform his elders, however, that Stephen Carl Linnaeus Gibson has taken gardening leave from his life's passion to pursue a career in stand-up comedy, they would most probably die laughing. Somewhere Stephen is aware of this, so for the time being he is keeping his schemes and aspirations well under wraps, whilst secretly 'dreaming on'.

Yet he also believes that he is becoming noticeably more amusing in everyday conversation. Wasn't it only last weekend that he overheard Noreen asking his Uncle Geoffrey if he had noticed anything funny about Stephen? He tells himself that it might be advisable to keep a reasonably tight lid on this development, for now, simply to avert suspicion and some tricky interrogation.

Curiously, Stephen finds he doesn't altogether mind that for once in his life he is a subject worthy of discussion. He has chosen, however, not to tell them that this afternoon he is attending the birthday party of a twelve-year-old boy.

***

It is the noise that strikes Stephen first.

It is like nothing he has ever heard nor anything he would wish to hear again. A mixture of the grindingly mechanical – with variations too unpredictable to allow any half-way tolerable rhythm to emerge – and the ecstatically or agonisingly human. Balls rattle and roll, skittles fall or resist, adults and children scream, machines rumble on.

People are manically running backwards and forwards, as if mimicking the trajectory of the bowling balls themselves, yet at the same time appear scrunched-up at the most uncomfortably contorted of angles, as if in desperate need of a toilet. They career with an alarming lack of inhibition, their arms either down to their knees or up in the air. Even when they have taken what is their shot or turn in the lane, they remain rooted in their own imprinted bowling position, with almost imperceptible twitches from side to side, apparently attempting to influence the direction of the ball by some form of grunting telekinesis.

The moment Stephen walks through the door, he finds himself wishing that he could return to the refuge of his silent greenhouse and leave this new hell to those who bizarrely appear to be rather enjoying it. Yet here he remains, rooted in the doorway, both fascinated and repelled.

As he rightly assumes that no-one will be searching madly for him, he resolves to make the effort and look around for Nathan and pals. Unfortunately, to the untrained eye, everyone this afternoon looks like they could be Nathan or a pal. Rarely having contact with children, Stephen would admit to some difficulty in distinguishing one from another, save by gender and even then he sometimes has problems. But show him two *Helianthus annuus*...

Eventually, he spots a small figure, awkwardly squatting and presumably poised to bowl, who looks like he could possibly be the birthday boy. As he approaches the lane, Stephen hears words which, whilst the context is unfamiliar, share an unmistakeable tone with memories from his youth. Recollections that he had assumed to be shelved and long-forgotten.

"Hoy, Isaiah, careful you don't dust the lane with your butt!"

The other children around the speaker laugh at this, but Stephen notices that Nathan, standing slightly apart from the group, simply smiles. The older man knows this smile. It has all the protective signs of acknowledgement, with barely a trace of amusement. He wonders what the significance of 'Isaiah' is. It sounds Biblical to him, but perhaps they've simply forgotten his name.

Nathan dispatches his ball at some speed. Unless Stephen has misunderstood the rules of this strange game, which is more than possible as he finds most sport quite beyond him, he has to assume that when one of these huge objects concludes its bumpy journey in a lane adjacent to the one in which it originally set off, this is not cause for celebration. Although the hapless bowler's so-called friends do appear to be treating it as such.

"My gerbil's got better form, Isaiah," yelps another lad, to more whooping from his gang. Comparisons with Stephen's first heckling session feel painfully obvious.

"Let's see *you* do it then," says Nathan.

Stephen envies the immediate comeback and swiftly jots down this pithy phrase for further use, adding a 'sir' or 'madam' to remain within the polite zone. Yet glancing back at the boy, he knows that the shades of red now colouring his small, freckled face and almost matching his hair are not entirely due to exertion.

"Me, bowl?" grunts the first boy, confusingly. "That's for tossers." So why are you here, silently wonders the eavesdropper. "We're only here cos there's free food and your mum's a bit hot," comes the unsolicited explanation.

Nathan suddenly launches himself at the boy, who is at least a head taller. Before he can make contact and most probably be demolished, Stephen steps between them, as if nothing untoward is about to take place.

"Hey, amigo!" he says, cheerily. "As in Spanish for 'friend'. Which you're not. Spanish, I mean. Not... *Happy birthday!*"

As the other kids stare at this weird newcomer, in his old-fashioned tweedy jacket and straggly tie, as if this is the sort of friend only a wuss like Nathan could possibly have, the birthday boy himself appears torn between continuing on his journey towards the most recent taunter or graciously accepting the huge, brown paper bag that Stephen has thrust towards him.

Nathan finally decides that a gift just beats a beating. He accepts the bag, which is far heavier than he had imagined, and staggers backwards to more snorts.

"*Jesus H. Christ!*" he exclaims, as he gently removes the giant plant from its protective covering. "Thanks, Stephen!"

"You got him a *plant*?" sneers the taller boy, in disbelief. "What kind of pansy are you?"

"If I were a pansy," explains Stephen, thoughtfully. "I'd probably be *Viola tricolor hortensis*, a hybridisation of—"

The kids roll their eyes back in their heads or make a zzzz-ing sound between their teeth. Yet nothing can dim the excitement emanating from the birthday boy himself.

"*This is a North American Trumpet Pitcher!*" he exults. "I'm right, aren't I, Steve?"

"Stephen... Yes, alright, Steve," he offers, in rare obeisance to the spirit of goodwill. "It is indeed, as you say, a North American Trumpet Pitcher, or *Sarracenia*. You know your carnivorous plants, Nathan." Stephen assumes, quite rightly, that these latter words will be totally lost on most of his audience.

"This is even better than a Venus flytrap!" exclaims Nathan, in delight.

"There's nothing in your fly to trap," says another of the boys, to general laughter, although none of them knows exactly what is being talked about.

"It eats flies!" explains Nathan. But now, warming to his theme, albeit cooling to his audience, he elaborates. "And rats and cats and Chihuahuas and—"

There is one young girl here, who looks as if she is only with the group under sufferance. Yet she appears quite enthralled. "How does it work, Nathan?" she asks.

Stephen is about to launch into an elaborate explanation of the entire process, when a voice deep inside tells him, in the immortal words of Tyler Watts himself, to shut the fuck up. The association makes him recall Kerry. He suddenly wonders where she is. Shouldn't she be attending to all this and doing what – he assumes – mothers are supposed to do on occasions such as these?

He looks around the massive, overly crowded hall and finally glimpses a small, hunched-over figure, in a corner of the cavernous room, most probably attempting to hear herself think above the frenzy. Or at least to make out whatever the other person is saying to her on her phone. Something appears to be upsetting her, whilst also making her more angry than he has ever seen her. And he has seen her pretty angry, especially towards him.

By the time his attention is refocused, Nathan is well into his explanation. To the boy's evident surprise, but not Stephen's, his audience is fascinated. Even players from other lanes are sneaking a look, as if they have never seen a robust, American carnivorous plant in a tenpin-bowling alley before.

"The prey goes inside," explains Nathan, "because it smells really nice in there."

"Like your mum," says the same boy who went on about Kerry earlier. Stephen tries to recall if he was interested in women when he himself was twelve, then realises he possibly only began to be seriously interested in them this May.

"And then SNAP! It closes," continues Nathan, ignoring the mum reference and startling the others. "Then it dissolves the creature *with its own acid*."

"Bollocks!" says the second boy.

"Them too!" says Nathan, undeterred. He smiles conspiratorially to Stephen, who – whilst not quite understanding – offers a warm and genuine smile back. "*Watch!*"

Very carefully yet precisely, with maximum drama, Nathan glides his hand into the trap, avoiding the obvious triggers. To his surprise, and most probably that of Stephen himself, the grown-up now takes over the commentary.

"Please. Nobody must move. Nobody should breathe. One false step and Nathan's hand is… is plant food."

The children are enthralled, as Nathan, showing not one milligram of fear, braves the lethal trap.

All that can be heard is the almost ear-splitting pandemonium echoing all around them. Yet somehow, in each of their raw, wholly occupied minds, this appears to be fading into nothingness. After a few nail-biting seconds, in which at least two of the observers do actually bite their nails, Nathan delicately withdraws his hand from the killer plant. He holds this same bold little limb aloft in triumph. Stephen would swear he can hear actual 'oohs' and 'ahhs' from most of the assembled kids.

"What a load of crap!" snorts one of the little cynics.

"You think, Ryan?" says Nathan.

Stephen can hear the young boy's mother so clearly in the way he speaks. Shoddy English, obviously, but not totally without appeal.

"Anybody can do that," continues the boy, then turns to his fellow scoffer. "Show him, Emmanuel."

"Who? *Me?*" exclaims the lad, with distinct unease.

"Now who's the *Viola tricolor hortensis*?" says Stephen.

No-one calls Emmanuel Grant from Year 7 a *Viola tricolor hortensis*. Very gingerly, he approaches the plant. He holds out a small and not awfully clean hand, which is shaking slightly. He eases it gently into the trap. Nothing happens.

"See, saddo." Ryan laughs, turning to Nathan. "Shitty old plant."

The trap closes on Emmanuel's hand.

"*It got me!*" he screams. "Fuckkkk! It got me!"

"Whatever you do, Emmanuel," says Nathan, quietly but urgently, "don't move your hand. Or it'll be so much worse." He moves even closer to the boy and stares into his frightened eyes. "Can you feel the acid burning into your skin, Emmanuel? Down to your bones? Not yet? Well, you will tonight. Really bad poison can sometimes take a few hours."

He looks at Stephen, who is just beginning to wonder if things are veering slightly out of control. The boy in the plant has gone quite pale. The other kids are either bouncing around, too spooked to stay still, or standing rigid, too transfixed to move.

"*Call an ambulance!*" urges Ryan.

"Too late," says Nathan. "He'll never jack the beanstalk again." Stephen has no idea what this means yet finds himself hoping it doesn't mean what it most probably does.

"Help! Help me, Isaiah – sorry, Nathan!" whimpers Emmanuel.

Players on neighbouring lanes are starting to feel that all this whining is putting them off their strike. Nathan senses that the fun he had never expected for one second to have this afternoon, but is relishing increasingly by the moment, may soon be brought to an abrupt foreshortening by the authorities. Or, even worse, by his own mother, if she ever gets off the phone.

He knows exactly to whom she's talking so animatedly, in that corner of the hall, yet right now he doesn't care. In this respect he is totally unlike Stephen, who hasn't a clue as to who might be at the other end of the phone, yet finds he has some genuine concern for the upset but still fiery person at this end.

Reluctantly, but with a certain élan, Nathan rips Emmanuel's hand swiftly out of the plant. The relieved boy examines it carefully, for any signs of corrosion or rot.

"I'm okay?" he concludes. "*I'm okay!*"

"Yeah. Except for that stain in your pants," points out Ryan, as only a friend can. If he is a little shit.

Stephen notices – in fact most of North-West London notices – the dark patch that has appeared on the front of Emmanuel's jeans. As the other kids start laughing and Emmanuel scoots off to find refuge, Stephen feels something for the mortified child. Something that he might find hard, or perhaps even painful, to explain. But he is gratified to see that the one child who isn't laughing is Nathan.

"So… who wants to bowl?" says the slightly torn birthday boy.

As the other partygoers raise their hands, with more enthusiasm than he had observed hitherto, Stephen slips away from the manic and near-hysterical activity that apparently passes for a perfectly normal Sunday afternoon in The Lanes.

He doesn't notice Nathan glancing briefly back at him. The young boy wears a curious look on his face that might almost be perceived as contrition, if not guilt. Which, were he to spot it, the oldest party guest might find just that bit troubling.

Totally oblivious, however, and still heady from all that just happened, Stephen bumps straight into Kerry. She is balancing a very large and well-iced cake, that proudly sports twelve as yet unlit candles. Tucked under her arm are several paper plates, with a sheaf of plastic forks peeking out above the pocket of a bright yellow gingham shirt. The gingham suddenly reminds him of Nigel Ngo's pullover collection, in that both appear to do something unsettling to his eyes. Yet he finds that he can't stop staring.

"Oh. Hi!" says Stephen, relieved to see her off the phone but saddened that her eyes are so red. And this time it can't be the pollen. (Especially as the clothes are his best and he just showered.) "Is that a carrot cake? It looks like and has the distinctive scent of a carrot cake."

"Okay…" says Kerry patiently. "I'm waiting."

"*Daucus carota subsp. Sativus* – cake. Yum yum!"

"The other shoe just fell. Hey, I saw what you did. With the kids."

"Oh. It was nothing."

"Yeah, it was, Stephen. That boy coulda been hurt."

"Oh. No, Kerry. The plant wouldn't hurt a fly. Well, that's not strictly—"

She shakes her head, resignedly. "Well, okay, you done good. Thank you, Stephen Gibson." She starts to move off. "Come on, I'll cut you a slice of *Daucus*."

"*Daucus* is just the genus. What you need to say is—"

"Bored now."

"Why do they call him Isaiah?"

She stops and again he catches that by now familiar look of such sadness. "You're the comedian. Can't you work it out?" Naturally, he can't even begin to fathom it. "They call him Isaiah," she explains, "because one eye's higher than the other." His puzzlement remains undiluted. "*Eye's higher?* Jesus! It's a very old English joke, apparently. Ha friggin' ha."

Finally, he nods then shakes his head. He follows her back to the kids. Before they have quite arrived at the lane and whilst the interminable noise can still muffle grown-up conversation, he asks Kerry if she is alright.

The cake wobbles slightly in her hands. "Sure. Why?"

"I saw you, over there – on the phone. You were..."

She seems a bit thrown for a moment, then attempts a smile that even Stephen can recognise as not being one of her best. "Oh. No. It was just... Nathan's dad promised he would come by this afternoon. But he got... this gig just came up. That he *naturally* couldn't refuse."

Stephen nods. "You don't have to tell me."

"You just asked."

"No. I mean about Sunday gigs."

She stares at him, wondering for one insane moment whether he could be joking, then moves towards the gang. Her face immediately lights up, like the cake she will soon be setting ablaze.

It is only later, when Stephen sits on one of the intensely uncomfortable plastic chairs, enjoying his allotted slice and watching the kids, that he notices the odd look of concern on Nathan's face. A look that he can't help feeling has nothing to do with the boy's fellow bowlers but everything to do with him. Yet when, on catching the man's questioning gaze, Nathan throws him a smile that is both friendly and carroty, Stephen resolves to let it pass and concentrate on how on earth the game of tenpin-bowling is played. And why anyone should wish to play it in the first place.

When taunter-in-chief Ryan throws up from too much cake, and a fully repaired Emmanuel gives his high-five to Nathan, they all decide it is time to call it a (pretty good) day.

TWENTY-SEVEN

Are you videoing me, sir?
Oh – just watching the match. Did we score?

Stephen Gibson doesn't have much on these days for which to rise early.

Notice has been worked at the place where he once enjoyed a day-job, and stand-up comedians are, of course, creatures of the night. Not that he actually is one, as yet. But an ever-growing clutch of cheque stubs and a costly pile of DVDs remind him that he's on his way.

So he is still dozing when he hears a knock on his bedroom door. Pulling up his leafy Royal Horticultural Society duvet to cover his matching pyjamas, he blearily bids whoever is outside – the choice being relatively limited – to come in.

He is quite surprised to find both Uncle Geoffrey *and* Noreen on his threshold. Especially as Noreen is carrying her open iPad, its unflattering glow highlighting the contours of her broad and clearly concerned face.

"Are you decent, Stephen?" she asks.

For a moment he wonders if she is questioning the nature of his material, until he recalls that neither she nor his uncle knows anything about this other, more secretive life. Of course, they soon will.

"I try to be, Noreen," he responds, cryptically.

He notices that the older couple are turning to each other. The discomfort on their faces is clear, even to Stephen, who has been known in the past to misread such things.

"We found this," begins Uncle Geoffrey, although he appears almost too overwhelmed to finish. He looks to Noreen for some – any – support. She says nothing but simply stares at the by now deeply puzzled young man, almost camouflaged in his verdant bed, who she thinks looks like a long, sprouting twig. Finally, she hits the iPad with a determined finger and sets it down to face him.

Stephen recognises the image instantly yet can't quite believe what he is watching. Or how on earth it ended up on his uncle's girlfriend's machine. Uncle Geoffrey and Noreen appear to be finding this equally unfathomable, although clearly they have already seen it at least once.

The onscreen Stephen is walking onto some nondescript stage, inexplicably furnished with an extravagantly curling staircase going nowhere. He moves with a certain modicum of confidence, already talking to an unseen audience. But, unfortunately, although his mouth is moving, we can't hear a single word that he is saying, because he hasn't as yet arrived at the ever-important microphone stand.

"...ibson," is what we eventually catch him saying, just before a voice from off-screen suggests that he is not a sodding miserable Norwegian playwright.

"Eh? ...Oh. Didn't you?" responds the confused, would-be performer, when he gathers what may have happened. "I'll start again, shall I?"

The unseen voice agrees that this would be a terrific idea. So the still-videoed Stephen trots off and after a good few seconds pads back, a tad more nervously, to the mic. But not before today's Stephen feels a jolt and looks around to find Noreen and Uncle Geoffrey flanking him on either side, reclined on top of, but certainly not relaxed into, his small single bed.

By now the featured artiste has the microphone grasped firmly in his hand. As he watches this, Stephen is rather relieved not to see the business where he is heckled to the ground and almost blinds himself in one eye. He now recalls, however, with a sinking stomach, what actually did evolve that same day, during his fateful afternoon session. The relief evaporates like a sigh.

"Hello, my name is... my name is... oh... *f-fungus!*"

Surely this can happen to anyone. In the heat of an anxious moment, you simply forget the name you were born with. As he thinks this – and perhaps even says it aloud – he wonders if he is absolutely correct in his assumption.

After a swift 'Christ on a bike!' – whatever that means – from the offscreen voice, the soundtrack continues with a tiny chorus of audience members kindly coming to Stephen's aid.

"*STEPHEN GIBSON!*" they cry, as one.

"Yes! Sorry. Thank you. How could I forget? It's not like it's a stage name! Well, not yet. When I go onstage, it will, of course, be *exactly* that."

He walks off the stage once more, microphone in hand, muttering his name over and over to himself for all to hear, like an amplified mantra.

"*Stephengibsonstephengibsonstephengibsonst...*"

When he strolls back onto that stage, it is with the confidence of a man who knows to the very last syllable what his own name is and requires no assistance from anyone. "Hello, my name is Stephen Gibson."

Stephen stops at this and stares out into the auditorium. And, of course, at anyone watching him on their iPad. He possibly feels, as indeed so many comics do at some stage in their act, that he can't honestly top what went before.

"*What the holy fuck are you waiting for?*" comes the voice of total frustration. Familiar, of course, to Stephen, as that of his well-paid mentor and sternest critic, Tyler Watts.

Yet this time Stephen has the answer, because he is a man who knows the very cornerstones of his craft. "It's called timing," he explains politely, but with a clearly discernible edge. "Okay. *Now!* My name is, of course, Stephen Gibson. And not 'fungus'. I don't have Tourette's Syndrome. Or Alzheimer's. Ha ha. Although, actually, I could have – they can do a blood test now. But would you *really* want to know—"

At this point, and perhaps fortuitously, there is a shriek of such ferocious feedback from the microphone that Stephen, for whom this ear-shattering phenomenon is totally unfamiliar and sounds like Ruislip is under lethal attack by forces unknown, immediately yelps, drops the offending object onto the ground and reels back in horror.

Unfortunately, in his manic retreat, his left foot catches on a corner of the mysterious staircase, causing Stephen to topple backwards against it with some force. This, of course, sends the entire structure gliding majestically but noisily into the wings, in a showstopper that not even his namesake Mr Sondheim could have orchestrated.

The young man in the bed stops the video.

Sufficient mortification for now, thank you very much. Although he does recall, with a shudder, that there is considerably more to come. He hands the offending machine back to Noreen.

"How did *that* get on… there?" he asks.

"This is what you've been doing with yourself?" says Uncle Geoffrey, which isn't really any sort of answer. "We thought you were on drugs. In fact, we sort of hoped—"

"I'm a stand-up comedian," says Stephen, not without some sort of pride. "Still learning my craft. Obviously."

Noreen looks over his head towards Uncle Geoffrey. "And you're certain this isn't genetic?"

With this unsettling comment, she brusquely shuts her iPad and leaves the room.

Uncle Geoffrey finds himself struggling. When he does finally address his aberrant nephew, he remains staring pensively out towards the closed bedroom door. The fact that he is still sitting on top of the duvet makes the bed's more regular occupant find it quite hard to move and rather impedes both breath and conversation.

"So this video, lad – it's your act?"

"*No!*" explains Stephen. "That was from a class, Uncle Geoffrey. A comedy class, that I signed up for."

Uncle Geoffrey nods for a few seconds, as he absorbs this new and extraordinary information. "Can you get your money back?"

Before Stephen can answer or protest, his phone rings. He wonders for one brief, reckless moment whether it could be Nina Hughes and recalls the flash he once had, long ago at that club, of her laughing so gaily. He doubts that her laughter, however bell-like and enchanting, is something he might wish to hear right now.

It isn't Nina Hughes.

Of course not, why would it be?

It is, in fact, the last person to whom Stephen might wish to speak this morning. Or, indeed, any morning. In any lifetime. Although he would have to admit that he has plenty to say to the man. So he steels himself.

"Hello… Tyler? …Yes, thank you, I just saw it. My uncle and his… I'm sure we shall all laugh about it in time. Ha flicking ha… *Where?!* …Yes, I do know the place, but… Okay, I will see you there. Thank you."

"That your teacher?" asks Uncle Geoffrey, with unexpected perception. Stephen just nods. "If it's any comfort, lad, I used to feel like killing my teachers too."

"Thank you, Uncle. And no, it isn't. Can I get out of my bed, please?"

Uncle Geoffrey would dearly love to know what had possessed his nephew to enter the one field of endeavour in which he is patently less suited than anyone in living memory. It would be like he, Geoffrey Gibson, auditioning for the lead-role in *Carmen*. Yet, as he shifts away from the duvet, he also wonders, rather guiltily, whether he should tell his closest kin that the video was, in its own excruciating way, rather funny. Albeit, unintentionally so.

Fortunately, he decides to keep his own counsel. On a brief but far from dispassionate glance, he has noticed the tears rapidly forming in the younger man's eyes.

TWENTY-EIGHT

Here, you'll laugh at this.
I'm not predicting now – I'm begging.

Not having a car, Stephen Gibson has had neither cause nor inclination to venture inside this particular multi-storey car park, even though it is attached to a major shopping centre very close to his home.

He decides he will cycle up the spiralling ramp to the open section at the very summit and is fortunate not to be immediately mowed down by an ascending shopper desperate to hit the mall running. (Although right now his feelings about being put swiftly out of his misery are a bit hit-and-miss.)

When he has finally pedalled his way to the very top, Stephen is quite naturally out of breath and more than a little sweaty. Yet he can't attribute the frenetic beating of his heart entirely to these exertions, as he is not an unfit man and far from overweight. Nor can he fully ascribe the bleakness inside his pounding frame to the soulless atmosphere that is the hallmark of every top floor of every multi-storey car park in the world.

None of these troubling sensations are alleviated by discovering Tyler Watts and Kerry leaning against a car, clearly awaiting his arrival. As they are facing the doors of the elevator and not the ramp, they are unprepared for the clattering of

Stephen's ancient bicycle, as it clanks to an outraged halt almost on top of them.

"*Ten storeys!*" he yells, as if the height is their fault alone. "You couldn't find a place on flat land!"

Tyler can't help but notice with some satisfaction that this last angry statement might just owe a debt to all the New York Jewish comedy his pupil has been learning by rote.

"Felt you might need some space," he offers. "It was a kindness – really."

"It was *you*, wasn't it? Who put it on the internet."

Tyler appears strangely conflicted. "Can't take all the credit," he mumbles. "It was..." He hesitates for a moment, looking, for some reason, towards Kerry. "It was Suzie's idea."

If Stephen isn't meant to notice Kerry knuckling her former brother-in-law really hard on the shoulder, the attempt fails miserably. He tries to gauge how she might be feeling about all this. Even with his limited antenna, Stephen reckons from her demeanour that she could be almost as angry as he is. And perhaps as sad, although this is hardly likely, as she is not the one who has been publicly humiliated. Hopefully, not that many people will have seen it. He realises, however, that he has completely failed to ascertain how Noreen and his uncle came across it in the first place. It's on his 'to do' list.

"But why, Tyler?" asks his victim, with genuine interest.

"Obvious, isn't it?" says Tyler, although it is clearly far from obvious to Stephen. "We... well, we thought it could be a good promo for Suzie's show. When it comes out. Or... when she possibly – maybe, who knows – sells it to a major broadcaster?"

"A major...? So it wasn't enough to ridicule me in front of the other students? You had to go..." He vaguely recalls a term Spike has mentioned in the past. "...contagious!"

"Viral," corrects Kerry. "But honey, we're not at that stage—"

"Yet," adds Tyler, which doesn't help. Nor does his subsequent justification, which Kerry believes can only be digging the man deeper into a mire of his own creation. "It *was* funny, Stephen! And you know the theory. You've scribbled it down enough sodding times. *Comedy is pain.*"

This time Kerry digs her elbow pointedly into her ex-relative's fleshy stomach. Yet the instructor's anguish is nothing compared to that which she can observe being slowly etched into his poor student's face.

"Maybe I just don't have a sense of humour," says Stephen. "Although, of course, I must have. *Because you shitting promised me one!*"

The shock of hearing Stephen Gibson employ language so alien to anything they've previously encountered – citing a pledge they don't actually recall being made – snatches any words from their contracting throats and sends them wispily into the toxic, petrol-fumed air.

But he hasn't finished.

"You *knew* about this?" he challenges Kerry.

She nods, sadly. "Uh huh. Too late."

Staring at her for one final, wretched and – from what she can judge – intensely sceptical time, he remounts his bicycle and turns shakily towards the ramp marked 'exit'.

"No career. No girlfriend. No self-respect," he mutters. "Well, it's downhill all the way from here. Isn't that fitting?"

Tyler beams at him. "Hey, not bad. You could use that, Stevie."

Stephen cycles off down the ramp and out of sight. "*Fucking Stephen*," comes a final, mournful cry.

"Don't see anyone doing that in a hurry," mutters Tyler. But Kerry is already running down the ramp, after the fleeing cyclist.

"Stephen. *Wait!* Be careful!"

"Let him go," calls Tyler. "The guy's a loser."

Tyler Watts knows, even as he says this, that his spiky little ex-sister-in-law is going to return very soon, after a fruitless chase, and probably kick him somewhere soft quite hard. She doesn't, but he finds himself almost wishing that she would.

Yet Tyler Watts also wonders when exactly his adored but tricky little nephew is going to admit that it was he who discovered the unreleased video on his uncle's laptop.

And sent it out into a cruel, rapacious world.

***

As Stephen Gibson cycles down streets he has known all of his life, back to the sanctuary that only a warm and eclectically stocked greenhouse can offer, he can't help noticing, through watery eyes, that people are staring at him.

He knows that he is a recognisable face to those many customers of Blooming Marvellous with whom he has dealt over the years. And who sadly will benefit no longer from his expertise. Yet the people who appear to be looking and pointing – and in some cases excitedly nudging their neighbours –don't resemble anyone whom he has had the privilege to assist. Nor do they seem like people who might willingly seek out that sort of unparalleled horticultural succour.

His confusion grows in almost direct proportion to the number of fingers directed, shoulders tapped and teeth exposed in gaping, awestruck mouths.

It is only when he passes a well-known showroom, with a giant screen in the window, that the penny – or perhaps, considering the scale of his shock, the meteor – drops. There he is, for Ruislip and most probably the rest of the civilised, or even less civilised, world to see.

Stumbling, stuttering, flapping and generally being an arse.

When a young couple in a taxi gleefully order their driver to follow him, he doubles down on his cycling and pedals breathlessly home.

TWENTY-NINE

I don't suffer from stress. But I'm a carrier.

Noreen has always assumed that her lover (and, hopefully, life partner, as she's getting 'too old to fanny around') is capable of sadness.

Yet, until recently, she has personally witnessed only the very occasional flash. This is usually when he has just missed securing a coveted artefact of absolutely no use to man or beast, because it has either disintegrated before he is able to lay his hands on it or the vendor has selfishly chosen to withdraw from the market.

This evening's sadness is of a different order.

"I've only seen this once before," mutters Uncle Geoffrey, in a voice so quiet and plaintive that Noreen finds herself torn between simply holding him tight, feeling the inevitable sobs as they start to wrack his solid frame, or asking him to speak up, as the noise from the greenhouse, on whose threshold they stand in awe, is almost deafening.

Water is splashing angrily and to no apparent horticultural purpose, against every pane of glass within the hopefully robust structure. And onto every living thing that cowers, sodden and shocked, in its demented orbit.

The older couple stand transfixed.

They can only watch in helpless horror as Stephen Gibson, usually so precise and methodical, runs totally amok down the narrow aisles, hose brandished in his ungloved hand like a fearfully random instrument of God-like wrath.

"*When* did you see it before?" asks Noreen, who frankly is a bit peeved she is having to get blood out of a stone. Then she realises, from the moisture in his eyes, what the occasion must have been. "Ah. Okay. When his mum and dad passed."

Uncle Geoffrey shakes his head. "When it looked like there could be a nationwide epidemic of European ash dieback."

"Oh, please!" says Noreen.

***

As Kerry walks down the numbingly dull suburban road once again, she notices that the skip she had briefly visited with her burrowing friend has now been carted off. She suspects that Eric the cat has also decided to move on. Defenestration is hardly a mixed message.

She doubts that this particular evening will be one for foraging or feline abuse. She also wonders why she is contemplating this with just a tinge of regret. Or, indeed, why she should be feeling so very anxious, as she returns to the oddest household she has encountered since crossing the pond.

Whilst Kerry is prepared for some truly appalling noises to greet her on the opening of the door, the sounds that cascade down the slightly less cluttered hallway this visit are surprisingly un-redolent of extreme fear or torture. The look on the face of the strange but rather sweet uncle, who stands there smiling sadly at her, warns that whatever is currently breaching their peace is clearly not 'direct to video'. Although she does suspect that a more recent and less finessed form of production might still be playing its part.

Uncle Geoffrey tactfully steps aside. "In the greenhouse, love."

As Kerry begins her journey, the man digs into the hollow elephant leg beside him and hands her a duck-head umbrella.

Accepting it graciously, Kerry weaves her way between the living-room towers, nodding to a solicitous Noreen without breaking stride. The older couple glance at each other, then tactfully withdraw into the kitchen. But not so deeply that they can't catch every word.

If Stephen hears his name being called, he shows no intention of pausing.

Whilst accustomed by now to an almost operatic strangeness, Kerry still can't quite believe what the man is doing. Yet, despite her usual, full-bodied antipathy to nature (and even with dynamic ricochets splattering all over her), the magnificent showing of exotic plants and shrubs in this relatively confined space manages to take her breath away. She realises, amidst the drenching, that she has never actually seen solid green evidence of Stephen's work.

Marvelling at the love that must have been so painstakingly lavished on all this greenery, she finds it hard to accept that the guy may have forever sabotaged his God-given calling. All for one lunatic and impossible dream. She can't bear to stand in this rainforest, watching him destroy his life's work and quite possibly himself.

"*STEPHEN!*" she yells. "Put that friggin' hose down!"

The manic sprayer stares in shock at his plants. "Oh my God. Who said that? Was it you, Ferdy Ficus?"

"*Who?* ...Stephen, it was me. Behind you."

Stephen turns at some speed and just misses water-cannoning Kerry, as she leaps away. Looking almost relieved that his plants haven't gone all bossy on him, he reluctantly powers down the hose.

"Oh. For a minute there I thought I was going insane."

"We all go a little mad, sometimes." Kerry can't see Uncle Geoffrey and Noreen, yet somehow she knows that they are listening and will be delighted by the Hitchcockian homage she has just afforded their nephew. On whom, naturally, it has dissolved like water on a thirsty ficus.

"Are you okay, Stephen?"

The young man pauses for a moment. He looks down at the limp hose in his hand, then at his saturated friends (or former friends). "No, I am not okay, Kerry. I don't believe I ever shall be okay. But I'll survive, won't I? There's plenty of work out there for laughable comics and… and jobless horticulturists, with toxic 'bloody' references."

"You're a lot more than… what you said."

Stephen suddenly looks at her in surprise. But it isn't her words that confuse him.

"How come you're not sneezing?"

"Took a pill on the way. Took quite a few, actually."

He looks at her, appreciating almost for the first time what it must have taken for her to come here and, of course, to Kew Gardens. "You should be careful with pharmaceuticals, Kerry. We had a neighbour who overdosed so badly on—"

"They're the non-drowsy kind. I'm fine, Stephen."

She walks around the greenhouse, angling her body through the narrow spaces between now-glistening foliage. A steely leaf with a lethal point just skims her ear. Now a drop of water lands on an eyelid, but she lets it rest there, scared that a stray arm might fatally dislodge some rare species. "I can't believe what you've done here, Stephen. It's… magical."

"Thank you," he says. "Would you like me to introduce you and tell you all their names?"

"That would be the icing on the cake – but not why I'm here."

He moves towards her, slipping nimbly down an aisle as if it's the Boulevard des Anglais. "Why *are* you here, Kerry? Haven't you had your fun?"

She shakes her head. "Stephen…"

Kerry doesn't complete her denial, however pressing, because a massive and debilitating yawn intervenes. Suddenly she starts to totter but feels it is more than her life's worth to grasp onto a frond for support.

Stephen watches her for a second or two, confused but fascinated. Finally, concern starts to set in. "Would you like to sit down?" he suggests.

He points her towards a chair at the front of the greenhouse, then computes that she might not manage the journey unaided. At least not without ploughing recklessly into some of his closest friends. Stretching out a bony arm somewhat tentatively, as if the slightest bodily contact might topple them both, he manages to lead her unsteadily to a chair, using just the tips of his fingers. He realises that he has never escorted a young woman, or indeed any sort of woman, to a chair before. Especially not one who has suddenly become so very groggy.

"Can I get you some water?" he says. "Or alcohol. I've heard that can sometimes help. Not entirely sure what type, however. Or what you have that needs helping."

"Sure, just hose me down with whatever." She looks up at him blearily, totally forgetting what she had intended to say before the dizziness set in. "Hey, Stephen, I'm fine. Thanks. Must just be PTSD." He stares at her. "Post-Traumatic Shrub Disorder."

He nods. He realises this is probably a joke, but he isn't in the mood and he doesn't honestly think Kerry is either, but it's almost like a condition with her and he has a feeling that it could be incurable.

She begins to rummage in her shoulder bag. He notices that her hands are shaking and wonders if she is scared of something and whether it might be him. "I brought you another note from Nathan. A thank-you note. For his gift and for coming to his party."

"You brought it yourself. In person. Why?"

"You didn't want to see me?" She notices that, despite her irritation, her words are struggling to come out and that her mouth is starting to feel like she has just been to the dentist for major root-canal work. She wonders if her lips are looking unduly thick and rubbery. Which reminds her of a joke about a Chinese waiter, but she can't quite recall how it goes.

"No. *Yes*. It's just… email is so much easier," he explains.

Kerry seems slightly put out by this, but he is at a loss as to why. She is of no help, as her eyes have begun to move erratically in their sockets and her head is bobbing like she can hear insistent music that no-one else is picking up. Stephen is confirmed in his belief that she really is a very strange person. Although he is not totally displeased by her visit.

He opens the flimsy note she has handed him and starts to read. "And with email you can utilise the spellcheck," he adds, but the response is just a weary sigh. "I bet he and his friends are jeering at me too. Along with all my neighbours. And my old customers. And everyone in the known world, so far as I can tell. I doubt I shall ever leave the house again." Before she can respond to this nonsense, he annoyingly changes tack. "Why does he write at the end that he is 'very sorry'? With one 'r'. In 'sorry'. 'Very' is fine. Sorry for what?"

"I dunno. He didn't say. Maybe cos he cares about you? And is just… sorry." She has a feeling that didn't sound as kind as it could have done.

"Because I come from Ruislip," he says. He realises that she has no idea what he is on about and is shaking her head. "Pathetic, aren't I?"

Kerry moans. She hates self-pity and would tell him so, were she certain she could still pronounce it. She rises very shakily from the chair and topples onto a triffid or whatever. "Fine. I'm going now," she says, attempting to struggle to her feet without committing planticide. "You can continue feeling sorry for yourself and shrubbing your drowns." He stares at her. "*What? WHAT?* …Oh. Drowning your shrubs. Whatever. I'll see myself out."

She staggers her way back towards the house, tripping over a set of watering cans, stumbling over the hose and banging into anything in her path. As she careers around, like a large, battery-operated toy running out of juice, she manages to miss the doorway on several occasions. Stephen can hear her muttering. "*Non-fucking-drowsy?* The first twenty-three, maybe!"

He watches her leave, totally confused by her visit and equally disturbed by her trajectory, yet he finds himself unable to help or support her. He returns to the hand-scrawled letter. "He got '*thank you*' right this time!" he calls after her, clutching at straws.

From the living room he hears a clatter, or rather the inevitable sequence of clatters, as a lifetime's junk from over-confident piles and obelisks cascades across the Gibson floor like a tsunami of crap. This is followed by a word that sounds like 'sorry' but not much like it, growing softer or simply being muffled by falling debris, as it is shakily repeated en route to the front door.

Stephen resumes his watering, yet somehow the initial fury has diminished. Voices inside his head – or perhaps it really *is* the plants themselves – are telling him that they truly are all he has.

He recalls an expression but can't think when he first heard it. School, probably. He always thought it couldn't possibly have been about him, because he didn't fit within the strict definition of either word. But now, somehow, as he steps outside himself to stare at whoever he is and whatever he has become, 'sad bastard' doesn't feel quite so far off the mark.

***

"*Three million and one!*"

The cry from the bedroom is ecstatic.

"Suzie! Get in here."

Suzie V pads in from the bathroom. She's patting her face with a small hand towel.

Tyler doesn't even allow her to speak. He simply raises the tablet he has been staring at.

"Look at this. Come. Look!"

She stares at it, until it makes sense. "*Jesus Christ!*" she cries. And this is not a religious person. "Three million and… OM fucking G!"

"Not very ladylike, but exceptional circumstances. I've got to call him! We're gonna be rich, kiddo! Rock rich! McIntyre rich! Richer-than-my-less-talented-but-extremely-rich-wanker-semi-brother rich!" He gives her a quick peck on the cheek. "Scratchy. You missed a spot."

He grabs for the phone.

PART FOUR

The Punchline

THIRTY

And the moral is: he who laughs last...
didn't get the bloody joke.

Stephen had never thought that he would see the house with the peeling blue door again.

Yet here he is, locking his bike beneath the bay window, as if it is an object worthy of theft. Perhaps he believes that there are other people like his uncle out there, for whom the lack of any conceivable value or resale potential is catnip.

He finds it even more difficult than he might have imagined to raise that familiar, tarnished knocker. Before he can steel himself, however, to announce his return to the scene of some of his most flagrant comedy crimes, the door opens and he is practically hoisted into the dingy hallway.

"Here he is. The hombre himself," says Tyler, dragging him warmly by his fraying sleeve into the all-too-resonant living room. He sees Suzie V sitting on the couch, in a disturbingly short, violet skirt, with her legs crossed but without her usual video camera. Stephen finds himself wondering whether staring at these long and far from unattractive legs makes him a womaniser or intimates that he's gay. He has no idea of the rules that apply.

He is almost relieved when Tyler opens his mouth and forces him to redirect his attentions.

"Stevie, have I got news for you, old son!" He waits for a second, because this is a man for whom timing is everything.

"Why are you asking me?" interrupts Stephen, a man for whom timing is a mystery. "You told me on the phone that you had some news. News that I had to hear in person straightaway. That's why I dropped everything."

"What did you drop, love?" asks Suzie V kindly, although still in that raspy voice.

"Well..." considers Stephen, who hadn't really been doing much that was droppable when his phone surprised him. Curiously, he had found himself rather pleased to have something to do, even though it involved the last people on earth he had believed he ever wanted to see again. But he isn't afforded time to elaborate on this black hole in his schedule, or his puzzling ambivalence, as Tyler is off and running.

"The world has seen Stephen Plantman Gibson and it has voted him..." No response. Not even a 'yes...?' Jesus! "*...Only the funniest thing on YouTube in the last month!*"

"I'm sorry?" says Stephen, in obvious puzzlement. "People thought I was funny?"

Both Tyler and Suzie nod. Stephen sits down on one of the plastic chairs. For some reason his legs feel wobbly.

"Not brain-dead or imbecilic? I made them laugh!"

"You did!" agrees Suzie V. "Apparently you made over three million people laugh their heads off. And Stephen, it's growing."

"I have a great sense of humour?"

Their hesitation fills the room like the smell of gas.

"Two out of three ain't chopped liver," says Tyler Watts, which is no answer at all.

"This is it, kid," enthuses Suzie, leaning towards him. He can detect a hint of cleavage just peeping out from her cerise v-neck jumper and tries to look anywhere else. "The comments people wrote online said they adore you. And they were kind, sweetheart, not cruel. They weren't trying to mock or ridicule you." She smiles at him in a way that she hopes will convey a similar sentiment. "There was real affection there. For what they saw, what they recognised. For what they *admired*. You can't fake innocence, kiddo. Well, not without a shitload of practise." She stares into his dumbstruck eyes and taps his hand. He is too absorbed even to flinch. "You've got something special, Mr Gibson. No – forget special – something totally unique."

"Don't need the—"

"Your fifteen minutes has started, Stevie," says Tyler, leaning earnestly towards him. "And we have got to grab it by the fuckin' horns." Stephen notices a hint of cleavage here also, above the fading T-shirt, but has no trouble looking away.

Yet he is not about to be lured in so easily. Especially not for just fifteen minutes. And not by the guy who betrayed him, made him a laughing-stock, even if that stock is perhaps moving in directions he never quite expected.

"What is it you want, Tyler?"

"What I want? God no, Stevie! It's what *you* want."

"It *is* also what we want," says Suzie V, who reckons Tyler is pushing the altruism a tad hard.

"Yeah. Okay," concedes Tyler Watts. "This is for all of us. So I booked you a gig for next Friday."

Stephen says nothing for a moment.

More than a moment. The words make no sense.

Tyler looks at Suzie V, as if wondering whether he had just segued accidentally into a language he doesn't actually speak.

Finally. "A gig," says Stephen.

"Yeah. It's like a spot. A set. A… performance."

"I know what it is!" says Stephen, although he is not entirely certain. At least not when it applies to him.

"And this is only the start, my friend. Only the beginning. We're gonna make deals, y'know, mega. For a DVD: 'Stephen Gibson – Live at the Laughter House!' A streaming video, TV, a tour, a book—"

"All of which I will produce, edit, direct and have an auteur cameo!" says Suzie V, getting even further ahead of herself than her over-excited friend.

Stephen shakes his head. Which doesn't halt the sensation of it spinning wildly. So he stops. "*Wait!* Please. Wait a moment. A 'gig' to do what? Exactly."

"Exactly what you did, babe."

"Only worse," adds Tyler, perhaps unnecessarily.

"Let me get this right," says Stephen, who may be uniquely innocent but isn't utterly deranged. "You want me to be – what do you call it – a jester? A clown. A fool. Using those..." He removes the much-used spiral notebook from his inside pocket and scrolls wildly back to the earliest entries. All, of course, transcribed from memory, when he was securely back home in his room and the notes safe from his teacher's destructive tendencies. How long ago does this seem? "...sprat falls and stupid one-liners and awful puns." He starts to read: "'*the lowest form of comedy, a stinking, putrid cesspit, without the least scintilla of observation, inspiration, truth or wit*', that you yourself warned all us students against."

"I got a one-word answer to that," says Tyler. "Jerry Lewis." Which means nothing to Stephen, as this person's DVDs were most certainly not on his watch-and-learn list.

Tyler glances at Suzie V, the desperation just starting to show. He attempts another tack. "Hey, Stevie – okay – sorry, *Stephen* – you need a job, don't you? A purpose in life. A goal. Not, y'know, having one. Currently." He looks at the bewildered, shell-shocked man and inspiration suddenly smacks him in his podgy face. "And I bet you, now you're famous, that Tina would show you her... appreciation."

"*Nina!*"

"Whoever!" Tyler ignores the looks Suzie V is hurling at him, although he senses that they could be inclining more towards the astonishment end of the continuum. "And I will *personally* make sure she's at the VIP table. Right at the front. Just tell me how to get hold of her."

For a moment, Stephen doesn't speak. He looks from Tyler to Suzie, then back again. Both manage to nod and smile, giving added veracity to this potent new element.

"You really think Ms Nina Hughes will come to my show?"

"A YouTube 'millionaire'? Who wouldn't?" smiles Suzie V, who hopes she's giving off the vibes of someone who knows women pretty damn well because she has felt and thought like one her whole life and now very nearly is one.

"Well, we had better start working, hadn't we?" says Stephen, the exhilaration on his face adding at least two bars of heat to the room. He can't quite compute why the pair are staring confusedly at each other, instead of beaming right back. Nor can he quite fathom why they are sitting so very close together on the sofa, their thighs and knees more than touching. He is not going there for the time being.

"Working?" says Tyler. "On what?"

"My act," says Stephen. As there is no response, or at least nothing verbal, he continues. "I do have *some* material, obviously. Stuff I've been honing between classes. But it needs refining. You know, polishing. Getting the – what is it? – the beats right."

Tyler and Suzie are both shaking their heads. They do this in unison, almost as if they have been to a class. Which, whilst vaguely perturbing, is not unpersuasive.

"Stephen, love," says Suzie, with a gentle smile. "What you've got can't be forced into the usual straitjacket of comedy rules and tropes and, well, basic competence. Even by pros like us. You're too… what's the word…?"

"Incurable," suggests Tyler.

"Natural," amends Suzie V.

"Spontaneous," adds Tyler.

"I am?"

They both nod.

"Now just go home and relax or you'll be no good to anyone," says Tyler. "Jot down this Nina's details and leave the rest to us. We'll stay in touch."

Stephen nods, too choked to speak. He scrawls down some numbers and addresses, clearly etched for life in his brain, then leaves without even remembering to say goodbye.

"Are we a pair of shits?" asks Tyler, of Suzie V, when the door has finally closed and they hear the ancient bicycle rattle off.

"Think we might be, babe. Unless, of course, we're the best thing that's ever happened to him in the poor guy's entire sorry little life."

"Yeah." Tyler Watts nods. "…Even so."

THIRTY-ONE

I'll have whatever she's having.

As Stephen Gibson has not once in his life been asked – or, indeed, instructed – to meet someone at a Starbucks, he is regarding this as a bit of an adventure. Even if it is only Kerry doing the asking. Or instructing.

When she had phoned him the previous evening, only hours after his life-changing chat with Tyler and Suzie V, he couldn't help thinking that she had sounded more brusque than excited. And possibly more earnest than friendly.

He would admit, however, that he is not the best person at interpreting feelings from tone of voice alone and assumes that this is a skill some people have, whilst others have different talents. Such as memorising entire plant encyclopaedias or making people laugh. I mean, come on, thinks Stephen, how could Kerry *not* be excited? He imagines that by now there must be at least four million mortals out there who know and love his work.

When he arrives, Kerry is already seated at a small table to the rear of the buzzing café, or coffee shop as he now knows to call them, checking her phone. In fact, everyone in the place appears to be on their phone, including the staff. Even toddlers in their buggies are happily tapping away, as their chattering mums just as happily ignore them. He wonders breezily if this might be a subject to include in his act. He feels certain that he can work something brilliant around this and its possible connection to brain tumours, with excessive caffeine being a potential contributory factor. Edgy but topical.

Despite Tyler's and Suzie's cautionary note, Stephen would have to confess that there has been a tiny bit of practising going on. In fact, it was going on rather successfully even as he walked here this morning. Had people paused to listen – and quite a few certainly stopped to point – they would have picked up random fragments of 'shtick', as his fellow stand-ups term it, for some impenetrable reason.

"*...And have you noticed – no, have you* observed – *that no matter how hard you flush, it just won't go down! It simply will not go down – how awful is that? Especially if you're in someone else's house... Like – oh, like your local vicar's... or rabbi!' No, imam! That is pushing the envelope, Gibster! Okay... 'So I was on the toilet at my local imam's...'*"

"HI, Kerry," he says, in his excitedly overloud voice. "Would you like a coffee? Or a biscuit of some sort? You can have BOTH, if you'd like."

"Oh, hi, Stephen. I've got, thanks. Well, a coffee. But get yourself one."

"I'm okay," he says, sitting down. "I had a tea with my breakfast." He realises, with a certain inevitability, that some of his public have recognised him, but right now he's more interested in what the unsmiling young woman in front of him has to say.

"I heard about your gig," she begins.

"I *know*! Isn't it exciting?" When she doesn't respond, he feels duty bound to explain to her in some detail just how exciting it is. With numbers included.

"They can't quite believe you're for real, Stephen. That's the draw."

He doesn't understand. "I'm sorry?"

She gently taps his hand. He jolts as he stares down at it, so she equally gently slides her fingers back to cupping her skinny cappuccino. "Stephen, sweetie, listen to me. This is going to end in tears. Trust me on this. And it won't be strictly from laughter."

"That is where you are *so* wrong, Kerry," insists Stephen Gibson, with a knowing smile. "It's the very fact I'm a complete amateur that makes me so professional." He notices her shaking her head. "It's true. Tyler said. I have an innocence, apparently, that some people work at for years and still don't achieve. Which I am told on good authority is totally unique – although, of course, we don't need the 'totally'. *Only perhaps this time we do!*" Kerry tries to speak but the man is clearly on a roll. "Just you come and watch me on Friday. I've been working on my act. But not too hard. Obviously."

A brilliant idea strikes him, as things so often do these days. "*You can sit with Nina!* You've already met her, so you won't be all on your own and feeling out of things. And, of course, your nose won't be running so much this time, so the contrast will be a bit less obvious. Tyler said he will make sure she'll be there."

"I don't doubt it. There'll be a full house. You're quite an attraction, but not for the..." She looks down into her coffee. "I won't be coming, Stephen."

"Oh. Won't you, Kerry? Okay." He finds his surprise at this is tinged with some disappointment. Rather a lot of disappointment, in fact, as he realises that Kerry usually has been there. But then, of course, it makes all the sense in the world. "You're still a bit jealous, aren't you? Of Nina."

"I'm dealing with it. Main reason this time, Stephen, is I've got a job. One that doesn't involve shooting children. Or comics. Same difference."

"Well, that's great, Kerry!" says Stephen. He notices that she isn't looking quite as thrilled as he might have expected. "Isn't it?"

"It would be in Sudan. Or The Sudan, as they used to call it."

Stephen isn't exactly certain whether he is shocked or saddened or both. Nor is he wholly convinced that his initial response accurately reveals either sentiment. "Lots of acacia trees and baobab—"

"Please don't. There's a rebel camp. Probably in those very trees. It's the sort of stuff I used to do, way back when. An agency needs me to cover for someone who's… who's got to come home."

"Was she shot?" asks Stephen.

"*He*. Not seriously."

"Being shot is always serious," decides Stephen, looking quite concerned. Kerry says nothing. This is patently not a conversational channel she is eager to dive into. Nor is what Stephen says next, which strangely she has expected even less. "What about Nathan?"

"*Nathan'll be fine!*" she says, swiftly. "He'll be good. His dad'll look after him. School will be more of a shlep, but—"

"The comic with the Barbie doll?"

"Well remembered. She's gone, actually. To do her GCSEs or something… Stephen, Nate will be okay. Really. And his father and I…"

Stephen wonders why she has stopped mid-sentence and is simply replacing whatever should come next with an unhelpful shrug. Kerry wonders why he is looking at her as if she has suddenly lost the plot.

"His father and you…?"

"Yeah, well. Who knows?"

Certainly not Stephen, who is quite confused. He hates it when people don't finish their sentences. It seems so lazy and inconsiderate. Yet he also finds himself feeling quite upset. Everything appears to be moving too fast these days, like a plant desperately accelerating in order to draw closer to the light it needs to survive. Sensing amidst the palpable excitement an unspecified harm, he finds himself wishing that someone could bring that nourishing light just a notch closer to home. What she says next makes him feel even further out of control.

"I fly out late Friday night. From Heathrow."

"*Friday?* That's almost – well, now. It's the night I'm doing my show."

"Yeah. Tough choice. They want me there to shoot a secret, all-out attack on the stronghold. You can read the details on Facebook."

"I'm not on Facebook. Can't it wait?"

"Insurrection season ends next week. We've got a window."

He stares at her for a moment, processing this. It is only the by now familiar raise of the eyebrows and jut of the chin that tells him she might not be totally serious. He finds himself torn between the realisation that perhaps he still can't get a joke and pure frustration that even at times like this she will insist on making them.

"*Can't you ever stop?*" He shakes his head, as if this will restore normal service. "So, that's it – you're gone? Just like that?"

"Yup." She looks up into his small, unblinking eyes. "As your late great Tommy Cooper would say – 'just like that.'"

"Isn't that bit irresponsible, Kerry? As a mother."

She glares angrily at him for a moment, a sudden fire in her eyes, but says nothing and returns to staring even harder into her coffee.

"Boys need their mothers."

He mumbles this last bit, almost as if he is having a conversation with himself. But she hears him.

"*Gotta go!*" she says, abruptly snatching up her phone. She rises from her chair, as if it were about to attack her. "Good luck with the gig. Which you really do not have to do, Stephen."

"Yes, I do have to, Kerry!" He looks up at her. "*What else do I have?*" Then, more quietly, as if this is something that has only just occurred to him. "I'll miss you."

"You'll always have Nina!" she calls back fiercely, as she stomps to the door.

Stephen wonders why she is suddenly so angry. A young man walks past the table, advertising on his T-shirt that he is a barrister, only he has spelled it wrong and Stephen doubts he has had any legal training whatsoever. He gazes at Kerry's barely half-drunk cappuccino. "Be careful," he says, but only to himself.

On the rim of the cup is a trace of the lipstick he now recognises that she always wears. How had he never noticed that it is the exact shade of *aeschynanthus pulcher*, the blossoms of the 'lipstick plant' itself? He turns the still-warm cup around and decides not to let it go to waste.

Although, in his far less tumultuous past, he was never one to attempt a coffee.

THIRTY-TWO

And his pal replies – he says you're gonna die!

"Hoy, Stevie!"

By now Stephen Gibson is quite accustomed to hearing his name yelled out, as he walks or cycles down Ruislip's busy High Street. Usually he ignores it or simply smiles to himself. Yet there is something about this particular voice that causes him to halt and swivel sharply in its direction.

It is only when he sets eyes on Spike again that Stephen realises how much he has missed the scrawny little Scotsman. Naturally the constant banter went way over his head and the flirting was an irritant, but the chirpier man's patent esteem for his colleague's professional expertise was never stinting or begrudging and without a hint of envy. What's more, wasn't it Spike who encouraged him to find his inner GSOH and win the heart of Nina? Which surely now isn't a million miles away from happening and quite possibly over four million viewers closer.

"Hi, bro Spike," he says. "How ya doin'?"

"Better for bumping into you, Mr Viral. I see you've got all the lingo."

"Lingo?"

"Aye. Okay. Well, you'll be pleased to know we've a wee party lined up for you on Friday."

"I'm not very good at parties, Spike," says Stephen. "Well, not yet. And actually, I'm doing a gig."

"That's what I'm telling you, daftie. A party – a wee group – to come see your spot in Harrow. Even Mrs Dave is coming!"

"Oh. I don't actually see Mrs Dave laughing much. Except when a rival nursery gets box-blight."

"Aye, well, enough said. But I know who you will be pleased to see in that audience."

"*Nina!*" Stephen says immediately. He can hardly breathe. His bicycle clips suddenly feel like shackles around his ankles.

"The very same. She was genuinely gutted to see you go, Stephen. I reckon it was her bosses who insisted on it. Surprise, surprise. The lady herself told me she's really thrilled you've picked yourself up so smartly. *And* found a new line of work. Who'd have thought you'd be famous! For something you can't even… who'd have thought!"

"How about my proposal?"

"You never fucking *proposed*!" Stephen just stares at him. "Oh, the Magnolia jobby. Went through unscathed. Zebra warts and all." The Scotsman seems really pleased at what he just did, although it wasn't nearly as off-the-cuff as he has made it sound.

"I certainly didn't recommend *Haworthia reinwardtii* – very bad choice – but I'm delighted my work will survive. It will look good on my bio."

"Yeah. Course it will. Maybe you can combine the two in your act."

Stephen just smiles. This less worldly man before him understands so little about the fine art of stand-up. And in truth, why would he?

"We won't sit too near the front," Spike reassures him. "Don't want to put you off. Mind you, with your act, that could work *for* you as much as agin you."

This is a bit too tortuous for Stephen. "I don't mind where you sit, Spike. So long as Nina's lime-green eyes and my conkerbrown ones meet across the darkness, because that's quite important, I gather. I believe I'm the first person on, so you won't have to hold your breath for too long."

"That's good to know. Actually, there's a sort of rumour goin' round that someone big is going to be on that night, but nobody knows who. Or, at least, they're no tellin'… Maybe it's you! Now I'd best leave you, old pal – to your practising."

"Tyler Watts of Killer Comedy, you remember him, the ugly fat one who got so angry at that club – actually, he still does get quite cross, but I think he means well – he's told me to keep it spontaneous. So that's what I'm working on."

"Aye. You do that." He touches his old colleague's arm. "One wee question. It *is* deliberate, isn't it? What you're up to? You can fess up to your old pal." The man thinks for a moment. "I mean, nobody can be *that*—"

"Oh, yes," says Stephen, whose thoughts have turned to Nina. To his surprise, he is finding it increasingly hard to picture her. She does have luminescent green eyes, doesn't she? Yes, he's quite certain she does. Well, green-ish. Like his thumb. He's not a religious person, but come on, that's a sign, isn't it?

"Great to see you, Stevie."

"Er – you too – *Spikie*!"

Stephen smiles to himself, as he pedals off. When did he get so sharp?

Yet beneath the only-to-be-expected nerves and apprehension ("Feel the fear and fucking do it anyway," instructed Tyler, in Module 8, which Stephen had found ridiculous at the time), he senses a vague, unfocussed sadness. A sadness that he can't quite fathom and seems different from others he has known.

He could well do without it.

THIRTY-THREE

The snail says, "What the hell was that all about?"

The comedy club is in the populous North-West London suburb of Harrow, just a few minutes' walk downhill from the famous public school, but not a straw boater nor striped blazer in sight.

Whilst its reputation is growing pretty fast, Ha Ha Harrow is not, as Tyler Watts explains to Stephen Gibson, quite yet the Mecca for aspiring comics. But nor, he adds with a rare smile, are there probably that many aspiring comics in Mecca. If this is the kind of remark guaranteed to uncoil the sheepshank nerves of a virgin stand-up, it isn't working on this one.

Yet, as Stephen stands at the side of the stage, peeking out in such a way that he can watch the evening's audience trickling in (and anyone in the audience bothering to look can see him), it is not stage fright that is making him quiver like a Cypress in a gale.

It must, as he tells himself, be love.

After all, for what other reason would he be putting himself through all this?

Then he reminds himself that he currently has no job, a YouTube following of millions, world (or, at least, adjacent boroughs of Hillingdon and Harrow) recognition and a unique chance to build and cement the last career on earth he ever dreamed of pursuing, considering that, until quite recently, he had no SOH whatsoever. Neither G nor not-very-G. Yet people are apparently finding him not merely funny but hysterically so, and it would appear that the less he actually gets right, the more people enjoy it.

As Tyler himself tells him, and as Spike had so astutely discerned, nobody quite knows whether his 'screw-ups' or wrong-footedness – and Stephen is not so stupid that he can't recognise these as the very bedrock of his current audience love-fest – are genuine inanities or breathtaking acts of deliberate calculation.

The slightly perturbing thing is that Stephen Gibson is no longer certain himself.

***

Tyler has now joined his 'boy' backstage but is still failing to drag him fully out of audience view and preserve what little mystique is available, in a rudimentary suburban comedy club, on a warm midsummer's evening. Although something is also telling him that this breach might just be the perfect teaser for what inevitably will follow.

Stephen's eyes flit excitedly from table to table, as the audience slowly but noisily take their seats, sometimes taking them several feet away from their original location, in order to accommodate the numbers in their particular party. The club, being in the barely decorated, or perhaps calculatedly informal, room above a pub, is amply equipped with the stuff that can either lubricate an audience into laughing at anything or intoxicate them to a state of unappeasable belligerence.

Despite the surging chatter and frenzied clanking of glassware, the words '*She's here!*' ring out from the wings and around the club. Nina is probably the only one who doesn't hear them, as she is already into a spirited conversation on her phone, simultaneously nodding and smiling to Spike, as he mouths something which is either vulgar or a drink suggestion.

Mrs Dave has seated herself strategically close to her newest client. She glances meaningfully around the crowded room, in order to announce her formidable presence, whilst simultaneously checking out whether any of her customers are frittering away their money on ephemeral comedy, rather than on blooms that could last for a matter of weeks. If she is in any way chastened by rocking up to watch a former employee, whom she has only recently and quite brutally let go, as he attempts to establish himself in a radically new line of work, she is making a valiant effort not to show it.

At a table conveniently close to the bar, Stephen is both touched and uplifted to spot his fellow alumni from The Killer Comedy Academy. All three are giving him the thumbs-up, which tells Stephen that they can, of course, see him and also that they are not as envious as he has feared they might be. He is aware that overnight success, such as he is currently enjoying, is, in all likelihood, something that will elude them for the remainder of their working and predictably unfulfilled lives.

Finally – or, at least, he assumes finally, as the audience now appears to comprise everyone he has ever known who still has a pulse and isn't too old or frail to make the journey – he spots his Uncle Geoffrey and Noreen. Only Tyler's firm arm around his wrist prevents him from leaping out and hugging the older couple, whose reaction to his new calling has, until this point, been lukewarm verging on Siberian.

He turns to Tyler in delight. "*Nina!*" he says first.

"Didn't I tell you?"

"*Jayson! NJ! Nigel!*"

"Lessons to be learned!"

"*Uncle Geoffrey and Noreen!*"

"Who the fuck are they?"

"Well, they're… I'm a bit nervous."

"It'll be fine," Tyler assures him, with as much conviction as he can muster. He has instructed Suzie V not to appear with her cameraman until Stephen is onstage, as they all reckoned that this could totally freak their subject – and possible meal-ticket – right out the park. "Remember Killer Rule Twelve," he smiles, "stack the audience with friends who will laugh their arses off at anything."

"Tyler, I can hardly breathe."

"Good. Hyperventilation works for you. There's a little room just along the corridor back there. We call it a 'green room', so you'll love it. Go and sit down and—"

"Prepare my act."

"Absolutely not. NO! Sitting would be fine. I'll go out there and check if… I'll go out there and mingle."

Stephen starts to move away. Then he turns back. "Is Suzie V your girlfriend? Or… something?" he asks.

The look that appears on Tyler's face is not one that Stephen recalls having noticed before, but he is aware yet again that looks aren't his specialty.

"Or something," mutters Tyler.

Stephen just nods, but Tyler can see that the man has gone deep into his own thoughts. He wonders for a moment what these might be, then decides he could be up nights and not fathom the workings of the Gibson mind. So he slips back into the audience and awaits the unimaginable.

The lights in the crowded room go down.

***

The small waiting room allocated to visiting comics makes the outer room appear like a triumph of interior design. There are a few mismatched chairs, a cracked mirror and a tiny three-legged table with a sad-looking plant dumped on it, to whose aid Stephen wishes he could come with at least some water. Never has a room, in his opinion, been less green.

Unfortunately, between him and the nearest available source of hydration, stands a large and very sun-ravaged man, with thinning grey hair that splays wildly in all directions, as if it has seen what is happening to his head and wants out. Under a worn black T-shirt, the owner proudly sports a paunch like he has just eaten the Christmas pudding for the entire orphanage. Stephen notices, on this person's sockless feet, flip-flops that have seen better days, as indeed have the feet within them. The man, who must be in his mid-fifties, seems to be bobbing up and down for no good reason that the younger man can discern and talking quite heatedly to himself.

From the stage can be heard the voice of a young and irrepressibly cheery comic, the MC for the evening. He is starting to warm up the already fairly jolly yet, as ever, potentially combative audience.

After a few moments, the anteroom's other occupant appears to notice Stephen and grunts something that sounds like a 'hi' but could as easily be a cough. The sound comes with an accent of some sort that Stephen can't quite distinguish. He offers a reciprocal 'hello', which can also happily function as a standalone, should it not, in fact, have been precipitated.

"What comes after post-modern?" says the man, which is clearly a sentence of sorts but makes no more sense than the opening grunt. Yet it does give Stephen a clue as the man's origins, which are American. Or Canadian. Or possibly Australian. New Zealand?

"I beg your pardon?" says Stephen.

The man, whose countenance, despite its initial fearsomeness, is not unkindly, just stares at Stephen through unexpectedly bright, pale-blue eyes, as if awaiting a further response, comic or otherwise.

"Don't recognise me?" says the man, with a slight smile. "That's cool."

This makes little more sense than the earlier question, but Stephen is picking up that this person may not be quite as 'cool' with the situation as his words convey. Never one willingly to upset anyone, he immediately glides into his professional apology mode.

"I'm so sorry, sir. You meet so many people in a garden centre." He tries to smile reassuringly. "I'm positive it will come back to me. Sometimes, you know, bumping into customers out of context..."

Noticing the air of total confusion, Stephen now has what he knows is a brilliant idea. One of many, these days, apparently. Picking up the wilting plant from the table, along with its dusty ceramic pot, he thrusts it as a bundle towards the larger man, who is too bemused to do anything other than accept it. Stephen continues to stare at him, cocking his head to one side then the other. He finally shakes it with equal vehemence in both directions.

Then suddenly it hits him.

"*Of course!* Tsk. What am I like? A fig tree for a south-facing garden!"

The man has had enough. Especially of plant-bearing. He thrusts the shabby combo back to this odd young person with some force. "*No, it fucking wasn't!* Fig tree? Garden centre! You shitting me? I'm Sandy Rosenzweig!"

Stephen nods, acknowledging that this must indeed be who the gentleman is, without being any wiser as to how he might have been expected to know this.

"Funny name," he says, because it is of a type he has never encountered before.

"Yeah. Well, I'm a funny guy. With me, now? *Huh?* I'm just trying out some stuff here. Seein' what pushes you guys' buttons, before the major UK gigs. Y'know – low key. And you can't get much lower than—"

"Oh, I am *so* sorry, Mr, er... I do get it now," says Stephen, a tad guiltily. "You're a comic, like me. Only a late starter. *Obviously*. Well, very best of luck."

"I am *not* a friggin' late starter," protests the older comic, wondering why he should be so incensed by this plant-bearing nonentity.

"Oh. Okay. Well, look at you, you persevered. Despite – well, clearly everything."

"Hey, guy, listen up. You really don't...? I been on TV, I been in movies, DVDs – you name it. I got awards comin' out of my... *Whaddaya mean 'clearly everything'?*"

At this moment, and perhaps fortuitously, Tyler Watts peers in. He does a double-take when he sees the older man.

"Oh my God! *Sandy Rosenzweig!*"

Stephen beams at the American. "You see, somebody *does* know you! Even if it's only Tyler."

The visiting comic gives the newcomer a despairing look, to which Tyler can only respond with a commiserating shrug, before turning to Stephen. "You're on next, mate. Just... y'know... be yourself." Ignoring the plant, he retreats back into the darkness.

Magnanimously, the older man offers Stephen a warm and even comradely smile. "Break a leg, kid."

Stephen is so horrified that for a moment he can't move. "*No!*" he protests. "Why would you say that?"

Sandy Rosenzweig is unable to respond – not that a suitable response comes readily to mind – because the voice from the stage has just grown louder.

"You've seen him on YouTube and you can't believe he's for real. But now he's right here in the Ha Ha room for fucking real. *But is he – or isn't he?* Yes, it's the world's favourite anti-comic – the one and only STEPHEN GIBSON!"

"That's me," says the opening act, somewhat unnecessarily.

***

As the Harrow audience goes wild in the semi-darkness, whooping and clapping, the one and only Stephen Gibson steps tentatively onto the tiny stage. Still mulling on the old comic's unexpected meanness of spirit, he has totally forgotten that he is holding the sorry little plant in his trembling hands. It doesn't occur to him, even when he is standing rigidly just a few feet away from the microphone, taking in the familiar and not-so-familiar faces.

A galaxy of smiles are beaming back at him, overlaid with anticipation, excitement and, in some cases, an almost quantifiable amount of dread. He can just about spot his fellow apprentices, seated at a small table already crowded with glasses, full, semi- and completely drained. They are all nervously but warmly giving him their trademark double thumbs-up. Dream on, sunshine!

Behind them, and ensuring that the loyal threesome are occasionally in shot, are Suzie V, her cameraman and an almost smiling Tyler Watts. Stephen had quite forgotten that this, his first proper set (if you discount Kew Gardens, which might more readily be termed a marketing presentation or a total disaster), would probably be filmed as part of Suzie's ongoing chronicle. Especially now that one pupil has unprecedentedly achieved fame on an almost global scale.

His glance shifts to Uncle Geoffrey and Noreen, who unsurprisingly seem a little out of place in this, his new milieu. Stephen finds himself almost wishing he could move down there, amidst his throng, to join the anxious couple, in order to make them feel more at home.

Perhaps there might indeed be time for some amusingly free-wheeling audience chit-chat. He has decided to play this by ear. "And you there, what's *your* name, Uncle Geoffrey?" That sort of thing, which is rather funny, in a way. He might even do some of his by now notorious Richard Pryor shtick with Noreen, who he feels would be a far more receptive audience than that elderly couple from Atlanta.

Finally, his eyes rest on the Blooming Marvellous table. To her credit, Mrs Dave is smiling benignly up at him, almost as if she has forgiven him for putting her in the invidious position of having to destroy his career. Spike, who is sitting a bit too close to their special guest for Stephen's liking, is raising his glass to his erstwhile colleague.

And, of course, there's Nina.

Nina, the glorious catalyst for all this, until it developed an extraordinary momentum of its own. Yet still the focus, the reason, the anticipated reward. Beautiful, entrancing Nina, whose exquisite face (with eyes that are most definitely green) is tilted up towards him, without rancour and with what he might almost interpret as – yes – admiration. And beyond this, something else, something far more potent. For the first time Stephen Gibson has an inkling of how celebrity, regardless of the form it might take, can affect those who can only touch it by association. The feeling is quite heady and is rendering him even more scared and speechless than he might otherwise be.

This speechlessness, however, whilst provoking the expected laughter, is just on the cusp of making his audience a little uneasy.

"Give us your name then!" comes a voice he doesn't recognise.

"Oh, I'm so sorry," says Stephen, who can't help feeling that something is slightly awry. Something hugely important, yet he can't quite assess what this is and now is hardly the time. "Hello, my name is—"

Before he can finish, the crowd is ahead of him. "StephengibsonstephengibsonSTEPHENGIBSONYAYYY!"

"I was just… I was going to say that! But thank you. Name recognition – very important. If it is, in fact, your name. Or your stage name, of course. Or indeed both."

"*Use the mic!*" comes the unarguably wise and not unkindly suggestion.

It is only now, as he moves towards the microphone stand and begins awkwardly to reach for it, that Stephen realises he still has the anteroom's flagging plant in his hands. He could, of course, make a thing of it – turn an encumbrance into an opportunity – perhaps even describe its genus in a particularly amusing way. Or he could simply put it down and continue with his 'set'.

He appears to select a third and possibly more theatrical option of allowing it to slip out of his perspiring hands onto the hard wooden floor. The makeshift bowl and equally inferior pot instantly smash to pieces, sending soil and sorry bits of plant in as many directions as possible, including onto those members of the audience unfortunate (or perhaps fortunate) enough to be perched in the very front row.

The microphone, having been dislodged from its stand during Stephen's futile struggle to contain the damage, topples with an amplified thud onto the newly soiled floor. Stephen sees no other available solution than to chase it before it rolls completely away and out of sight.

The audience is in hysterics. Beer and dry white wine are being spilled, snorted and unwillingly regurgitated, as mortals known and unknown raise the roof.

Smiling happily, whilst still apologising profµsely to an unseen management for damage to their foliage, ceramics and infrastructure, Stephen picks up the mic and deliberately sticks it in his eye. Or, more accurately, onto his right eyeglass, as he has omitted to remove his spectacles for the duration of his set.

The opener is on a roll, as he performs to the increasingly entertained – whilst justifiably mystified – audience.

He tells bad jokes, that are hardly jokes at all under all the universally accepted international definition, including of course the imam toilet joke, which he feels ticks a lot of boxes in this, Britain's most multicultural borough. He makes a big thing of losing the notes he has made, because he has, in truth, lost the notes he has made. Although he suddenly and publicly recalls that he left them in his other brown corduroy trousers, which look identical to the ones he is currently sporting, so it's such an easy mistake to make. He just hopes they haven't shredded too badly in the wash, the notes not the trousers, which are pretty resilient even after all these years, the trousers not the notes, because then he'll have to spend forever picking tiny bits of soggy paper off his clothes and also perhaps from some of Noreen's woollier garments and massive undergarments, sorry, Noreen, sitting over there on the far corner table. Which leads him into some inspiredly observed washing-machine-and-soiled-laundry shtick that he hadn't, until this actual moment of delivery, known he had in him.

Talk about spontaneous.

Stephen finds it quite exhilarating that he has the audience with him. Somehow he knows that he can say anything now and they will laugh like drains. He tries it and he's right. They do. He actually hears one man in the very front, wiping tears from his eyes, saying to his wife or partner, "*I don't know why I'm fucking laughing!*" which has to be praise indeed.

Before he finishes, because he knows all good things must come to an end and that you should leave your audience craving more, he snatches one final look at Nina. She is glowing. And it is all for him.

"Well, that's my time," says Stephen, because this is what you say. "Thanks so much for coming out on a night like… well, actually, quite a pleasant night. Although watch out for some possible squally showers on your way home, *especially* if you live in the north. And are maybe here, visiting. Or on business. My name is—"

"*Gibsonstephengibsonstephengibsonste…*"

Stephen bows graciously and, after a final, lingering look at Nina, begins his journey off the stage. On the way, just before a barman, armed with a broom, can deftly sweep a path for him, he manages inevitably – yet perhaps even deliberately – to skid on some of the spilled soil and pot fragments.

And thus tonight's barnstorming opener disappears from the arena, fortunately without breaking anything, including his leg. (Despite what that strange foreigner with the antic hair and unhealthy paunch had wished on him.)

Even before Stephen has fully disappeared, the bemused but indefatigably jolly MC is back. "And let's hear it one more time for Mr Stephen Gibson, the most laughable stand-up in the comedy universe!"

The crowd roars with delight. Stephen peeks in once more from the wings and throws his fans a friendly wave, reminding some in the audience of their own child in its first Nativity play. From offstage they just manage to hear a contrite, "So sorry about the plant, but I'm afraid it was on its last leaves anyway."

By the time Stephen returns to the smaller room, he is shaking with excitement. He discovers Sandy Rosenzweig, keen but clearly envious foreign comic, rooted to the spot. The larger man stares at him without blinking.

"Different," is all the American says, when he has regained the power of speech.

"Between you and me, I was rather nervous," concedes Stephen. "Quite a few things went Conference Pear-shaped. And, confidentially, not all of them deliberate."

"You serious?"

"I am. Forgive me, Mr… er… I've forgotten your name."

"Sandy. Sandy Rosenzweig."

"That's quite a mouthful. If you don't mind a piece of advice, from someone whose name people *do* appear to remember—"

"'*Rocky*' Rosenzweig?"

Stephen shakes his head. He realises it's a lost cause, so he doesn't pursue it.

"Why are you doing this, kid?" asks the man, his voice softening and an unexpected element of sweetness confusing the mix. Stephen is rather thrown.

"Why am I…? Well, I do realise this is not what I was born to do, Mr, er… but did you see that lady out there? The one in the *dianthus grantantiapolitensis* blouse?"

"Say what? Oh, near the front? I sure did. *She's* who you're doing it for?"

"Yes! Her name is Ms Nina Hughes and she's Welsh. Women go for men with a GSOH. Well, 94.6 per cent, by current reckoning. It means Good Sen—"

"Whoa! Lemme get this straight – you're doin' stand-up for a *woman*?"

"For a lady. Nina. Hughes. Yes."

The older man starts to walk – or flip-flop – around the room, which isn't easy, as it is rather tiny and stuffed with hard chairs. But, of course, minus a plant. He suddenly swings back towards Stephen, as if he wants to shake him violently, like a rag doll, but hopes that swift, well-chosen words might just do the trick. "Jeez! Kid, *women don't want an act!*"

"Don't they?" says Stephen, who can't for the life of him see where this is leading or why the scruffy American wobbling his head almost in Stephen's face should, in any way, be an authority. "What *do* they want?"

"Furs… diamonds… alimony." He stares at Stephen, who is clearly processing this. "Er… I'm kidding? Stephen, is it?" Stephen nods. "Steve, trust me, they want – well, shit, they want honesty. Y'know, truth. Kindness. Sincerity. Yeah – go figure." He puts a brawny arm around Stephen, which makes the younger man uncomfortable yet oddly reluctant to stem the flow. "Kid, they want who you *are*, not your set. Especially not *your* set."

The skinny English guy in the bear-like grip of Sandy Rosenzweig and still sweating from his onstage exertions, appears bewildered. "All my research proves that today's women want – possibly even *demand* – a Good Sense of—"

"You told me. Hey – who knows? Maybe you'll end up with just one single, solitary person laughing – or, in your case, smiling caringly. But if she's the *right* person, ain't she all the audience you'll ever need? Unless, of course, you're playing Madison Square Garden, then you'll look kind of an asshole. By the way, I stormed the place – go buy my friggin' DVD."

Stephen appears thoughtful but then notices Sandy Rosenzweig's pale eyes suddenly light up. The older man is no longer looking at him.

Stephen turns. To see Nina standing in the doorway.

"Hello, Stephen."

A voice from outside suddenly bellows. "And now, ladies and gents, someone you never expected to see. Someone I never expected to see. And someone Ha Ha Harrow sure never expected to see. Making a secret appearance – but now the secret is out – direct from the Big Apple and before his sell-out UK arena dates. The one – the only – the legendary Sandy Rosenzweig."

For a moment the audience is quiet. As if they can't quite believe their good fortune. And then they begin to cheer and stamp and whoop.

"Gotta go," says the legend, smiling admiringly at Nina Hughes. He turns to Stephen. "Hey, maybe I'm the shmuck!" He makes for the stage. Passing Nina, he says, "*You* know who I am, don't you?"

She laughs and nods. The laugh still trills in his ears, as the audience goes berserk.

"Nina! Hi!" says Stephen. He notes with some satisfaction that her eyes tonight are greener and more sparkly than ever, if indeed this is possible. "Did you… did you enjoy the show?"

"Er. Yeah. I did. Yes, Stephen. It was… quite unique." Before he can interrupt: "I know – 'unique' will suffice." She laughs again. "Not sure or even *totally* sure what this was all in aid of, or exactly how 'knowing' you really are, Mr Gibson, but you're certainly very… I dunno, courageous?" She smiles that extraordinarily wide, gleaming smile, as if amongst all The

Lord's munificent bounties he had blessed her with an extra set of teeth. "And you're mingling with the rich and famous now. Who would ever have thought!" Stephen says nothing. He just keeps staring.

"Stephen…?"

For some inexplicable reason, Stephen Gibson finds that his mind is wandering.

Back to earlier events, different conversations. Random incidents. He appreciates that this must be due to performance adrenaline suddenly quitting his body in a torrent, like water out of one of his hoses, leaving him totally drained. What else could it be, with *the* Nina Hughes standing right here before him? Tall, Welsh and plant-loving. The object of his aberration.

Yet he is vaguely puzzled that this current encounter, one that he has so vividly imagined and 'dreamed on sunshine' for so long, isn't sending a new and even more powerful surge of adrenaline whirling in utter frenzy round and round his buzzing head, like those dizzying fairground attractions he was always far too scared to ride.

Early days.

His new fan rests an elegant hand on his shoulder. So gently that he can hardly feel it. He notices that her impeccably manicured nails exactly match her lipstick. Whilst neatly complimenting her eye-shadow. How clever is that?

"Stephen," she smiles warmly, "I know it's not quite July 28th, but do you still want to take me out?"

He stares at her, looking deep into those gorgeous, glimmering eyes, slightly moist and, yes, just as breathtakingly lime-green as his precious Green Trick Dianthus. Two dianthuses in one! And not just the eyes. Topping to perfection that exquisitely svelte and enticing body, like the very first flowers of spring after a taxing winter, are this young woman's tantalising, *Pseudoplatanus* lips.

"I'll call you," he says.

"Excuse me?" says Ms Nina Hughes, of the eyes and lips.

Stephen Gibson rushes past his startled visitor, knocking over a chair, and pelts out of the tiny room. Right onto the stage and past a bemused Sandy Rosenzweig. Which gets the biggest laugh of the evening, so far.

"Lock the fucking doors," snarls Sandy Rosenzweig. "Next Brit tries to leave – I break *both* his friggin' legs!"

THIRTY-FOUR

Khartoum Network.

Stephen is relieved to see that his bike is still parked where he left it, down a darkened side road near the club, leaning against a wall. In his excitement, he had forgotten that he normally padlocks it when foraying into central Harrow (although he has found, on previous, less neglectful occasions, that thieves have left the bike but stolen the padlock).

He can hear laughter coming from inside the club and is rather pleased that the acerbic yet somehow rather kind American gentleman is finding a sort of success, after all his years of struggle. He can't help thinking about the man's closing words to him. Not the rubbish about performing to huge crowds in some sort of 'garden' – who does comedy in gardens? – (although, wouldn't Stephen be *terrific* at that!) but the less delusional, personal stuff.

"*Hey! Stephen! Where are you going?*"

The familiar voice stops him, as his body is mounted half-way across his bike. He turns to see a hallucinatory jumper with Nigel somewhere inside it, darting at speed towards him like a flickering neon light, alongside his less psychedelic but equally motivated classmates. NJ is clearly struggling to keep up.

"Hello, Nigel. Thank you for coming to my show. No time to talk. Got to go!"

"Where you off to in such a rush, Stevie?" asks Jayson.

Stephen realises that until this moment he has had no clear idea exactly where in the world he is off to. But now, to his surprise, he does.

"The Sudan," he says.

"Nah. Don't know it," says Jayson Spliff, shaking his head. "But there's a real pub downstairs in *this* place, if you don't want to hang about up there. Which I can sort of understand."

"It's not a pub, Jay," explains Nigel. "Who'd call a pub The Sudan? It's that new Indian restaurant in Wealdstone. Right, Steve?"

"It might be, Nigel. Or Sudanese restaurant, possibly. If there is such a… considering they're starving. But I was talking about the actual country. You know, in Africa."

"On your *fershtinkeneh* bicycle?" says NJ, shaking her head and puffing at the same time. "Even Jesus Christ couldn't—"

Stephen stares at her. "No, of course not, NJ." He looks down at his bicycle, as if this has been the main instigator of his shaky decision-making. "Just to the airport. Heathrow," he says, unsurely.

"Why, Stephen?" asks NJ.

"It's personal, NJ."

The woman nods. She understands personal.

Jayson takes in the expression on his comrade's face. Suddenly he is off and away from them, scooting down the road, long legs flying. "*Wait there!*"

They watch him go. Stephen just wants to get back on his bike, but he feels that this could be impolite. Especially after his friends have been so gracious in their support of him, without rancour or totally justifiable envy.

"You really killed tonight," says Nigel.

"I did, didn't I, Nigel?" says Stephen, "if it's what I think you mean." He smiles. "I certainly *killed* a plant!"

"To own an entire room by dissing all the rules. Takes a special kind of genius, boychik." NJ gives him a big hug, which doesn't bother him quite so much as he might have expected, although it does cut off his breathing for a while.

"Was it everything you dreamed of?" asks Nigel Ngo, wistfully.

"Actually, Nigel, no," admits Stephen, adding for clarity, "No, as in not yes, as opposed to your name. Ngo."

They suddenly hear a sound that is familiar to all of them, but not normally associated with this time of the night. With lights flashing and 'Torna a Surriento' blaring from an external speaker, a large ice-cream van tears down the bumpy suburban side road towards them, as if someone has just hit 999 for an emergency bunny-eared double vanilla cone *with* sprinkles and chocolate sauce.

On the van, the name '*Antonioni and Son*' is emblazoned in script the colour of a raspberry ripple. A window on the driver's side opens and Jayson sticks his head out.

"All aboard for the Sudan! Wherever the hell that is."

"So this is what you do all day?" says NJ. "You told us you had your own business."

"Well, I do, sort of."

"When Antonioni dies?"

"When son dies."

Stephen suddenly feels rather guilty for never having asked Jayson – or, in fact, anyone – what they did other than aspire. He doesn't even know anything about Spike or what brought him down from Scotland. Or what Noreen did with her life before meeting his Uncle Geoffrey, or even what she wants to do now. He only knows about Kerry because she let him into her world. And now she has let him out again.

He suddenly allows his bike to drop onto the ground, opens the driver's door and yanks Jayson smartly out. "You've been drinking."

Jayson shrugs and walks round to the passenger side. Lugging the discarded bike, Nigel and NJ clamber clumsily into the body of the van. Even Stephen feels that the glee on the face of the larger passenger can't entirely be attributed to a prospective trip to the airport.

Stephen finds the key and starts the car. They hear a grinding of gears as the old machine leaps onto the nearby pavement. Jayson stares at him.

"Can't drive, can you?"

Stephen slides out of the van once more and Jayson resumes his familiar place behind the wheel. When Stephen slips in beside him, they both just shrug. No apology necessary.

As they pass the entrance to the club, within which he assumes the deceptively wise and dogged American is still in full flow, Stephen can just make out his uncle and sort-of auntie on the pavement, looking around for their famous nephew with a certain puzzlement. He waves to them from the window of a passing ice-cream van, which doesn't relieve their puzzlement one jot.

NJ has found the way to dispense ice-cream before the van has even reached the first set of traffic lights.

"Feed a cold, starve a fever," she explains to Nigel, from her cramped position. Her mouth is poised directly underneath the funnel and locked onto open.

"Do you have a cold, NJ?"

"Not yet, Nige. But I will by the time I've hoovered all this sodding ice-cream."

"You're gonna pay for all that!" calls Jayson, from the front. "And it's not fresh." They can almost feel the shrug of indifference from the rear. Jayson turns to his most important passenger. "Uh, Stephen – you're not really going to Sudan, are you?"

"I am, Jayson. I've just realised. I need to tell her how I feel."

"Nina? But we all saw her, didn't we? She was right there in the club, and very nice too. You couldn't take your eyes off her."

"Not Nina!" his passenger calls out loud, above the roaring of the engine and the ice-cream machine that has just switched on. "Kerry."

The reaction is unanimous. Jayson's van begins to swerve. "*KERRY?!*"

"Did I miss an episode?" asks Nigel. Whilst NJ's mouth opens even wider, which is actually good news for her. "Does Tyler know?"

"No," admits Stephen. "And I see no reason why he should."

"Gotta be careful in this next stretch," says Jayson, as they turn a sharp corner. In light of the current conversation, this doesn't make sense to any of them. "Rival ice-cream territory," explains Jayson. "Ferrante and daughters. We could start another Dessert Storm. See what I did there?"

"We saw," mutters NJ. "Can't you just ring her, Stevie?"

"Stephen. *No!* Some things you can only say face to face, NJ. Although, to be quite honest, I really have no idea what I want to say."

"If you're done with Nina, can I have her?" asks NJ.

"Er, I don't actually think she's—"

"Jewish? Hey, nobody's perfect."

Before he can correct her, although really what's the point, Stephen spots the first road sign directing them towards Heathrow.

He finds that he can hardly breathe.

***

As the van comes screeching to a musical halt outside terminal three, from which Stephen has ascertained that planes for Sudan occasionally take off, a group of excited new arrivals to the United Kingdom quit their precious places in the taxi queue and rush to order their very first, late-night UK ice-creams. When

Jayson Spliff aka Julio Antonioni tells them to piss off, he's not a vanilla vendor, they happily put this down to local colour and the unique British sense of the absurd about which they have heard so much.

Barely pausing to thank the first true 'posse' he has made in his entire life, although he knows that he will love them dearly for the rest of time, Stephen jumps out of the thrumming van and dives into the terminal.

"We'll wait here as long as necessary," says NJ, who finds the delivery of freshly dispensed ice-cream far less problematic in a stationary vehicle.

"No need," says Stephen, with supreme confidence.

Jayson notices policemen and security guards moving towards him at some speed, as if he is a major terrorist risk or they desperately crave a swift on-duty cone. He isn't waiting to find out. "If you say so, Stevie. Good luck," he cries, careering off.

Exactly five minutes later, Stephen Gibson slumps out of the airport and makes his way to the end of the line at the cab rank.

Five and a half minutes after this, he hears the by now familiar Neapolitan melody blaring out of a large white van, as it nips ahead of an approaching taxi.

"Get in, schmuck," cries NJ, who looks like she is foaming vanilla at the mouth.

"Plane left, did it?"

Stephen nods. "Next one isn't until Sunday. She could be anywhere by then. She could be lying shot and dead by a baobab tree."

"And they say you've got no sense of humour," says NJ.

"Who says that?" asks Stephen, sharply, as if he has been struck once more.

Jayson Spliff turns up the music, so that a conversation no-one really wishes to have becomes impossible.

Children in the London borough of Hillingdon will talk in hushed tones for many years to come of how they were awakened early from their slumbers by the sound of a phantom ice-cream van, hurtling through the dark, midsummer night.

THIRTY-FIVE

And the cannibal eating the comedian says,
"Does this taste funny to you?"

Stephen Gibson spends most of the following forty-eight hours either in bed, with his eyes disturbingly open, or sitting in his greenhouse, lids yearning desperately to close. He barely touches a Krispie all morning, or a slice of buttered bread at lunch, let alone one of his plant-based health drinks, which look like bottled slime and which Uncle Geoffrey occasionally buys for him, if he's passing 'that hippie shop' off the High Street. Nor do his beloved plants receive the nourishment he has unfailingly provided and which they have come unquestioningly to expect.

It would be clear to anyone that the sad young man has begun the process of wilting, but he stubbornly refuses to talk about it. Not to his nearest or dearest, nor even, in the world of humans, to his Uncle Geoffrey and Noreen.

This, of course, doesn't prevent the concerned couple from discussing it between themselves. The performance, if this is what it was, at the comedy club, has left them reeling. Yet they tell each other that they should have been quite prepared, having tortured themselves with the YouTube video more times than they would care to admit. Seeing their very own Stephen onstage, however, in the mortifying flesh, was a spectacle more horrific than anything they could possibly have selected from their creaking movie shelves.

Uncle Geoffrey is quite certain it is the inevitable realisation that people are laughing, however good-naturedly, *at* his poor nephew rather than with him, that has propelled Stephen into such a downward spiral. And, of course, losing the job that he has loved forever and was surely born to do. Not simply born but predestined by his very DNA.

Noreen, however, has no such blinding certainty as to the root cause of the young man's decline. She is quite as perturbed as her partner that Stephen has allowed his manifestly obvious gifts to evaporate, or at least be shelved for an indeterminate period, in order to concentrate on a career for which he is as suited as Ayatollah Khomeini. Yet her own intuition is leading her to wonder whether there might not be another, even more seismic, element involved in this sudden slump. After all, hadn't he appeared pretty elated at the conclusion of his first-ever comedy club 'set'? Buoyed up by the evident joy being hurled back at him and bolstered, at least for now, by the universal disbelief that anyone could be so naturally and instinctively rubbish.

Whatever the reasons, these grown-ups, as they regard themselves, are in the noblest sense his guardians. They can't just sit by and watch their poor charge go under.

It is Uncle Geoffrey who finally comes up with the solution. He is aware that it is radical and will involve almost strong-arming Stephen into doing something he has never done, nor shown the least inclination even to attempt. Yet needs must.

"Stephen, lad," the older man calls into the greenhouse, "come sit here in the living room. Right between me and Noreen on the old chaise...."

Stephen Gibson stares at his uncle, as if the man has just invited him to share their bed. Geoffrey merely shrugs to his partner, who has already shifted her position to the lumpier end of the furniture.

When the weary young man understandably fails to move, Uncle Geoffrey gently but firmly yanks him from his trusty greenhouse chair and plonks him, like a cushion that could do with some plumping, right in the centre of the chaise-longue and directly in front of the massive TV screen.

"Please don't show me another YouTube video," says Stephen. "I've already seen the one somebody posted from my Harrow debut."

"Your hair looked nice," says Noreen, who sees something positive in everything.

"And you *were* a palpable hit," adds Geoffrey. Realising swiftly that he is going to achieve little by false praise or further conversation, he grabs his well-thumbed remote control and presses the PLAY button.

To his credit, Stephen Gibson says barely a word and moves nary a muscle during the entire experience, as if sensing that the kindly older couple diligently bookending him are, in their own way, simply attempting to do the right thing. Although he can't for the life of him understand why watching a film called *The Silence of the Lambs*, which doesn't have a single lamb in it and precious little silence, is relevant to anything in his miserable life right now. It isn't funny and certainly isn't a love story. In fact, it is one of the most horrific and terrifying things he has ever seen.

"Can I go back to my plants now?" he asks shakily, as the seemingly endless list of people involved in this unspeakable project scrolls down the screen.

"I hope you do," says Uncle Geoffrey, switching off the machinery with a certain reluctance, as he and Noreen usually enjoy a double bill. "That was the object of the exercise." He appears quite satisfied by this.

"I'm sorry?" says Stephen.

"That movie," continues Uncle Geoffrey, "which, by the way, was a massive critical and commercial success, *and* a multiple

Oscar-winner, was about a man who knew what he was good at – what he was *expert* at – and he just went out and did it."

"He killed people!"

"*Forget the minutiae!*" Uncle Geoffrey shakes his head and sighs. "Okay, granted, it isn't horticulture, but every man to his last. Look at the bigger picture, Stephen, heart. The message, if you will. It's about having a God-given gift. Something a feller was born to do. And his being duty bound to use it."

"He was a murderer. He ate a census-taker! He bit a sergeant's face off! He made a prisoner swallow his own tongue!"

"*He can't abide rudeness!*" says Uncle Geoffrey, who is starting to become a bit frustrated. Surely this isn't a difficult concept to grasp. "I didn't have any movies about sodding plants!"

"There's *Day of the Triffids*," says Noreen. "He liked that one, didn't he?"

"Yes, okay, Noreen," grumbles Uncle Geoffrey, "but it didn't exactly make my point, did it? Anyway, I swapped it with a guy in Purfleet for *Saw III*."

"*You SWAPPED* Day of the Triffids*?*" yelps an outraged Stephen. "The *original*? I was saving that for Nathan!"

At his own mention of the little boy, Stephen's eyes begin to tear up. The couple look at him sympathetically, unused to seeing such a swell of emotion on his normally unrevealing face.

"It's okay, sweetheart," says Noreen gently, tapping his knee. "To… you know… like this guy Nathan."

"He's a twelve-year-old boy."

Fortunately Stephen's phone rings before the unsettled woman can draw them all into further complications.

He rises with some discomfort from a posture he hasn't been able to adjust for over two chilling hours. The older couple remain seated, attempting to glean what they can from at least one side of this rare, incoming phone call. And hoping, against hope, that it won't be more comedy news. Or, indeed, a twelve-year-old boy.

"Stephen Gibson," he announces.

The ordinary listener might believe a voice could not sound more miserable, until it suddenly sinks into a new slough of despond.

"Oh, hello, Tyler, how are you?" The couple are once again struck by their nephew's innate courtesy, irrespective of how he is feeling. "...No, I'm quite aware that I haven't been answering your calls. Sorry, I just didn't feel like... What am I doing? I just watched *Silence of the Lambs*, if you must. ...*No, it isn't for my act!* How could a man who eats people be for... and I'm not *doing* another act. I'm not doing anything. Well, I suppose I'm moping, but that isn't actually a career. Although I bet you could sell me a course to make it one."

Stephen looks very much to Uncle Geoffrey and Noreen as if he is about to put his mobile down, or even destroy it, so they are rather surprised when he stands there, the phone still active in his hand, with a look of total shock on his face.

"Excuse me? *Another gig!*"

At this the couple on the sofa spring up as one, madly shaking their heads and hands and remotes at the younger man, as they frantically mouth, "*No, no way... Are you mad...? Jesus Christ!*" Etc... etc.

"What do you mean – do it for *you?* I've lost my job, my self-respect, my... never mind... What *exactly* do I owe you?" He can sense his concerned relatives nodding and giving two very relieved and approving thumbs-ups, so he is not surprised to feel their bodily reaction to his follow-up question shaking the already sagging floorboards beneath his feet. "Where is it this time? ...*Birmingham?!* ...O-kay. I'll be ready."

He takes his time fitting the phone back into his pocket, knowing that it is a few precious seconds in which he doesn't have to face the disappointed glares of the older couple, rooted to the spot just a few feet in front of him.

Finally, he explains. "The poor man was almost begging me." He's clearly not getting through. "He had tears in his voice,

Uncle and Noreen. Real tears." Nothing. "Apparently, he had already *promised* the person whose club it is that I would be there. Signed a proper contract… Tyler says this club owner can get quite violent… *Very* violent… It's the Midlands!"

"Oh, Stephen, lad," says Uncle Geoffrey, with such sadness, "the bugger's using you. It's what people do to other people, who don't understand what the real world is like."

"And *Birmingham*?" says Noreen.

THIRTY-SIX

What is this, an audience or an oil painting?

Stephen Gibson has never been to Birmingham.

Yet those heights of anticipation he might reasonably have expected to reach over this, his first Midlands foray, are somewhat clouded by the fact that Tyler Watts appears to be totally bypassing the city centre. And, of course, that the newcomer himself is still struggling over why he has agreed to come here in the first place.

Tyler is far too busy mocking the posh voice of his sat-nav to pay Stephen's concerns too much attention. Occasionally, however, he does try to dispel what he deduces to be troubling thoughts in his new client's head.

"It'll be fine, matey. Even *you* can see the audiences sodding love you. And after this, you don't have to do any more gigs. That's a Tyler Watts promise."

"What's so special about this place?" asks Stephen, ignoring any temptation to quantify the value of a promise from Tyler Watts.

"Not a thing. Like I said, I owe the owner a favour. Well, a few. A lot, actually. Remember that photo on my wall?"

"So it's all about you, again."

"And the continuing use of my legs. Squat as they may be. Not everyone in this game is as nice as me, Steve. Especially if you let 'em down." He shivers. "Repeatedly. And hey, you still want to win the heart of lovely Lena, don't you?"

Stephen seems quite alarmed. "Nina! *She's not going to be there, is she?*"

"Course she's fucking not. Birmingham?"

Stephen is silent for a while. Finally, he has to speak. "Tyler – you haven't heard from Kerry, have you? Since she—"

"Kerry? Yeah, she's ok," says Tyler Watts. "You know Kerry."

They are silent until they reach the club. Except for that posh bloody know-all on the sat-nav.

***

The Hydeaway Comedy Club is actually in a rather smart, inner-city suburb of Birmingham, not so far off the beaten track but without the business rates a beaten track might incur.

Stephen can't quite understand why, with full benefit of a snooty but highly proactive sat-nav, they have still managed to arrive at the club in darkness, when the MC is already onstage in front of a full house, warming up Stephen's audience.

Fortunately, there are no American comics, struggling or otherwise, in today's small but reasonably well-appointed green room. Or languishing plants. Only Tyler, who appears to Stephen (a person who doesn't normally notice these things with dazzling perspicacity) unusually nervous. Almost as nervous as Stephen himself, who is in no immediate danger of clubland violence but has commenced, for some reason, to shake like a leaf. He thinks he knows why but is finding it hard to admit the truth to himself, because he has never really failed at anything before, not having attempted anything even a gnat's arse beyond his comfort zone, and seems now to be making up for it big time.

They listen in silence to the MC. Even Stephen concludes that the man on stage is rather sharp and funny, although this realisation is still arrived at by gauging the scale of audience reaction rather than in actually comprehending the material.

"Tiny word of warning," says Tyler, seconds before Stephen's intro. "The guy out there's the owner. And a complete penis."

"Well, that's not very nice," says the already unconfident opening act. Although he does understand now why they had waited until he was safely on stage.

Tyler Watts doesn't respond. He just keeps rubbing his legs.

***

"Thank you. Very kind. Now, I hope you'll continue to be a great audience and not let me or yourselves down. Cos we have a real Hydeaway surprise for all you people tonight. You've seen him do... what he does... on YouTube and maybe even, God help you, in a comedy club. This guy is on the rise, on the net and, likely as not, on the spectrum. So please give a big Hydeaway welcome to comedy's latest flash in the pan – is he this year's enfant terrible or just a terrible infant? Ladies and gents – Stephen Gibson!

Just a few seconds after he recognises his name, Stephen stumbles out of the room and onto the tiny, dazzlingly lit stage. As they pass, he nods to the MC, a slim, good-looking man in his late-thirties, without even noticing the disdainful look behind the gleaming, professional smile.

Stephen Gibson realises, as indeed he has for some time, that he has absolutely nothing prepared. More alarmingly, he is now pretty certain that whatever he has diligently prepared on past occasions is, basically, nothing. Hence the evening's mounting fear. But he tells himself that he is helping out a friend, or sort of friend, which is apparently what sort of friends do. (He can't be totally certain of this, because he has no empirical evidence.)

Adding to this, of course, is the simple truth that he is in Birmingham, a city where nobody knows him and which, with all due respect, he very much doubts that he will ever see again.

And this is most definitely his final gig.

So what the hell!

Those lights really are glaring.

He discovers all too swiftly, as he makes for the microphone stand, that the beams are focussed directly into his eyes. Stephen wonders whether it is simply that his rather thick glasses are taking a particularly high-end, megawatt-hammering or, more perturbingly, that someone is deliberately aiming the venue lighting onto him at full squint, in order to maximise his discomfort. With hilarious consequences.

Whatever.

At least this time he can't see the audience, which has to be a bonus. Even if he can hear the hush of anticipation all too loud and clear. All he wants now is to get this show on the road, be a bit stupid and absurdly amateurish, leave everyone laughing at him then scoot back down the M40 or whichever route Tyler's bossy lady decides.

"Hello," he begins nervously, before even reaching the microphone stand, "my name is Stephen—"

He doesn't even complete his intro – although this has itself in the past proved a labour of Hercules – before the first heckler strikes.

"*Gibsonstephengibsonstephengibsonste…*" yells out the wit, from somewhere in the mote-ridden gloom, to cheers and laughter from the well-warmed up Brummie crowd.

Stephen, whose fledgling stand-up career has thus far been relatively free of audience participation, other than cheers, laughter and a comparatively soundless incredulity, is slightly thrown.

"…Gibson. Er. Right," says Stephen. "Stephen Gibson. Thank you."

He leans in towards the microphone, still with little idea of what he is about to say. Yet he knows with some certainty that he is not the only comic who feels this way – it's apparently what gets the adrenaline surging. Or when you start to shit yourself, as his friend Jayson Spliff, aka Julio Antonioni, is fond of saying. And, if God's on your side, the shit'll soon come out your mouth, as NJ is equally fond of adding.

"*Do the mic-in-your-eye thing!*"

He has no idea who is suggesting this, but it appears to be another younger man, seated in a different part of the crowded room. Amidst the clatter-clink of glasses and laughter, he catches requests slowly building for one of his greatest hits. "Yeah… Go for it… In your fockin' eye."

Stephen believes that there is an expression 'give the people what they want', although he has no idea where he first heard it, nor its origin. Political, most probably. So he simply acquiesces to their plea with a knowing nod. Remembering this time to remove his glasses, he is about to wrench said microphone brutally from its socket, in the hope that he doesn't actually blind himself, when he hears it.

The sound appears to be coming from somewhere in the very centre of the house.

Ah-choo!

He stands completely still, hand on the still-lodged microphone, staring into the darkness. Then he shakes his head. He mustn't allow himself to be distracted. He almost smiles at his foolishness. In fact, he believes he does smile. In the middle of a comedy set. *Stephen!*

"You were saying?" This from Heckler One, who is sounding just the slightest bit impatient.

Stephen remains silent for a few more uncomfortable seconds, looking blindly into his dark, expectant crowd. He can hear vague stirrings of unease beneath the usual drinking buzz.

The silence is becoming distinctly angry.

Very tentatively, and possibly to his own surprise as much as that of his audience, he begins to talk.

"Sorry. For the… well, for the delay. Yes. I know that some of you – actually about four million, three hundred thousand and six of you, when I last looked – have already seen me making a tit of myself. Not my language – something our window cleaner said the other day. Mr Popescu, Rumanian. Nice man. Not that it matters. Or that he said 'teet'. I think he meant it kindly. And that's because I'm the only stand-up comedian in the country – on the planet, probably – *without* a GSOH. That means Good – or, possibly even – Great Sense of Humour. I'm not joking."

"We're not laughing." This is from a lady heckler, middle-aged and quite jolly, by the sound of her. She receives the chortles she was probably going for. A natural.

"Especially the 'G' bit," continues Stephen, undeterred. "Which is what I thought you had to find to make a girl like you."

"More like the G-spot!"

Hello again, Heckler Two. This time the audience roars. The world is back on track.

"You see – I don't even understand the heckles!" explains Stephen, almost apologetically. "Maybe that's because, until very recently, the only living things I ever talked to – *really* talked to – were plants. Seriously. Because... well, they always listened, didn't they? They never walked away or rolled their eyes or changed the subject. Or talked about themselves instead. Or, indeed, about other plants. And I only had to put my lips close to them to make them grow tall and strong."

"*Works for me!*" yelps the lady contributor, with some audible success.

"Yet I couldn't talk to women. Well, not about anything un-botanical. And I... I still can't."

He pauses for a moment and takes a deep breath. He knows the audience is out there: he can hear them; he can almost smell them. In fact, he *can* smell them. Yet somehow, whilst intensely present, they're taking on the guise of spirits. Or – perhaps – trees, in a sepulchral forest.

"It never really mattered," he continues. "At least, not until now. Because now... well, now there's one young woman in particular who – whom – I'd really like to tell my feelings to. To whom." He utters a sigh that reverberates around the room. "But I'm talking to a roomful of strangers instead."

"Not as strange as you, pal."

Stephen doesn't recognise this voice. Heckler Three. Clearly someone new to contend with, sporting a broad and unfamiliar accent, which is probably local. As expected, this most recent contributor does attract a measure of appreciation from his neighbours. Yet possibly not quite as wholehearted as that of his predecessors.

"You're right, sir. I am strange," says Stephen. "I can tell you're a fellow sufferer."

The gush of delighted surprise from the audience at this medium-sharp riposte is matched only by Stephen's astonishment at what he just did. Yet he can't allow this to throw him.

"Thank you. Now I imagine," he continues briskly, "that most of you out there remember the way, as a small child, you would make your mummy and your daddy laugh, most probably with the silliest, stupidest stuff. You know, daft faces, terrible jokes – knock knock! Who is it outside the door?– ridiculous songs." He is sure he can sense at least a couple of nods in the darkness, but it could just be bored heads seeking solace in and out of pint glasses. "For reasons I won't go into right now, I never really had that... that audience. At least, not that I can recall. So I never really learned how to make someone laugh. Can you *believe* it? Which is why, in my late twenties, I went on a stand-up comedy course. Not to make *you* laugh. Or people just like you, but with different accents. I don't even know any of you."

He pauses, just for a second, staring into the light. When he resumes, it is quieter, chattier, almost as if he is telling his story to somebody right next to him, perhaps over a cup of tea and a Jaffa Cake. "It was to make one *particular* someone laugh. That's all. Just the one. And if you think that's, well, laughable – wait for the punchline: *she was totally the wrong particular someone!* Sorry – don't need the 'totally.'"

The sound he hears now is the most extraordinary sound he has ever heard. It is the sound of an audience trying not to make a sound.

Suddenly the silence is broken. By another sneeze.

Ah-choo!

Stephen looks into the crowd. As if he is searching. As if no-one ever comes to a comedy club with a cold. Or hay-fever. Or consumption.

"Bless you, sir. Or madam," he says, politely. "Anyway, my comedy teacher – who is an excellent teacher, by the way, albeit permanently angry and emotionally stunted – he told us that the essence of comedy is truth. He told us this a lot. But with plenty of swear words that I would never use. Like 'fucking' or 'arsehole'. But what if… what if the truth just *isn't* funny?"

By this time, Stephen appears to be talking only to himself. Yet for once, miraculously, his microphone technique is working. And he hasn't stumbled over any hidden obstacles, other than perhaps his own tongue. "What if the truth is that, for the first time in my life, I've discovered – okay, yes, I've discovered love?"

Stephen pauses, as if no-one could be more shocked at these words than he himself. He waits, slightly stunned, for the inevitable, diminishing heckle. Especially from jolly, Number Two woman. Yet, to his surprise, none comes. So he carries on.

"I mean love for someone whose special, unusually crinkly smile you could spend the rest of your life just staring at. Like the best kind of botanical garden in the world. Which is, in fact, Kew. In my opinion. Although Jardim Botanico in Rio is apparently excellent. But you can't. Spend the rest of your life, staring at it. At her. Big lesson."

The audience is very still. There comes another sneeze.

For the first time, Stephen appears genuinely confused. He actually believes that he *recognises* the sneeze. But, of course, this is impossible. For one thing, a sneeze is a sneeze. Isn't it? And, for another, she's thousands of miles away. Or maybe even worse by now. And yet…

"And yet… and yet she could be in this very room. Possibly. No. I wonder. Not sure how. Or why. *Birmingham?*"

The tension in the room is palpable. Even the possible slur on their fair city doesn't alter the atmosphere. Stephen himself finds it pretty hard to bear. So he puts his glasses back on and points to one of the only people he can make out through the electric fog. A blonde woman at a small table in the front row.

"*It's you!*" he cries.

Laughter tinged with relief embraces the room.

"No, it's not," he continues, with a disarming smile. "It's really not." He adjusts his glasses, as the perspiration now flooding his body causes them to glide down his nose. "I'm sure you're with someone nice, madam. Or going home to someone nice. Or maybe both. Which would be nice too."

He doesn't even wait for the appreciative laughter to fade, because his mind has leaped straight back to the main event. "But if she *were* – by some extraordinary miracle – to be here, right now, tonight, in this room, I would just want to tell her how very stupid I was. And still am. Stupid for not once mentioning to her how much I actually *enjoy* her company. Even her weird and, to be frank, rather incessant jokes. Which, naturally, I don't understand, yet sort of like anyway, because they're part of her. And, of course, her son, who is a big part of her too and is going to be this amazing young man. If he doesn't poison someone first and go to some sort of remand home or institution for young offenders."

Stephen removes the microphone from its stand with unexpected dexterity and no permanent facial injury. This appears to be for no other reason than that he patently can't stand still any longer and has to wander, even if right this minute his wandering room is severely limited.

"And when I heard that she'd left the country, ladies and gentlemen – I felt like my heart had been ripped into tiny pieces. For only the second time in my life. Like one of those tricks with newspaper that the strange man, Tommy Cooper, does. '*Just like that – ha ha ha!*' Only this time the torn paper doesn't come out whole again.

"Oh, say what you like, I know I can't change anything. It's way too late for that. So, obviously, I didn't pay attention to *that* bit of Tyler Watt's Killer Comedy course – you know, the big lesson about timing. But I have to find *some* way just to tell her. And maybe – well, who knows, maybe this *is* it. Although probably not. Even just to *thank* her. Yes! For having been a good listener – and an even better friend. I mean, we climbed into a skip together, for heaven's sake. So she's a… a rubbish friend!"

On this admittedly baffling note, Stephen Gibson appears to have reached some sort of conclusion. Or at least his busy mouth has stopped moving. The room remains disturbingly silent. Both laughter and heckle-free.

The MC immediately leaps back onto the stage, clapping his hands frenetically, desperate to relieve the dangerously funereal mood. His mouth is open, ready to take over and, please God, be funny.

"*And do you know something – even plants do it!*" continues Stephen Gibson.

"Oh, you are shitting me!" says the thwarted MC. "Well, thank you, er…"

Stephen stares at this angry intruder, who isn't moving, and then beyond him, to the side of the stage, where his erstwhile mentor and tormentor, Tyler Watts, is actually smiling delightedly. So perhaps the threat of broken legs has passed.

From the audience there comes an unexpected sound. Like the gentle whisper of the sea against a shingly shore. They are telling the frustrated MC to shushhh.

"... *Yes!*" says Stephen Gibson. "Different species of plants can be really good companions and even facilitate each other by improving growth. No, I'm really not joking." They're really not laughing. "Basil – that's *ocimum basilicum* – positively enhances the germination rates of chilli seeds – *capsicum annuum*. I know! I didn't believe it either!" He stares out plaintively into the gloom. "But what's this guy Basil got that I haven't?"

The MC, irascible at the best of times, and apparently violent at others, has clearly had enough. He wrenches the sweat-soaked microphone from Stephen's hand. Manfully ignoring the surprisingly green thumb, he pushes the younger man aside and moves to the front of the stage.

"And let's give it up for the Emeritus Professor of Tedium!" He whispers to Stephen: "Go – *GO*! Fucking vanish! Can we have the house lights up, guys? NOW would be good!"

The lights in the crowded room go up, removing the dazzle from Stephen's moist eyes and revealing the night's heaving Hydeaway crowd for the first time.

He hears a sound that pierces him to his soul.

Stephen Gibson looks to the appalled MC and then at an astonished Tyler Watts, as if for confirmation.

The entire audience are still seated at their tables.

And they are gently sobbing.

The men, of course, pretend that they're not. They all appear to have something in their eye. A speck of dust, a splash of beer. The women aren't pretending at all.

Stephen can also see, amidst the tears and the shuffling, the full extent of his foolishness. Kerry isn't there. Whoever was sneezing, it certainly wasn't direct from Sudan.

"*Jesus wept!*" says the MC, who feels that he will never live this down. Unless, of course, there is a burgeoning market for tragedy clubs and he is only just catching up with the curve.

Stephen's initial feeling is one of guilt. Terrible, overpowering guilt. He has somehow managed to send an entire comedy-bound audience, primed one and all for a fun evening out, into a state of mass depression. Which, in itself, has to be quite some achievement.

"Oh dear... I am *so* very sorry," he says. "I really hadn't intended... *Shit*! Er... 'We're all doomed!'... 'Oh, grow up!'... '*Muthafucker!*'... Thank you. Thank you so much. I was Stephen Gibson. And still am, of course. Sorry again. That's me."

He walks off the tiny stage, past an incensed yet oddly intrigued MC, to a weepy sort of semi-silence. No applause, no cheering. Almost as if this might appear unseemly.

Ignoring the gentle yet patently heartfelt pat on the back from an embarrassingly wet-faced Tyler Watts, Stephen makes blindly for the rear exit. The microphone is still clamped tightly in his hand.

Stephen Gibson just wants to go home.

PART FIVE

The Sign-Off

THIRTY-SEVEN

Say goodnight, Stevie.

In the alley beside the Hydeaway, he begins to pant.

Wondering what the hell he has just done.

He also wonders, peripherally, why all comedy clubs appear to have alleys. Is it so that humiliated, ridiculous, no-hoper stand-ups can slink away unnoticed into oblivion and almost certain despair? Or is it simply where the essential beer barrels can be most readily unloaded?

"*Told you it'd end in tears.*"

There is no mistaking the voice. He feels like spinning round yet discovers that his body is reluctant or even powerless to move.

"I did wonder if it was your sneeze," he tells the empty alleyway. "But I thought I was just imagining it."

Kerry moves round so that they can talk more sensibly. After the disorienting brightness of the club, Stephen finds it quite comforting to see a human face in a more natural light. Especially this human face. He still can't fathom how he could have failed to appreciate the loveliness of this young woman. Even now, with the first traces of snot just beginning to glide from both delicate nostrils.

"Jesus, you *do* bathe in pollen!"

"No," says Stephen, because he doesn't. "It must just cling to my clothes."

"For dear life… It was quite an act, Stephen."

"What was? Oh, you mean just now. I had the audience crying, didn't I? But not in a good way."

"I enjoyed it. In a good way."

"I thought you'd gone to Sudan."

"Ticket sales were poor for the rebellion. They had to cancel." He just stares at her, trying to work this out. She shrugs almost apologetically and, curiously for her, appears slightly embarrassed. "I heard what you said, Stephen."

"What – just now? I'm so sorry, Kerry—"

"*No!* No, Stephen. Well, I heard that too. But I meant in Starbucks. About Nathan. Y'know, me needing to be a responsible mom. Kinda like the one you never got to have." He realises, with unusual tact, that he should remain silent, so he just nods. But he is not displeased. "And, well, the MC tonight – guy who owns the place—"

"He was a bit unkind. Tyler says he's a penis… anyway, I can see why he might have been cross."

"He's my ex. Eamon Hyde… *Hydeaway*?"

"Oh," says Stephen, as the dots begin to join. "Tyler's far more successful half-brother."

"Yeah. They're not close."

"No." He seems even more puzzled. "So why did Tyler insist I do this show? To get back at him?" When she says nothing, in the hope he might do the math, he simply looks blank. Finally: "You asked him to?"

"*Me?* No – I wouldn't do that to you. Or him. Your little comedy pals told Tyler about the ice-cream run to the airport, so the nut-job decided he would play matchmaker. *And* maybe shaft his sibling. Go figure."

"But why did *you* come here, Kerry? To Birmingham."

"To see if the flame still burned." He says nothing. She stares at him for a moment, as if willing him to speak. Then a few more moments. "You're supposed to say, 'And did it?'"

"And did what?" He knows that he is sounding, in Tyler's charming phrase, as thick as pig shit, but this is all moving far too fast for him. Transitions are not his thing, as he is starting to realise. And tonight's feels like a biggie.

"Jesus, Stephen, get with the programme! 'And did the flame still burn?'"

"Oh. Then what do you say?"

"Well, I could say my ass is on fire. Or I could say, 'If you kiss me, then maybe I'll know.'"

"Then what do I—"

"Just bloody kiss me, Stephen."

As no-one has ever asked Stephen Gibson to just bloody kiss them, he is slightly paralysed. But, fortunately, not for long. As he holds out his trembling arms and she slips into the warm space between, he drops the microphone he now realises he has been clutching throughout their conversation, in order to kiss her with all the passion he can muster. And with a sudden, overwhelming love that doesn't take much mustering at all.

She sneezes almost into his mouth.

For once, in matters of the heart, Stephen is ruthlessly proactive. Swiftly removing his tweedy jacket and tie, he proceeds to rip off his best shirt and favourite Marks & Spencer vest then hurls the pollen-ridden lot of them, with what can only be called abandon, against the wall of the alley.

He is about to remove further items, like a Salome of Solihull, when Kerry holds him even tighter. Stephen Gibson is not certain whether this is in total reciprocation of the sudden cataclysmic swell of emotion he is feeling or simply to keep him decent and halt his almost immediate, helpless shivering.

Whatever. It works for him.

It also works for the remainder of the Hydeaway audience, now pouring into the alleyway, who stop to clap, cheer, pretend to vomit (Tyler) or just go teary all over again.

OKAY. SO IT'S EIGHTEEN MONTHS LATER AND...

THIRTY-EIGHT

And I've been Stephen Gibson!

The sign on the new, purpose-built structure reads 'PHOTOGRAPHIC STUDIO AND SCHOOL'. The building, nestling amongst tall trees, is not large, but its warm colours and slightly asymmetrical shape have proved to be both reassuring and welcoming, especially for the younger subjects. So far no-one has needed their feet superglued to the floor.

Kerry pops her head out to find Nathan still sitting with his friend Emmanuel, beside a sunlit patch of garden. Plants are just starting to grow, each one neatly labelled with its full Latin name, below a professionally printed skull and crossbones.

"Time to go, Mister Borgia," says his mother.

"Mum," asks Nathan, seriously, "what was the name again of that weird guy from the garden centre? Y'know, the dorky nerd who really liked you and turned up one night out of nowhere?"

For a moment his mother's slightly swollen face takes on a sad and thoughtful look. A voice makes them turn.

"*That was me!*"

They smile tolerantly at the man, who has walked through the compact but expertly stocked nursery. Behind him is the rear entrance to a smart new garden centre, with a sign that reads 'THE GREEN THUMB'.

"Can you still not get a friggin' joke?" says the boy.

"*Language!*" say Kerry and Stephen together.

"We'd better get ready," says Kerry. "Takes me a bit longer these days."

Stephen comes over and strokes her huge belly. She suddenly sneezes and touches her bump, as if something is ever so imminent and exposure to just a few more dahlias could give the place another water feature. The couple exchange a look.

"I feel guilty leaving the shop in the middle of the week."

"It's one afternoon, Stephen! You can wear your hair shirt under your best suit if you want." Stephen just looks baffled. "Never mind. Hey, your uncle and Noreen and Spike can handle things. You've got them well-trained. And invested!"

"You don't think Mrs Dave…?"

"What – will torch the place while we're out?"

"I was thinking more spreading aphids."

"The great Ruislip Garden Centre Wars." She shakes her head and looks serious. "Well, since you poached Nina Hughes' business, but happily not her tall, histamine-free, Welsh heart, the gardening gloves are off. Talking of which…"

Stephen removes his trusty apparel and gives his wife an unexpected and rather vivid thumbs-up. "Come on, you guys," he says, in some excitement, "we've got a wedding to go to! Not you, Emmanuel."

***

The room in which Tyler Watts and Suzie Vernon have chosen to exchange their vows is not a conventional venue. But neither is their wedding a conventional ceremony.

Whilst there is no legal status to a marriage conducted in an Asian social club two days after Diwali, by a man who is himself a moderately successful stand-up comedian, it has a special resonance for at least one of the parties concerned. In former days it was the small, neighbourhood pub above which Tyler Watts performed his first-ever professional gig. He is hoping the marriage will be a touch more joyful.

The celebrant for today's event had been the MC that memorable night. As Stephen assists Kerry to a seat, the man is already warming up the assembled guests. Kerry finds herself wanting to cover both of Nathan's ears, until she realises that he has probably heard far worse at school or at home. And location-specific gags about things beginning to *sag* and supposing a *Bombay duck* is out of the question only contribute to the festive atmosphere.

Stephen is surprised to be greeted so warmly by so many people. The place is, of course, full of stand-up comedians, who know him only by repute. From that period when, for one brief, shining moment and with due thanks, as he now knows, to his YouTube savvy stepson, he was a global mega-dick. But there are also people for whom Stephen has a huge amount of affection, a sentiment that is readily reciprocated.

Jayson Spliff is there. He tells Stephen that, whilst still helping out his family in their ice-cream business, he is also gigging quite regularly. The man wants to introduce his old mate to his new love, who is sitting happily beside him. "You know how you don't find *anything* funny?" says Jayson. "Well, this one came to one of my gigs and she couldn't be more different." Stephen hasn't actually required an introduction – he could hear Clova's laugh even before he entered the room. She gives him a glorious smile and tells Kerry that 'your guy is hysterical', then adds her distinctive bray as endorsement. Kerry just nods and gives Stephen a look he decides to ignore.

Just in front of Stephen and wearing what, even by his own standards, is a particularly exuberant pullover, is Nigel Ngo. He is happily signing to the older couple sitting beside him, but his parents – as this has to be who they are – appear more shocked than amused. Stephen wonders for a moment whether his dexterous friend is substituting his own material for that of the man actually talking.

Beside them, and laughing with every part of her body, is NJ, dressed in a gleaming, midnight-blue tuxedo and seated very close to a small and rather attractive woman, whom she introduces as Rabbi Hirschfeld. Stephen has never met a rabbi before and clearly has lots of questions he would love to ask. Kerry, who fears that one of them might be whether she is there in her capacity as a religious leader or as a lesbian, uses her bump to steer her husband to a harmless seat near the back, just in case an early exit is required.

It is barely forty-five minutes later that the theme music from *The Good, the Bad and the Ugly* echoes mysteriously around the room and the bride, on the arm of a diminutive and considerably older man, strolls confidently down the aisle. Stephen has to admit that Suzie V, *the* Suzie V, looks endearingly and convincingly feminine in her tightly fitting cream silk trouser suit and drop-dead heels, encasing what have to be the largest feet he has ever seen, at least on a woman.

Waiting proudly for his wife-to-be, in a kilt with the pattern reminiscent of the McDonald's arches repeated in tartan (for reasons that are as inexplicable as the music but clearly resonate with the couple) and wearing a gentle smile that is almost more surprising, is Stephen's instructor, friend and now sort-of relative, Tyler Watts.

The ceremony itself is rather fun and charming. The laughs that envelop it are heartfelt and sincere. It is only when the happily 'married' couple turn and walk back down the makeshift aisle that the distinctive nature of the guest list truly asserts itself. Instead of smiles, flowers or confetti, the crowd begin to throw heckles.

"*I've seen better legs on a Chippendale. And I'm talking furniture.*"

"*You changed your sex. But you still wake up with a dick!*"

"*You can tell who wears the trousers in this marriage.*"

"*Show us yer tits – Tyler!*"

"*Don't open the fridge tonight, Suzie – he'll start telling jokes.*"

Kerry has to explain this last one to Stephen. About comedians being always 'onstage' and lights going on, as a fridge does when you... In fact, she has to explain all the heckles to Stephen.

"*It's the children I feel sorry for.*"

"*If he says, 'And that's me, Tyler Watts!', tell him you were expecting another ten minutes.*"

Finally, after a slow, appreciative and very contented saunter, they arrive at Stephen. This time they simply halt. And stare down at him. And wait.

And wait.

Finally, Stephen announces, in an over-loud voice that projects around the attentive hall. "I hope... I HOPE your life will be as rich and colourful as a *prunus serrulata*." The congregation sigh. "May your cherry always flower."

The assembled audience stands up and cheers. The bride and groom both kiss this standalone guy, this sweetest of green-thumbed men and their final well-wisher, before leaving the room.

"That was kinda funny," says Kerry, giving her husband's hand a squeeze.

"I knew that," says Stephen Gibson, with an enigmatic nod. He tries to ignore the sceptical look from his young stepson.

Kerry finds suddenly that she can't stop laughing. Her eyes begin to water. Her stomach heaves. It becomes almost uncontrollable.

The baby, a girl, arrives at 3.14 the following morning. They call her *Amaryllis Minerva.*

ACKNOWLEDGEMENTS

Having worked with performers, writers and directors blessed with that precious gift of comedy for so many years, I hope at least that some of their skills have rubbed off.

I would particularly like to thank the wonderfully talented and gracious Paul Alexander, Keith Farnan and Alan Moskowitz for their helpful advice when this concept was in a much earlier and very different incarnation.

My thanks also to Tammy Mendelson for some diligent reading, judicious editing and even more valuable encouragement.

Undying gratitude to the generous audiences to my comedy series, who have thankfully proved to me you don't always have to add the laughs on afterwards.

And finally to my late mother, who sat in the front row of my first ever sit-com episode and sobbed throughout, whilst all those around her appeared to be having fun. (Which slightly threw the cast but I believe I understood.)

ABOUT THE AUTHOR

PAUL A MENDELSON is the BAFTA-nominated creator of several hit BBC comedy series, including 'May to December', 'So Haunt Me' and the long-running 'My Hero', starring Ardal O'Hanlon as the hapless superhero Thermoman. He co-created 'Neighbors From Hell' for DreamWorks Animation and wrote the acclaimed ITV drama 'Losing It' starring Martin Clunes.

Paul's first novel, In the Matter of Isabel, was published in 2017 and is being developed as a movie with a major Hollywood company.

Paul has written two books for children, Losing Arthur and The Funnies, which was praised as 'Orwellian but with laughs'.

His most recent 'grown-up' book, The Art of Listening, a collection of humorous shorter fiction, was called 'compelling and often disconcerting' by The Independent.

Paul lives in North-West London and is married with two daughters and four grandchildren.